Praise for Elly Griffiths

'A wonderfully rich mixture of ancient and contemporary
. . . A welcome addition to a great series'
Guardian

'A memorable, breathless race against time . . . One of the
most cinematic finales in recent British crime novels'
Daily Telegraph

'Griffiths weaves superstition and myth into her crime
novels, skilfuly treading a line between credulity and
modern methods of detection'
Sunday Times

'Griffiths' excellent series is well informed and original'
Literary Review

'The perfect ratio of anticipation, shock and surprise'
Independent

'A palpable sense of evil . . . Perfect for dark winter evenings'
Financial Times

'A sinister, life-threatening mystery that grips to its end'
Woman and Home

'The characters are constantly engaging - particularly the
vulnerable Ruth - the writing is perceptive, as well as wryly
humorous . . . This is recommended'
Spectator

Elly Griffiths was born in London, and worked in publishing for many years. Her bestselling series of Ruth Galloway novels have three times been shortlisted for the Theakston's Old Peculier Crime Novel of the Year, and twice for the CWA Dagger in the Library. Her new series is based in 1950s Brighton. Elly lives near Brighton with her husband, an archaeologist, their two children and her cat.

Also by Elly Griffiths

THE DR RUTH GALLOWAY MYSTERIES

The Crossing Places
The House at Sea's End
A Room Full of Bones
Dying Fall
The Outcast Dead
The Ghost Fields
The Woman in Blue

THE STEPHENS AND MEPHISTO MYSTERIES

The Zig Zag Girl
Smoke and Mirrors

and coming soon
The Blood Card

ELLY GRIFFITHS

The Janus Stone

A Dr RUTH GALLOWAY MYSTERY

Quercus

First published in Great Britain in 2010 by Quercus
This paperback edition published in 2016 by

Quercus Editions Ltd
Carmelite House
50 Victoria Embankment
London EC4Y 0DZ

An Hachette UK company

A CIP catalogue record for this book is available
from the British Library

PB ISBN 978 1 78648 212 9
EBOOK ISBN 978 1 84916 776 5

10 9 8

Printed and bound in Great Britain by Clays Ltd, Elcograf S.p.A.

For my nieces and nephews: Francesca,
William, Robert, Charlotte and Eleanor

The Janus
Stone

1st June,
Festival of Carna

The house is waiting. It knows. When I sacrificed yesterday, the entrails were black. Everything is turned to night. Outside it is spring but in the house there is a coldness, a pall of despair that covers everything.

We are cursed. This is no longer a house but a grave. The birds do not sing in the garden and even the sun does not dare penetrate the windows. No one knows how to lift the curse. They have given in and lie as if waiting for death. But I know and the house knows.

Only blood will save us now.

CHAPTER 1

A light breeze runs through the long grass at the top of the hill. Close up, the land looks ordinary, just heather and coarse pasture with the occasional white stone standing out like a signpost. But if you were to fly up above these unremarkable hills you would be able to see circular raised banks and darker rectangles amongst the greens and browns – sure signs that this land has been occupied many, many times before.

Ruth Galloway, walking rather slowly up the hill, does not need the eagle's eye view to know that this is an archaeological site of some importance. Colleagues from the university have been digging on this hill for days and they have uncovered not only evidence of a Roman villa but also of earlier Bronze Age and Iron Age settlements.

Ruth had planned to visit the site earlier but she has been busy marking papers and preparing for the end of term. It is May and the air is sweet, full of pollen and the scent of rain. She stops, getting her breath back and enjoying the feeling of being outdoors on a spring afternoon. The year has been dark so far, though not without unexpected bonuses, and she relishes the chance just to stand still, letting the sun beat down on her face.

'Ruth!' She turns and sees a man walking towards her. He is wearing jeans and a work-stained shirt and he treats the hill with disdain, hardly altering his long stride. He is tall and slim with curly dark hair greying at the temples. Ruth recognises him, as he obviously does her, from a talk he gave at her university several months ago. Dr Max Grey, from the University of Sussex, an archaeologist and an expert on Roman Britain.

'I'm glad you could come,' he says and he actually does look glad. A change from most archaeologists, who resent another expert on their patch. And Ruth is an acknowledged expert – on bones, decomposition and death. She is Head of Forensic Archaeology at the University of North Norfolk.

'Are you down to the foundations?' asks Ruth, following Max to the summit of the hill. It is colder here and, somewhere high above, a skylark sings.

'Yes, I think so,' says Max, pointing to a neat trench in front of them. Halfway down, a line of grey stone can be seen. 'I think we may have found something that will interest you, actually.'

Ruth knows without being told.

'Bones,' she says.

Detective Chief Inspector Harry Nelson is shouting. Despite a notoriously short fuse at work (at home with his wife and daughters he is a pussy cat) he is not normally a shouter. Brusque commands are more his line, usually delivered on the run whilst moving on to the next job. He is a man of quick decisions and limited patience. He likes doing things: catching criminals, interrogating suspects, driving too fast and eating too much. He does not like meetings, pointless discussions or listening to advice. Above all, he does not like sitting in his office on a fine spring day trying to persuade his new computer to communicate with him. Hence the shouting.

'Leah!' he bellows.

Leah, Nelson's admin assistant (or secretary, as he likes to call her), edges cautiously into the room. She is a delicate, dark girl of twenty-five, much admired by the younger officers. Nelson, though, sees her mainly as a source of coffee and an interpreter of new technology, which seems to get newer and more temperamental every day.

'Leah,' he complains, 'the screen's gone blank again.'

'Did you switch it off?' asks Leah. Nelson has been known to pull out plugs in moments of frustration, once fusing all the lights on the second floor.

'No. Well, once or twice.'

Leah dives beneath the desk to check the connections. 'Seems OK,' she says. 'Press a key.'

'Which one?'

'Surprise me.'

Nelson thumps the space bar and the computer miraculously comes to life, saying smugly, 'Good afternoon, DCI Nelson.'

'Fuck off,' responds Nelson, reaching for the mouse.

'I beg your pardon?' Leah's eyebrows rise.

'Not you,' says Nelson, 'This thing. When I want small talk, I'll ask for it.'

'I assume it's programmed to say good morning,' says Leah equably. 'Mine plays me a tune.'

'Jesus wept.'

'Chief Superintendent Whitcliffe says everyone's got to familiarise themselves with the new computers. There's a training session at four today.'

'I'm busy,' says Nelson without looking up. 'Got a case conference out Swaffham way.'

'Isn't that where they're doing that Roman dig?' asks Leah. 'I saw it on *Time Team*.'

She has her back to Nelson, straightening files on his shelves, and so fails to see the sudden expression of interest on his face.

'A dig? Archaeology?'

'Yes,' says Leah, turning round. 'They've found a whole Roman town there, they think.'

Nelson now bends his head to his computer screen. 'Lots of archaeologists there, are there?'

'Yes. My uncle owns the local pub, the Phoenix, and he says they're in there every night. He's had to double his cider order.'

'Typical,' grunts Nelson. He can just imagine archaeologists drinking cider when everyone knows that bitter's a man's drink. Women archaeologists, though, are another matter.

'I might have a look at the site on my way back,' he says.

'Are you interested in history?' asks Leah disbelievingly.

'Me? Yes, fascinated. Never miss an episode of *Sharpe*.'

'You should be on our pub quiz team then.'

'I get too nervous,' says Nelson blandly, typing in his password with one finger. Nelson1; he's not one for ambiguity. 'Do me a favour, love, make us a cup of coffee would you?'

Swaffham is a picturesque market town, the kind Nelson drives through every day without noticing. A few miles outside and you are deep in the country – fields waist high with grass, signposts pointing in both directions at once, cows wandering across the road shepherded by a vacant-looking boy on a quad bike. Nelson is lost in seconds and almost gives up before it occurs to him to ask the vacant youth the way to the Phoenix pub. When in doubt in Norfolk, ask the way to a pub. It turns out to be quite near so Nelson does a U-turn in the mud, turns into a road that is no more than a track and there it is, a low thatched building facing a high, grassy bank. Nelson parks in the pub car park and, with a heart turn that he does not want to acknowledge as excitement, he recognises the battered red Renault parked across the road, at the foot of the hill. I just haven't seen her for a while, he tells himself, it'll be good to catch up.

He has no idea where to find the dig, or even what it will look like, but he reckons he'll be able to see more from the top of the bank. It's a beautiful evening, the shadows are long on the grass and the air is soft. But Nelson does not notice his surroundings; he is thinking of a bleak coastline, of bodies washed out to sea by a relentless tide, of the circumstances in which he met Ruth Galloway. She had been the forensic archaeologist called in when human bones were found on the Saltmarsh, a desolate spot on the North Norfolk coast. Though those bones had turned out to be over two thousand years old, Ruth had subsequently become involved in a much more recent case, that of a five-year-old girl, abducted, believed murdered. He hasn't seen Ruth since the case ended three months ago.

At the top of the hill all he can see is more hills. The only features of interest are some earthworks in the distance, and two figures walking along the top of a curving bank: one a brown-haired woman in loose, dark clothes, the other a tall man in mud-stained jeans. A cider-drinker, he'll be bound.

'Ruth,' calls Nelson. He can see her smile; she has a remarkably lovely smile, not that he would ever tell her so.

'Nelson!' She looks good too, he thinks, her eyes bright, her cheeks pink with exercise. She hasn't lost any weight though and he realises that he would have been rather disappointed if she had.

'What are you doing here?' asks Ruth. They don't kiss or even shake hands but both are grinning broadly.

'Had a case conference nearby. Heard there was a dig here.'

'What, are you watching *Time Team* now?'

'My favourite viewing.'

Ruth smiles sceptically and introduces her companion. 'This is Dr Max Grey from Sussex University. He's in charge of the dig. Max, this is DCI Nelson.'

The man, Max, looks up in surprise. Nelson himself is aware that his title sounds incongruous in the golden evening. Crime happens, even here, Nelson tells Max Grey silently. Academics are never keen on the police.

But Dr Grey manages a smile. 'Are you interested in archaeology, DCI Nelson?'

'Sometimes,' says Nelson cautiously. 'Ruth . . . Dr Galloway . . . and I worked on a case together recently.'

'That affair on the Saltmarsh?' asks Max, his eyes wide.

'Yes,' says Ruth shortly. 'DCI Nelson called me in when he found some bones on the marsh.'

'Turned out to be bloody Stone Age,' says Nelson.

'Iron Age,' corrects Ruth automatically. 'Actually, Nelson, Max found some human bones today.'

'Iron Age?' asks Nelson.

'Roman, we think. They seem to have been buried under the wall of a house. Come and see.' She leads them down the bank and towards the earthworks. Close up, Nelson sees that the land is full of these strange mounds and hills, some curving round, some standing alone like large molehills.

'What are all these bumps?' he asks Max Grey.

'We think they're walls,' replies Max, his face lighting up in the way that archaeologists have when they are about to bore the pants off you. 'You know, we think there was a whole settlement here, we're fairly near the old Roman road but, from the surface, the only signs are some brown lines in the grass, crop marks, that sort of thing.'

Nelson looks back at the smoothly curving bank. He can just about imagine it as a wall but the rest just looks like grass to him.

'This body, you say it's under a wall?'

'Yes. We just dug a trial trench and there it was. We think it's the wall of a villa, quite a sizeable one, by the looks of it.'

'Funny place to find bones, under a wall,' says Nelson.

'They may have been a foundation sacrifice,' says Max.

'What's that?'

'The Celts, and the Romans sometimes, used to bury bodies

under walls and doors as offerings to the Gods Janus and Terminus.'

'Terminus?'

'The God of boundaries.'

'I pray to him whenever I go to Heathrow. And the other one?'

'Janus, God of doors and openings.'

'So they killed people and stuck their bodies under their houses? Funny sort of luck.'

'We don't know if they killed them or if they were dead already,' says Max calmly, 'but the bodies are often children's'.

'Jesus.'

They have reached the trench which has been covered by a blue tarpaulin. Ruth peels back the covering and kneels on the edge of the trench. Nelson crouches beside her. He sees a neat, rectangular hole (he often wishes that his crime-scene boys were as tidy as archaeologists), the edges sharp and straight. The trench is about a metre deep and Nelson can see a clear cross-section of the layers as the topsoil gives way to clay and then chalk. Below the chalk, a line of grey stones can be seen. Next to the stones a deeper hole has been dug. At the bottom of this hole is a gleam of white.

'Haven't you dug them up?' asks Nelson.

'No,' says Ruth, 'we need to record and draw the grave and skeleton on plan so that we can understand its context. It'll be really important to check which way the skeleton is lying. Could be significant if it points to the east, for example.'

'The brothers used to tell us to sleep with our feet to the east,' says Nelson suddenly remembering, 'so that if we died in the night we could walk to heaven.'

'An interesting survival of superstition,' says Ruth coolly. Nelson remembers that she has no time for religion. 'Churches,' Ruth goes on, 'are nearly always built east to west, never north to south.'

'I'll remember that.'

'And sometimes,' cuts in Max, 'men are buried facing west and women facing east.'

'Sounds sexist to me,' says Nelson straightening up.

'And you're never sexist,' says Ruth.

'Never. I've just been on a course all about redefining gender roles in the police force.'

'What was it like?'

'Crap. I left at lunchtime.'

Ruth laughs and Max, who has been looking disapproving, smiles too, looking from Ruth to Nelson and back again. Clearly more is going on here than he realised.

'We're just off to the Phoenix for a drink,' Ruth is saying. 'Do you want to come?'

'I can't,' says Nelson regretfully, 'I've got some sort of do to go to.'

'A do?'

'A ball in aid of the festival. It's being held at the castle. Black tie and all that. Michelle wanted to go.'

'How the other half lives,' says Ruth.

Nelson's only reply is a grunt. He can't think of anything worse than poncing around in a monkey suit in the company of a load of arty-farty types. But not only his wife but his boss, Gerry Whitcliffe, were insistent that he should go. 'Just the sort of PR the force needs,' Whitcliffe had said, carefully not mentioning that it was Nelson's handling of the

Saltmarsh case that had left the local force so in need of good publicity. PR! Jesus wept.

'Pity,' says Max lightly, his hand just hovering around Ruth's shoulders. 'Another time perhaps.'

Nelson watches them go. The beer garden of the Phoenix is filling up with early evening drinkers. He can hear laughter and the clink of glasses. He can't help hoping that Leah's uncle has run out of cider.

CHAPTER 2

Ruth drives slowly along the A47 towards King's Lynn. Although it is past eight, the traffic is never-ending. Where can they all be going, thinks Ruth, tapping impatiently on her steering wheel and looking out at the stream of lorries, cars, caravans and people carriers. It's not the holiday season yet and it's far too late for the school run or even the commuter traffic. What are all these people doing, heading for Narborough, Marham and West Winch? Why are they all trapped on this particular circle of hell? For several junctions now she has been stuck behind a large BMW with two smug riding hats on the back shelf. She starts to hate the BMW family with their Longleat sticker and personalised number-plate (SH3LLY 40) and their horse riding at weekends. She bets they don't even really like horses. Brought up in a London suburb, Ruth has never been on a horse though she does have a secret fondness for books about ponies. She bets that Shelly got the car for her fortieth birthday along with a holiday in the Caribbean and a special session of Botox. Ruth will be forty in two months' time.

She'd enjoyed the drinks in the pub, though she'd only

had orange juice. Max had been very interesting, talking about Roman burial traditions. We tend to think of the Romans as so civilised, he'd said, so outraged by the barbaric Iron Age practices but there is plenty of evidence of Roman punishment burials, ritual killing and even infanticide. A boy's skull found in St Albans about ten years ago, for example, showed that its owner had been battered to death and then decapitated. At Springfield in Kent foundation sacrifices of paired babies had been found at all four corners of a Roman temple. Ruth shivers and passes a hand lightly across her stomach.

But Max had been good company for all his tales of death and decapitation. He'd been brought up in Norfolk and obviously loved the place. Ruth told him about her home on the north Norfolk coast, about the winds that come directly from Siberia and the marshes flowering purple with sea lavender. I'd like to visit one day, Max had said. That would be nice, Ruth had replied but neither had said more. Ruth had agreed to visit the dig next week though. Max has a whole team coming up from Sussex. They are going to camp in the fields and dig all through May and June. Ruth feels a rush of nostalgia for summer digs; for the camaraderie, the songs and dope-smoking round the camp fire, the days of back-breaking labour. She doesn't miss the lack of proper loos or showers though. She's too old for all that.

Thank God, SH3LLY 40 has turned off to the left and Ruth can see signs for Snettisham and Hunstanton. She's nearly home. On Radio 4 someone is talking about bereavement: 'for everything there is a season'. Ruth loves Radio 4 but there are limits. She switches to cassette (her car is too old for a CD player) and the air is filled with Bruce Springsteen's heartfelt all-American whine. Ruth loves Bruce Springsteen – the open road, the doomed love, the friends called Bobby Joe who've fallen on hard times – and no amount of derision is going to make her change her mind. She turns the sound up.

Ruth is now driving between overhanging trees, the verges rich with cow parsley. In a moment, she knows, the trees will vanish as if by magic and the sea will be in front of her. She never tires of this moment, when the horizon suddenly stretches away into infinity, blue turning to white turning to gold. She drives faster and, when she reaches the caravan site that marks the start of her road home, she stops and gets out of the car, letting the sea breeze blow back her hair.

Ahead of her are the sand dunes, blown into fantastic shapes by the wind. The tide is out and the sea is barely visible, a line of blue against the grey sand. Seagulls call high above and the red sail of a windsurfer shimmers silently past.

Without warning, Ruth leans over and is violently sick.

Norwich Castle, a Victorian icing covering a rich medieval cake, is now a museum. Nelson has been there several times with his daughters. They used to love the dungeons, he remembers, and Laura had a soft spot for the teapot collection. He hasn't been for years though and as he and his wife Michelle ascend the winding pathway, floodlit and decorated with heraldic banners, he fears the worst. His fears are justified when they are met by serving wenches. The invitation did not mention fancy dress but these girls are very definitely wenches, wearing low-cut, vaguely medieval dresses and sporting frilly caps on their heads. They are proffering trays of champagne and Nelson takes the fullest glass, a fact not wasted on Michelle.

'Trust you to take the biggest,' she says, accepting a glass of orange juice.

'I'm going to need alcohol to get through this evening,' says Nelson as they walk up to the heavy wooden doors. 'You didn't tell me it was fancy dress.'

'It isn't.' Michelle is wearing a silver mini-dress which is definitely not medieval. In fact, Nelson feels that it could do with a bit more material, a train or a crinoline or whatever women wore in those days. She looks good though, he has to admit.

They enter a circular reception room to be met by more champagne, someone playing the lute, and, most disturbingly, a jester. Nelson takes a step backwards.

'Go on,' Michelle pushes him from behind.

'There's a man in tights!'

'So? He won't kill you.'

Nelson steps warily into the room, keeping his eye on the jester. He has ignored another danger though, which advances from the opposite direction.

'Ah Harry! And the beautiful Mrs Nelson.'

It is Whitcliffe, resplendent in a dinner jacket with an open-neck shirt, which he presumably thinks is trendy. He's also wearing a white scarf. Wanker.

'Hallo, Gerry.'

Whitcliffe is kissing Michelle's hand. The jester is hovering hopefully, shaking his bells.

'You didn't tell me there'd be people dressed up funny,' says Nelson, his northern accent, always evident in times of stress, coming to the fore.

'It's a medieval theme,' says Whitcliffe smoothly. 'Edward does these things so well.'

'Edward?'

'Edward Spens,' says Whitcliffe. 'You remember I told you that Spens and Co are sponsoring this evening.'

'The builders. Yes.'

'Building contractors,' says a voice behind them.

Nelson swings round to see a good-looking man of his own age, wearing faultless evening dress. No white scarf or open-neck shirt for him, just a conventional white shirt and black tie, setting off tanned skin and thick dark hair. Nelson dislikes him instantly.

'Edward!' Whitcliffe obviously doesn't share this feeling. 'This is Edward Spens, our host. Edward, this is Detective Chief Inspector Harry Nelson and his lovely wife, Michelle.'

Edward Spens looks admiringly at Michelle. 'I never knew policemen had such beautiful wives, Gerry.'

'It's a perk of the job,' says Nelson tightly.

Whitcliffe, who isn't married (a cause of much speculation), says nothing. Michelle, who is used to male admiration, flashes a wide but slightly distancing smile.

'Nelson,' Edward Spens is saying, 'weren't you the copper involved in the Saltmarsh affair?'

'Yes.' Nelson hates talking about his work and he particularly dislikes being called a 'copper'.

'What a terrible business.' Spens is looking serious.

'Yes.'

'Well, thank God you solved it.' Spens pats him heartily on the back.

Thank Ruth Galloway as well, thinks Nelson. But Ruth has always wanted her involvement in the case kept as low-key as possible.

'Luckily cases like that don't occur very often,' he says.

'I'll drink to that!' Spens pushes another glass of champagne into his hand.

Nobody has seen Ruth throw up so she simply kicks some dirt over the vomit and gets back in the car. Bruce Springsteen is telling the improbably named Wendy that they are born to run. Ruth backs the car out of the caravan site and heads for home.

Her cottage is one of three on the edge of the Saltmarsh. One cottage is empty and the other is owned by weekenders who visit less and less now that their children are growing up. The isolation does not bother Ruth. In fact, as she gets out of her car and drinks in the wide expanse of marsh, the distant sand dunes and the far-off murmur of the sea, her enjoyment is enhanced by the thought that this view is hers and hers alone. Smiling she opens her front door.

Ruth's ginger cat, Flint, has been lying in wait and now advances, complaining loudly. He has food in his bowl but it is obviously out of the question that he should eat it. He purrs around Ruth's legs until she gives him a fresh bowlful, heaving slightly at the smell. Then he sniffs it fastidiously and goes out of the cat flap.

Ruth sits at the table by the window to check her answerphone messages. One is from her mother asking if Ruth is still coming to stay at the weekend. Her mother always expects Ruth's plans to change at the last minute, despite the fact that Ruth is actually extremely punctual and reliable. The second message is from her friend Shona, burbling on about her married boyfriend Phil. The third is from Max Grey. Interesting.

'Hi Ruth. Just to say how much I enjoyed our chat. I was just thinking about our body. If the head is missing, that could be evidence of a head-cult. Have you heard of the Lankhills excavations in Winchester? Seven decapitated bodies were found in a Roman cemetery, including a child's. Could that be what we've got here, I wonder? Anyway, speak soon.'

Ruth thinks how strangely archaeologists speak sometimes. 'Our body'. The bones found buried under the Roman foundations have become 'our body', linking Ruth and Max in some strange, surreal way. They both feel a sense of ownership, even sympathy, towards them. But is this enough reason for Max to leave this message? Did he really just want a cosy chat about decapitated bodies or did he, just possibly, want to talk to her again?

Ruth sighs. It's all too complicated for her. Besides, she has other things on her mind. Tomorrow she has to drive to London and tell her mother that's she's pregnant.

'So, you see, we're developing three key sites in the heart of Norwich. The old tannery, the Odeon cinema and the derelict house on Woolmarket Street.'

'Woolmarket Street?' Whitcliffe cuts in. 'Didn't that used to be a children's home?'

'I believe so, yes,' says Edward Spens, spreading butter on his roll. 'Are you a local Norwich boy, Gerry?'

That explains a lot, thinks Nelson, as Whitcliffe nods. Nelson was born in Blackpool and would be back there like a shot if it wasn't for Michelle and the girls. It had been Michelle's idea for him to take the Norfolk job and, deep down, he still resents her for it. The girls don't like Blackpool; everyone talks funnily and you eat your supper at five o'clock. And it's too cold for them, although the local girls seem to wear miniskirts all year round.

They are at the 'banquet' stage now; roast pork disguised as suckling pig. Michelle has left most of hers. She is sparkling away at her neighbour, some goon called Leo wearing a pink shirt and ridiculous glasses. Nelson's neighbour, a regal woman in blue satin, has ignored him completely, which has left him listening to Edward Spens' relentless sales pitch.

'It's a family company,' Spens is saying. 'Built up by my father, Roderick Spens. Actually it's Sir Roderick, he was knighted for services to the building trade. Dad's supposed to be retired but he still comes into the office every day. Tries to tell me how to run things. He's against me developing the Woolmarket site, for example, but it's a prime piece of real estate.' He laughs expansively. Nelson regards him stonily. *Real estate*. Who does this guy think he is?

'Harry!' Nelson is aware that his wife is actually speaking to him, twinkling charmingly from across the table.

'Harry. Leo was talking about the Roman settlement that they've dug up. The one near Swaffham. I was telling him that we've got a friend who's an archaeologist.'

Michelle and Ruth, rather to Nelson's surprise, hit it off

immediately. Michelle likes boasting about her intellectual friend. 'Honestly, she doesn't care what she looks like.' Michelle will be delighted to hear that Ruth hasn't lost any weight.

'Yes,' says Nelson guardedly, 'she works at the university.'

'I'm writing a play,' says Leo earnestly, 'about the Roman God Janus. The two-faced God. The God of beginnings and endings, of doorways and openings, of the past and the future.'

Janus. Something is echoing in Nelson's head but is having trouble fighting through the champagne and the suckling pig. Of course, it was Ruth's know-all friend, the one from Sussex University. *Janus, God of doors and openings.*

And suddenly Nelson realises something else. It is as if he is seeing a film rewound and, in the second viewing, recognising something that was there all the time. He sees Ruth walking towards him, her loose shirt blown flat against her body. She hasn't lost weight. In fact, she may even have put some on.

Could Ruth possibly be pregnant? Because, if so, he could be the father.

CHAPTER 3

'What do you mean you're pregnant? You're not even married.'

This is one of the times when Ruth just wants to lift up her head and howl. She has made her disclosure on a Sunday afternoon walk in Castle Wood, hoping that the open-air setting might dissuade her mother from having hysterics. Fat chance.

'You don't need to be married to have a baby,' she says.

Her mother draws herself up to her full height. Like Ruth she is a big woman but majestic rather than fat. She looks like Queen Victoria in M&S slacks.

'I am aware of that, Ruth. What I mean, as you know very well, is that God has ordained marriage for the purpose of having children.'

Well, she might have guessed that God would come into it somewhere. Ruth's parents are both Born Again Christians who believe that unless Ruth too is Born Again, she faces a one-way trip to eternal damnation. A location that, at present, seems preferable to Eltham.

'Well I'm not married,' says Ruth steadily. But the father

is, she adds silently. She knows this piece of information will not help matters at all.

'Who's the father?' asks her father, rather hoarsely. Ruth looks at him sadly. She usually finds her dad a bit easier than her mother but he seems about to work himself up into Victorian father frenzy.

'I'd rather not say.'

'You'd rather not say!' Ruth's mother collapses onto a tree stump. 'Oh, Ruth, how could you?' She starts to sob, noisily, into a tiny lace handkerchief. Other Sunday walkers look at her curiously as they tramp past. Ruth kneels beside her mother feeling, despite herself, extremely guilty.

'Mum, look, I'm sorry if this has upset you but please try to look at the positive side. You'll be getting a grandchild. I'll be having a baby. Isn't that something to be happy about?'

'Happy about having a bastard grandchild,' rumbles her father. 'Are you out of your mind?'

Obviously, thinks Ruth. She must have been out of her mind to assume, for one second, that her parents would be happy at the news. That they would rejoice with her. That they would accept that, while their daughter doesn't have a partner, she does have a baby and that the baby is, if not planned, desperately wanted. How desperately, Ruth does not like to admit even to herself. All she knows is, the moment when her suspicions crystallised into that thin blue line on her pregnancy kit, her heart went into overdrive. It was as if every heartbreak and disappointment in her life, to say nothing of the traumas of the past few months, had faded into nothingness, leaving only a boundless blue contentment.

'I hope you'll change your minds,' is all she says. She stands and helps her mother up from the tree stump.

'We never change our minds about anything,' says her mother proudly. 'That's not the sort of people we are.'

You can say that again, thinks Ruth. Being Born Again has only increased her parents' already well-developed sense of infallibility. After all, if God has chosen you, how can you ever be wrong again? About anything. Her parents found God when she was a teenager. Far too late for Ruth, although she had, for a time, accompanied them to services. She has never found God but, then again, she isn't about to go looking.

Her father gestures dramatically towards Severndroog Castle in the background.

'Our values don't change. They haven't changed since that castle was built in the Middle Ages.'

Ruth does not add that the castle is, in fact, an eighteenth-century folly or that the Middle Ages were presumably rife with illegitimate babies and unmarried mothers. She only says, 'Well I hope you'll feel differently when the baby's born.'

Neither of her parents answers but, when they cross Avery Hill Road, Ruth's father takes her arm in a protective way, as if being pregnant has seriously impaired her traffic sense. This Ruth finds obscurely comforting.

Sunday afternoon in a King's Lynn suburb. Cars are being washed, fresh-faced families set out on bike rides, dogs are walked, newspapers are read and the smell of Sunday lunch permeates the air. After his own lunch (roast lamb with vegetarian option for Laura) Nelson announces his intention of mowing the lawn. Michelle says she'll go to the gym (she's the only woman in the world who wants to go to the gym on a Sunday afternoon) and Laura says she'll go too, for a swim. That leaves Nelson and sixteen-year-old Rebecca, who immediately disappears upstairs to plug herself into her iPod and computer. This suits Nelson fine. He wants to be by himself, performing some mundane domestic task. It's the way he thinks best.

By the time he has got out the lawnmower, found that it has run out of petrol, fetched the spare can from the boot of his Mercedes, dropped the garage door on his foot, fixed the broken clutch cable and moved Michelle's washing line, he's thinking furiously. Is Ruth pregnant? Is it his baby? They spent one night together, back in February, but, at the same time, he knew Ruth was seeing her ex-boyfriend, Peter. It's possible then that the baby is Peter's. And what about Erik, Ruth's old tutor? He always thought Ruth was very close to Erik. Could they have been sleeping together? It's a funny thing but he thinks of Ruth as somehow existing on a higher plane than most people. The night they slept together had seemed removed from the ordinary motivations of lust and desire, though those had played their part. He and Ruth had come together as equals who had just been through a terrible experience together. It had just seemed ... right. The sex, Nelson remembers, had been incredible.

Somehow, remembering that sense of rightness, Nelson feels convinced that Ruth did conceive that night. It seems almost preordained. Jesus – he gives the mower a vicious shove – he's thinking like some crap women's magazine. It's highly unlikely that she got pregnant; she was probably using birth control (which was never mentioned; they didn't talk much). He's not even sure that she is pregnant. She has probably just put on weight.

'Dad!'

Rebecca is leaning out of an upstairs window. With her long blonde hair and serious face she looks oddly accusatory, like a Victorian picture of a wronged woman. For one stupid moment Nelson imagines that his daughter knows all about Ruth, is about to tell Michelle . . .

'Dad. It's Doug on the phone. He says do you want to go to the pub tonight.'

Nelson pauses, breathing hard. The smell of mown grass is almost overpowering.

'Thanks, love. Tell him no, I'd rather spend the night in with my family.'

Rebecca shrugs. 'Suit yourself. But I think Mum's going out to the pictures.'

That evening, as Nelson and his daughters sit in front of an old James Bond film (Michelle has indeed gone to the cinema with a girlfriend), Ruth is mindlessly watching the same movie in her parents' sitting room. She loathes James Bond, thinks he's sexist, racist and almost unbearably boring but her parents seem to be enjoying the film (although was there ever anyone less Born Again than James Bond?) and the last thing she wants to do is argue with them. The arguments about her baby have continued, wearily, all afternoon. How could she? Who's going to look after it when she goes to work? Hasn't she heard that families need fathers? What's the poor little mite going to do without a father, without a family, without God? 'You'll be its family,' Ruth said, 'and you can tell it about God.' Although, she adds silently, I shall tell it my own version. That God is a made-up fairy tale, like *Snow White* only nastier.

Now, mercifully, her parents are silent, happily watching James Bond beat up a scantily dressed woman. When Ruth's phone rings, they both look at her accusingly.

Ruth walks out into the hall to answer it. 'Phil' says the message on the screen. Her boss. Head of the Archaeology Department at the University of North Norfolk.

'Hallo, Phil.'

'Hi, Ruth. Not interrupting anything am I?'

'I'm visiting my parents.'

'Oh . . . good. Just that something's come up on one of the field sites.'

The university employs field archaeologists to work on sites that are being developed, usually for building. The field archaeologists nominally report to Phil and are the bane of his life.

'Which one?'

'Woolmarket Street, I think.'

'What have they found?'

Though, of course, she already knows the answer.

'Human remains.'

4th June
Festival for Hercules Custos

Working all day today, translating Catullus. She distracted me, which is Wrong. I heard the voices again last night. I used to think that I was going mad but now I know that I have been Chosen. It's a great responsibility.

It is not only the Lady who talks in my mind but the whole army of saints who once occupied this place. The martyrs who died for the Faith. They speak to me too. This is my body. This is my blood.

Death must be avenged by another death, blood by blood. I understand that now. She will never understand because she is a woman and women are Weak. Everyone knows that. She is too attached to the child. A mistake.

I sacrificed again last night and the result was the same. Wait. But she grows bigger. She is walking and soon she will be talking. I'm not a cruel person. The Gods know I would never willingly hurt anyone. But the family comes first. What must be done, must be done. Fortes fortuna iuvat.

CHAPTER 4

It is afternoon by the time that Ruth reaches the site on Woolmarket Street. She has no lectures on a Monday so took the opportunity to have a lie-in at her parents' house (she is still being sick in the mornings – and evenings too, for that matter). Her mother made her porridge because that is meant to be good for morning sickness. Ruth could only manage a few spoonfuls but was dimly aware that her mother was trying to be kind. No other mention was made of the bastard grandchild.

Woolmarket Street is one of the oldest in Norwich, one of a maze of narrow, medieval alleyways interspersed by new, hideous office blocks. As Ruth drives carefully through the one-way system, city map open beside her, she sees part of the old city wall, a lump of flint and stone, looking as if it has grown there rather than being built. Opposite this land-mark is a massive Victorian house, set back from the road behind iron gates. A sign on one of the gates declares that Spens and Co are building seventy-five luxury apartments on this site.

From the gates, the house still looks impressive. A tree-lined drive, sweeping and gracious, leads up to a looming red-brick façade. Through the trees Ruth can see curved windows, archways, turrets and other displays of Victorian Gothic grandeur. But as she gets closer she realises that this is only a shell. Diggers and skips have taken over. The outer walls of the house still stand but inside men in hard hats scurry busily along planks and hastily constructed walkways, trundling wheelbarrows along what were once corridors, drawing rooms, kitchens and pantries.

Ruth parks at the front of the house. On what would once have been the front lawn there is now a prefabricated hut and a portaloo. Mounds of sand and cement cover the grass and the air is full of noise, the clang of metal against metal and the relentless grind of machinery.

Grabbing her site gear, she gets out of the car. A red-faced man comes out of the hut.

'Can I help you?'

'Dr Ruth Galloway,' says Ruth, holding out her hand. 'I'm from the university. I'm here to see the archaeologists.'

The man grunts, as if his worst suspicions have been con-firmed. 'How are my boys ever going to get any work done with archaeologists cluttering up the place?'

Ruth ignores this. 'I believe the lead archaeologist is Ted Cross?'

The man nods. 'Irish Ted. I'll get someone to fetch him.' He hands her a hard hat saying, 'You'll need to wear this' and disappears back into his hut. Ruth knows Irish Ted slightly from previous digs. He is a heavily built man in his late forties, bald and heavily tattooed. There is, to the outer eye at least, nothing Irish about him.

Ted greets her with a grin, showing two gold teeth. 'Come to see our skeleton have you?'

'Yes. Phil rang me.'

Ted spits, presumably at the mention of the head of department. 'This way,' is all he says.

He leads the way towards the main entrance of the house. Standing on its own, impressive and slightly surreal, is a massive stone archway. As they pass underneath Ruth sees that an inscription has been carved into the stone: *Omnia Mutantur, Nihil Interit*. Ruth is a comprehensive-school girl: she has never studied Latin. 'Omnia' means all or everything, doesn't it? 'Mutantur' sounds like 'mutated' so maybe it means transformed or changed. What about the rest of it? 'Nihil' has a nasty, final sort of sound, like 'nihilism'.

Behind the archway, wide steps lead up to an impressive portico: columns, pediment, the lot. Ruth walks through the stone porch (the door has been taken down) and finds, on the other side of the wall, utter desolation. The interior of the house has vanished, leaving only rubble and churned-up stone. The occasional staircase and doorframe still stand, looking unreal, like stage scenery. Here and there, Ruth can see patches of wallpaper on half-demolished walls and stray pieces of furniture, washed up like flotsam and jetsam: a filing cabinet, a ceramic bath, a fridge door still sporting its jaunty magnets, 'You don't have to be mad to work here', 'There's no I in Teamwork'.

'Building work's well advanced,' she says.

'Yeah,' Ted smiles sardonically, 'Edward Spens is in a hurry. He doesn't like archaeologists slowing things down.'

'The arch is very grand.'

'It's staying apparently. Going to be a feature in the new building. Spens reckons it gives the place class.'

'Any idea what the inscription means?'

'Are you kidding? I went to school in Bolton. Watch your step here.'

Behind the doorway the ground drops away sharply. All that remains of what must have been the entrance hall is a narrow ledge, still paved with black and white tiles, chipped and discoloured. In front and directly underneath the doorstep is a trench. Ruth recognises archaeologists' handiwork at once. The sides are perfectly straight and a red-and-white measuring pole marks the depth. A young woman in a hard hat is standing in the trench, looking up at them.

'This is Trace,' says Ted, 'one of the field archaeologists.'

Ruth knows Trace by sight. She's a familiar figure on summer digs and she also works at the museum. She is just the sort of woman who makes Ruth feel inadequate – whippet-thin, wearing a sleeveless jerkin, her muscles standing out like whipcord. The hair protruding from the hat is dark purple.

'Where are the bones?' asks Ruth.

Trace points to the far end of the earth wall.

'Right under the main doorway,' says Ted, reading her thoughts.

She sees it at once – the grave cut. Below the stone doorstep (still in place) and a thin layer of cement, the earth has been churned up. Normally you would expect to see a layer of brick followed by foundation rubble, but here sand, stones and earth are mixed together like builder's soup. These layers have been disturbed, not that long ago, and the line cutting through them is called – Ruth realises for the first time how ominous the name is – the grave cut. And, sure enough, below the disarranged earth lie the bones.

Ruth kneels down. They are human, she sees that at once. 'Have you called the police?' she asks. 'The coroner?'

'No,' says Trace, rather sullenly. 'We thought we'd wait for you.'

'What do you think?' asks Ted, leaning over her shoulder.

'They're human, they look like a child's. Hard to tell the age.' Recently unearthed bones are fairly easy to date but after that, as Ruth knows to her cost, analysis is a difficult business. Though the grave cut is recent, the bones could be anything from fifty to several hundred (maybe even thousand) years old. She is looking at a cross-section, the bones suspended in the side of the trench. They appear to be crouched in a foetal position. She looks at Ted. 'No skull,' she says.

'No,' he says chattily, 'we noticed that.'

All of a sudden, Ruth knows she is going to be sick again. She lurches away from Ted and retches violently in the corner of the trench. Trace looks at her with horror.

Ted, though, seems undisturbed. 'Are you all right?' he asks. 'Would you like some water?'

'Yes please.' Ruth's head is pounding and she knows that she is shaking. Why did this have to happen here? It will be all over the department by tomorrow. She crouches down, trying to control her breathing.

'Here.' Ted has returned with a battered-looking water bottle. Ruth takes a cautious sip and feels her insides settle slightly. She must stay calm. Breathe.

'I'm sorry,' she says, 'must have been something I ate.'

'Motorway food,' says Ted sympathetically.

'Yes,' says Ruth, straightening up. 'We'd better call the police.'

'Shall I dial 999?' asks Trace, sounding animated for the first time.

'I've got a number,' says Ruth, getting out her mobile phone and dialling.

'Ruth!' says a surprised voice, 'why are you calling?'

'We've found some bones, Nelson,' says Ruth. 'I think you'd better come.'

By the time Nelson arrives the builders have gone home, leaving only the very irritated foreman. 'Edward Spens wants this site clear by the end of the week,' he keeps saying.

'I'm sure he wouldn't want to get in the way of a police inquiry,' says Ruth tartly. The foreman looks as if he isn't so sure about this.

Ruth hears Nelson's Mercedes screeching around the curved driveway. She is not sure how she feels about Nelson. She likes him, more than likes him, but she knows that as her pregnancy becomes more obvious things are going to get very difficult between them. Still there is no reason for Nelson to suspect for a few weeks yet. Lucky she has always worn baggy clothes.

Then Nelson himself appears, framed briefly in the doorway. At his shoulder is a policeman called Clough, whom Ruth knows by sight. Nelson speaks briefly to Clough and then strides along the narrow walkway, jumping lightly into the trench. This is Ruth's main memory of him; always hurrying, always eager to get on to the next thing. But she knows that he can be patient when it comes to an enquiry. Almost as patient as an archaeologist.

'Who's in charge?' is his first question.

'Me', Ruth wants to say, but the foreman bustles forward.

'Derek Andrews,' he says, 'foreman.'

Nelson grunts and looks past him, to where Ruth is standing.

'Where are the bones?'

'Here,' says Ruth. During the wait she, Ted and Trace have exposed more of the bones and she has photographed them, using the measuring pole as a scale. The skeleton is now protruding like a macabre mosaic. Nelson squats down and touches a bone gently with the tip of one finger.

'Are you sure they're human?' he asks.

'Pretty sure,' says Ruth. 'There may be animal bones mixed in there but I think I can see tibia and fibula.'

'Are you going to take them out?'

'I want to expose the whole skeleton first,' she says. 'Remember what I said on the Roman site, about context?'

Nelson straightens up. 'How do we know these bones aren't Roman?' he says. 'Or bloody Stone Age, like the other ones.'

'Iron Age,' says Ruth, through gritted teeth. 'We don't know for sure,' she continues coolly, 'but the grave looks fairly recent. See the lines cutting through the strata? I guess the body was buried when the walls were built.'

'When was that?' asks Nelson.

'Well, the house looks Victorian. About a hundred and fifty years ago maybe.'

'You call that recent?'

'What was on this site before?' asks Clough.

'Children's home,' says Nelson briefly. 'Run by the Sisters of the Sacred Heart.'

Clough gives a sharp intake of breath.

'What?' Nelson asks irritably.

'Well, it was run by nuns, wasn't it?' says Clough. 'And you know what they're like. This could be some poor kiddie they killed.'

'No I don't know what they're like,' says Nelson, his face darkening, 'and you, Sergeant, would do well not to jump to conclusions.'

'We think there was a medieval churchyard on this site,' cuts in Ted. 'That's why we're excavating here. County archaeologist insisted we do a dig before the new build goes up.'

'Edward Spens was furious,' says Derek Andrews, 'says you're costing him thousands of pounds a day.'

'Well, we're not being paid thousands,' says Trace sulkily. 'Every brickie on site gets paid more than we do.'

Nelson ignores this, turning to Ruth. 'Could the bones be medieval?'

'It's possible,' says Ruth, 'but the context looks modern. Of course, they could be medieval bones that have been buried relatively recently. But I think it's unlikely. The skeleton looks intact, as if it was buried fairly soon after death.'

'Well,' says Nelson decisively, brushing soil off his trousers, 'we need to close the site until you've finished your investigations.' He raises his hand. 'And I don't want to hear what bloody Edward Spens thinks. This is a police matter now. You did well to call me, Ruth, and not the local boys.'

Nelson, Ruth knows, is in charge of something called the Serious Crimes Unit and resents any interference from 'uniforms'. She is ashamed of how pleased she feels at the praise. Nelson turns to her now, ignoring Trace who obviously hates being outranked like this.

'How long will you need, Ruth?'

'A few days, at least. We'll have to see if there are any more. Also, the head is missing.'

'The head?'

'Yes, it looks as though the skeleton is missing its skull. It could be buried somewhere else on site.'

'Is it a child?' asks Nelson. 'The skeleton?'

'I think so. We'll be able to tell more when we examine the bones. Children's bones have growing ends on them, called epiphyses. As they get older, these fuse with the main part of the bone. Of course,' she adds, seeing Nelson looking glassy-eyed, 'examining the skull is the best way of determining age.'

'You mean because of the teeth?'

'Yes and the growth patterns.'

'Will you be able to tell its sex?'

'It's very difficult if the skeleton is pre-pubescent. Though there was a case recently in Sussex where archaeologists were able to sex foetal skeletons using DNA analysis. Of course, if it's older, the skull should give us a clue.'

'Why?'

'The brow-ridge is more pronounced in post-pubescent males.'

Nelson smiles faintly. 'You mean we're all Neanderthals?'

'Neanderthal man died out,' says Ruth, 'but, yes, something like that.'

'OK.' Nelson turns to Clough. 'We'll need to get the scene-of-crime boys down here.'

Over the last few minutes, Derek Andrews has been looking ready to explode. 'What shall I tell Mr Spens?' he says at last.

'Tell him this is a suspected murder enquiry,' says Nelson, climbing out of the trench. Andrews mutters something incomprehensible.

Ruth follows Nelson along the raised path. She is still feeling sick and slightly dizzy. The black and white tiles merge unpleasantly before her eyes. She stops, breathing hard. Nelson looks at her sharply, 'Are you all right?'

'Yes,' she says lightly, forcing herself to straighten up. 'Why wouldn't I be?'

'You tell me.'

There is a slightly awkward pause. Ruth sees Clough looking at them curiously.

'I'm fine, Nelson,' says Ruth. 'This is my job, remember.'

Nelson looks at her for another long minute, frowning. 'Rather you than me,' he says at last and heads off back to his car without saying goodbye.

CHAPTER 5

Ruth drives slowly back along the Norwich ring road. She has stopped feeling sick and now feels ravenously hungry, a common pattern over the last few weeks. She stops at a garage and buys a baguette and some mineral water. Plain carbohydrate is what she needs. That and water. She drives along stuffing pieces of bread into her mouth. She's going to put on several stone with this baby, she can see it now. This has been one of the very best things about being pregnant though; not worrying about her weight. Ruth has been overweight since school. How many years of her life has she spent dieting, worrying about her body-mass index and trying to stand on the scales in a way that makes her four pounds lighter? She has been to WeightWatchers and Slimming World and has had several bloated weeks on the cabbage soup diet. In the last few years she has stopped dieting, which has had no effect on her weight but has made her feel, if not happier, at least resigned. She is never going to be one of those women who boasts that they can eat what they like and not get fat ('it's just my metabolism; I'd give anything to have curves'). She's never going to look good in a bikini or vest top. But, by and large, she doesn't care. She wears anonymous, baggy clothes and only looks in the mirror to check that she hasn't got spinach in her teeth. But now, hallelujah, she has an excuse for being fat. She can drink a non-diet Coke without having a chorus of invisible voices berating her: 'Did you see the size of her? Shouldn't she be drinking the diet version?'

Has Nelson noticed anything? She doesn't think so. He was fairly abrupt but that is what Nelson is like when he is on an investigation. And he had deferred to her, asked her how long the excavations would take, much to the annoyance of Trace and the foreman. She wishes she hadn't been sick though. Irish Ted had been nice but she doesn't trust Trace not to tell all her field archaeology friends. Had it been the car journey and the exertion of clambering over the site? Or had it been the skeleton, the foetal position, the thought of the head separated from the body? She remembers Max's talk of head rituals in Celtic mythology. Celts were head hunters. Celtic warriors would cut off their opponents' heads in battle and hang them from their horses' necks. After battle, the heads would be displayed at the entrance to the temple. The severed head is a recurring theme in Celtic art.

Is the building-site body Celtic or Roman? Is it medieval, a relic from the long vanished churchyard? Maybe, but Ruth is still convinced that it was buried fairly recently, in the last couple of hundred years. The disturbance of the earth under the door suggests that it was buried when the door was put in place. How old was the children's home? She will have to ask Nelson to look at the title deeds and planning history.

She is passing the Swaffham road and, on impulse, makes a sharp turn, earning her a furious hoot from the car behind. She will stop off at the Roman dig, have a word with Max. If nothing else it will be good to be out in the open air after a day spent in the car. The earlier rain has stopped; the air will be sharp and pure at the top of the hill.

To her surprise she finds a coach parked awkwardly at the foot of the grass bank. The driver is still inside, eating a sandwich and reading the *Sun*. As Ruth parks her Renault beside the bus, she notices a group of elderly people approaching. They are dressed in tweeds and waterproofs and some are carrying guidebooks. The slope is steep and some of them are leaning on sticks and breathing heavily, while others sprint along like teenagers. Ruth spots Max bringing up the rear, offering his arm to a large grey-haired woman. Some of the elderly people smile and wave at Ruth and she waves back, although she has no idea who they are. They seem friendly anyway. When everyone is inside the bus, the driver puts down his paper and the wheels churn slowly in the mud. Max waves heartily until they are out of sight.

'Hi!'

Max jumps. 'Ruth. I didn't see you there.'

'Who were the visitors?'

He grimaces. 'The Conservative Association.' Ruth starts to regret waving. 'We've had quite a few groups now. It was the Scouts earlier.'

'Jesus. Two paramilitary organisations in one day.'

Max grins. It's the oldies who scare me most. Did you see that woman walking with me? Looked just like the Emperor Vespasian.'

Ruth laughs. 'I just came to have a look round but if you've had enough for today . . .'

'No, no.' Ruth is flattered by Max's eager denial. 'I'd love to show you round. We found something interesting today actually.'

They climb the hill, Ruth trying to disguise how out of breath she is. Jesus, at this rate she'll be immobile at nine months. The trouble was, she wasn't terribly fit before.

At the top of the hill, Max bounds off towards the furthest trench. Ruth follows more slowly. She can see that, even before his students arrive, Max has been busy. There are now three trenches radiating outwards like spokes on a wheel. The furthest trench is the deepest, and as she gets closer she can see the layers, topsoil then the telltale layer of chalk which indicates that once, thousands of years ago, this whole area was under water. Cut into the chalk line she sees a wall, the mix of flint and mortar with a thin line of bricks distinctly Roman. And, below the bricks, a silver-grey orb, faintly translucent in the evening light.

'A skull?'

'Yes. Can't see any more just yet.'

'Do you think it could be a foundation sacrifice?'

'Yes I do.' Max gestures towards the bricks. 'I think this may have been the corner of a room, which could be significant. Remember the bodies at Springfield? They were buried in all four corners of the temple.'

'Is this a temple then?' Ruth looks round at the trench, with its neat earth walls open to the sky; her archaeologist's eye seeing instead a stone temple with statues, altar and incense burning.

'Again, it's possible. We've found some pottery. They could be amphorae. But it could also be a private house.'

Ruth knows that all Roman houses would have had shrines to the domestic gods. The head of the house – the paterfamilias – would have been, to all intents and purposes, the high priest of his own household religion. And at the hearth, the symbolic centre of the home, there would have been a fire sacred to the goddess of fire. What was she called?

'Vesta,' supplies Max. 'Just think of the matches. Her Greek name was Hestia. The women of the house would be responsible for making sure the fire didn't go out and for making offerings to her.'

'Haven't there been instances of bodies being found buried inside Roman houses?' asks Ruth.

'In early Roman times it was quite usual for a dead family member to be buried inside the house,' says Max. 'We often find the letters DM by these tombs. *Dii Manes* – the spirits of the dead or The Good.'

Ruth shivers, thinking of the little body buried under the door in Woolmarket Street. *The Good*. Children are good, by anybody's reckoning, and innocent. But this does not seem to stop people from doing dreadful things to them.

'Children's bodies have been found too, haven't they?' she says.

'Yes. In Cambridge in the seventies twelve newborn babies were found buried under a Roman building. We don't know if they had died naturally, maybe even stillborn, or if they were sacrifices.'

'The field team have found a body on a building site in Norwich,' says Ruth slowly. 'I think it's headless.'

Max looks at her with interest. 'Modern?'

'I don't know. We haven't done carbon dating yet. But the grave cut looks fairly recent.'

'The bones could still be old though.'

'Yes,' agrees Ruth. 'But the skeleton looks intact. I think it was buried when the doorway was built.'

'When was that?'

'Well, the house is Victorian but the entrance and portico could be later, I suppose. It used to be a children's home.'

Thinking of the children's home reminds her of something else. She gets her notebook out of her pocket. 'Do you know what this means?' she asks. 'It was an inscription found at the site.'

Max looks down at the words and, for a second, his face seems to darken. Ruth wonders if she has offended him. 'I couldn't understand it myself,' she says, rather nervously. 'I didn't go to the right kind of school.'

'*Omnia Mutantur, Nihil Interit*,' says Max slowly, 'It means: everything changes, nothing perishes.'

'Oh ... thanks. Did you learn Latin at school then?' He has a rather public-school look to him, Ruth thinks. Maybe it's the curly hair. Or the Range Rover.

Max smiles, his laid-back charming self again. 'No, but I've learnt a good deal of Latin over the years. The Romans are my speciality after all.'

'Everything changes, nothing perishes,' repeats Ruth. 'What sort of a motto is that?'

'The perfect motto for an archaeologist,' says Max, clambering out of the trench.

*

Nelson drives back to the police station, trying to ignore Clough who is noisily eating a packet of crisps. When out on a case Clough eats almost constantly: crisps, sweets, innumerable takeaways. It's a wonder he's not the size of a house, thinks Nelson sourly. In fact, Clough has less of a gut than he has. There's no justice.

'Do you think it's a murder?' asks Clough, crunching away. The smell of cheese and onion is making Nelson feel sick. Perhaps I've got morning sickness, he thinks. He suffered psychosomatic pains with both Michelle's pregnancies. But Ruth may not be pregnant and, even if she is, the child might not be his.

'I've got no idea,' he says shortly. 'And you had no business speculating.'

'Come on, boss, you know what those nuns and priests are like. I read a book once, set in Ireland, and the things they did to those poor kids.'

Nelson is silent, thinking of his own schooling in Catholic establishments. The brothers had been strict, he remembers, strict but fair. And he'd been no angel at school, probably deserved everything he got. He remembers the parish priest, Father Damian, a slight, insignificant man, worshipped by Nelson's mother who was forever ascribing dogmatic opinions to him. 'Father Damian thinks, Father Damian says . . .' He couldn't remember Father Damian himself ever offering an opinion about anything, except about the horses. He'd been a betting man he remembers.

'Lots of those books are bollocks,' he says, taking a corner too fast. 'Authors make everything up just to make money.'

'Nuns are creepy, though,' says Clough, unabashed. 'Those

black robes, those headdresses. Spooky.'

'My aunt's a nun,' says Nelson, to shut him up. In fact, Sister Margaret Mary of the Precious Blood is his great-aunt, his grandmother's sister. He hasn't seen her for years.

'You're joking! You a Catholic then?'

'Yes,' says Nelson, though he hasn't been to church since Rebecca's first holy communion, eight years ago.

'Bloody hell, boss. I wouldn't have had you down as religious.'

'I'm not,' says Nelson. 'You don't have to be religious to be a Catholic.'

CHAPTER 6

Ruth and Max are in the bar of the Phoenix. Ruth is ragingly hungry once again. She has torn open a packet of crisps (plain) and is having to force herself even to put up a pretence of sharing them with Max.

'No thanks.' Max waves the crisps away and takes a gulp of beer. In celebration, Ruth puts four into her mouth.

'I'd like you to have another look at the bones when we've excavated them,' says Max. 'Is that possible?'

'Of course,' says Ruth, blushing and crunching.

'After all, that's your area of expertise isn't it?'

Ruth agrees that it is, trying to sound like an expert and less like a contestant in a crisp-eating challenge.

'I'd like to know how and why the body was decapitated,' says Max. 'Whether it was before or after death.'

'Do you think it could be evidence of a head cult?' asks Ruth.

'It's possible. Head cults are more Celtic than Roman but there have been Roman examples. Of course, heads were often preserved as holy relics in medieval times. Think of St Hugh of Lincoln. They cut off his head so it could perform miracles on its own. St Fremund too. There's a legend that he was seen washing his severed head in a well. Of course, afterwards the well had miraculous powers.'

Max's voice is interested, even amused, but Ruth has little time for miracles. Her parents, of course, despise anything to do with relics and shrines, seeing them as sinister papist practices. Ruth thinks of the children's home and of Nelson's defensiveness about the nuns. He was brought up a Catholic, she knows. She thinks of Cathbad, her friend and sometime Druid. He'd love all this.

'They think there was a medieval church on my Norwich site,' she says. 'That's why the field team was there in the first place.'

'You know what Norwich is like,' says Max, still sounding amused. 'There are churches everywhere.'

'A church for every week of the year . . .'

'And a pub for every day,' concludes Max. They both laugh. For some reason Ruth feels relieved, as if they have somehow moved away from dangerous ground. Max's eyes meet hers and she feels herself blushing. Then the moment is ruined as her stomach gives a thunderous rumble.

'Would you like something to eat?' says Max. 'The food here's pretty good.'

Ruth assents eagerly.

It is pitch black by the time she gets back to the Saltmarsh. She drives slowly; the road has ditches on either side and one false turn of the wheel could send her plunging into the darkness. Nothingness. The flat marsh land has disappeared into the night, her headlights the only light for miles.

Has the rest of the world ceased to exist? It feels like that sometimes. She drives on in her circle of light, Radio 4 muttering soothingly in her ear.

Her cottage is dark but, as she starts down the path, her untidy garden is suddenly flooded with harsh, white light. Nelson insisted on fitting this security light after the Lucy Downey case. Ruth hates it. She is always being woken up because a fox has wandered across her garden and is caught in the spotlight. She doesn't mind the dark but the light can be terrifying.

Thank goodness Flint comes hurrying to meet her, purring loudly. Since the death of her other cat, Sparky, Ruth becomes morbidly worried if she doesn't see Flint as soon as she comes home. What will he do when he has to share my attention with a baby, thinks Ruth, spooning out cat food. But the idea of a baby in the cottage is still unimaginable. Intellectually, she knows she is pregnant and that in six months or so she will have a baby. But she keeps catching herself wondering where she will go on holiday next year and if she might be able to take a sabbatical and go digging in the Virgin Islands. I'll have a baby by then, she tells herself, but her imagination just can't cope. Bring pregnant is enough to be going on with; the reality of a baby is, at present, too much for her.

She'd hoped that telling her parents might make it more real but instead their melodramatic response has made the whole thing seem fantastical. Did her father really say, 'I'll kill the scoundrel?' Surely not. Did her mother really weep and say that her worst fears had been realised? Did she really declare that Ruth had been living an immoral life and this was her reward? Language like this belongs in films and not in real life. Being churchgoers her parents are used to talking about death, destruction and the wages of sin. Ruth is used to scientific facts, soberly presented. presently. She is simply not equipped to cope with the vocabulary.

She will have to tell Phil soon. She can't have people guessing at work and she is sure that Trace will tell everyone that she was sick on the site. Phil will be fine, she's sure. He's a new man, always boasting about changing nappies and helping with housework. Of course, now he's having an affair with Ruth's friend Shona, which doesn't do his perfect husband and father image much good. But Ruth is not supposed to know about that. She will tell Phil and sort out her maternity leave. Perhaps then she will start to believe that she is really going to have a baby.

Somehow she is hungry again and she forages in the kitchen for some biscuits. Then she sits at her desk to check her emails, scrolling down through the requests from students for extra time on their assignments, the supposedly amusing jokes sent from a colleague in the chemistry department, the new timetables for next year. Incredible to think that the academic year is almost at an end.

She is just about to delete another email from the chemistry department when she sees the name of the sender.

From: Michael Malone
Date: 19 May 2008 17.30
To: Ruth Galloway
Subject: Imbolc

Michael Malone, also known as Cathbad, sometime Druid, also employed as a lab assistant in the chemistry department. Strange that she had been thinking about Cathbad only that evening, sitting in the pub with Max. But, on second thoughts, maybe not that strange. Cathbad has a habit of appearing just when he is needed. Cathbad would say that this is his sixth sense, his extraordinary sensitivity to the world around him. Ruth prefers to think of it as coincidence. As far as she is concerned, the jury is out on Cathbad's sixth sense.

Light a fire to celebrate Imbolc [reads the email], the Gaelic festival of the coming of spring. Join us on Saltmarsh beach on Friday 23rd May at six o'clock. Light a fire for Brigid, the goddess of holy wells, sacred flames and healing.

Below, in rather less high-flown language, Cathbad has written:

Imbolc is traditionally celebrated on 2nd Feb but the weather's been so bad I thought we'd wait. I don't expect Brigid will mind! Do come, Ruth.

He finishes with a Gaelic verse to which he has kindly added a translation.

Thig an nathair as an toll
La donn Bride,
Ged robh tri traighean dh' an t-sneachd
Air leachd an lair.

The serpent will come from the hole
On the brown Day of Bride,
Though there should be three feet of snow
On the flat surface of the ground.

Ruth looks at this email for a long time. On one hand it is Cathbad doing what he does best, combining Celtic mysticism with an opportunity for binge drinking and dancing round a fire. On the other hand . . . She points her cursor at the words 'goddess of holy wells'. It seems strange, even sinister, that this email should come just after her discussion with Max. Ruth wonders about the term 'holy wells'. Brigid seems distinctly pagan – in what sense were her wells holy? And what's this about 'sacred flames'? Is Brigid another fire goddess? Sacred, holy – it is the language of the Church but she knows that there will be nothing Christian about the celebration on Saltmarsh beach.

On impulse, she types 'St Bridget' into her search engine. Immediately, she comes up with a Wikipedia entry for St Bridget, or Brigid. St Bridget, she reads, is considered one of Ireland's patron saints, along with Patrick and Columba. Her feast day is the first of February.

Imbolc, according to Cathbad, is usually held on the second of February. Does the holy Bridget (a nun, she discovers) have anything to do with the earlier, pagan feast day? She reads on. Bridget founded Kildare monastery, which is sometimes called 'the church of the oak' after the large oak tree which grew outside Bridget's cell. The oak, Ruth knows, is highly important in Norse and Celtic mythology. The word Druid even comes from the Celtic word for oak 'derw'.

Another story concerns 'St Bridget's cross'. Apparently, Bridget made a cross out of reeds and placed it beside a dying man in order to convert him (might have been more useful to have called a doctor, Ruth thinks). Anyway, traditionally, a new cross is made every St Bridget's day and the old one burnt to keep the maker's house safe from fire. Clearly there is a thin line between the pagan Brigid's fire and the saintly Bridget's burning cross.

Max would be interested in this, thinks Ruth. Should she invite him to Cathbad's Imbolc celebration? Max did say that he wanted to see the Saltmarsh. And it is interesting, too, from an archaeological perspective. Ten years ago, Ruth's ex-tutor, Erik, discovered a Bronze-Age wooden henge on Saltmarsh beach. That was where Ruth first met Cathbad. He was one of the Druids fighting to stop the henge's timbers being removed to a museum. The Druids had lost, even though Erik had sympathised with them, and now all that is left of the henge is a slightly blackened circle of sand.

Ruth has Max's email address. She'll send a casual invitation to the Imbolc thing. Cathbad won't mind, she's sure. Druids aren't exactly hung up on numbers and table settings. And he would like the chance of converting another academic to the 'old ways'. Thinking of Max's face as he described St Hugh and St Fremund, Ruth thinks that he may well be a closet Christian. Well, that won't deter Cathbad. He is open to any form of ritual, though he does tend to alienate the more devout by referring to Jesus as 'the great shaman'.

Ruth starts to type when suddenly a light comes on, making her momentarily shield her eyes. After a second she realises that it is the security light. She goes to the window and looks out. The garden is flooded with the glare, each blade of grass sharply defined, white against black. But there is no living creature to be seen.

8th June
Day consecrated for Vesta

The proper thing to do is to sacrifice nine black puppies to Hecate. I worried about this because, owing to my asthma, I don't have even one puppy. And I do like to do the right thing. In the end, I killed a cat. I didn't like doing it because I'm fond of animals. But it was old. A scrawny black cat who used to sleep in the sun outside my window. I think it belongs to some old lady in the alms cottages. Anyway, yesterday when the domus was deserted I crept out and cut its throat. It screamed and scratched and I realised that I should have hit it on the head first. Oh well, tamdiu discendum est, quamdiu vivas. We live and learn. I chased it into the bushes, caught it by its tail and finished the job. Then I hacked off the head. It was hard work but I found an axe in the outhouse which did the job admirably. The axe will be useful later so I hid it in the usual place. There was a hell of a lot of blood. Too much really. I got a bucket of water and cleaned the pathway and I buried the cat beneath the laurel bush. I was exhausted after all that and had to lie down. I just hope Hecate is satisfied.

CHAPTER 7

Nelson is in his car, one of his favourite places, doing one of his favourite things, driving to interrogate a suspect. Of course, Whitcliffe would say that he is 'merely popping down to have a chat' with Father Patrick Hennessey, ex-principal of the Sacred Heart Children's Home. There is, as yet, no crime. Ruth's skeleton has, as yet, no age and no sex. But Nelson has been a policeman long enough to smell wrong-doing. As soon as he looked into that trench ('grave' is how he thinks of it), as soon as he saw the bones, so small and oddly vulnerable curled up in the foetal position, he knew. He knew that he was looking at a murder victim. And, if the bones do turn out to be medieval, or even bloody Iron Age again, he knows that he will still be right. That body, that child, was murdered.

When Nelson is asked what's the worst thing about being a policeman, he sometimes answers 'the smell'. It is partly meant as a rather grim joke but, in fact, it conceals an even grimmer truth. Villains, the feral, rat-like kind, do smell. As a young policeman, Nelson once had to accompany a convicted paedophile from court to prison. Being locked in the back of a van with this scum for a sixty-mile journey was one of the worst experiences of his life. Nelson remembers the man had actually tried to talk to him. Had even, incredible as it seems, wanted to be friendly. 'Don't. fucking. talk. to. me.' Nelson had spat, before they had even reached the outskirts of Manchester. But it is the smell that he remembers most. This man would obviously have had a shower in prison but he absolutely *stank*: a fetid, rotten smell that reeked of unwashed clothes, windowless rooms, of fear and unspeakable obsession. When he got home that night, Nelson had washed and showered three times but sometimes, even today, he can still smell it. The stench of evil.

Places smell too. The downstairs loo where he once found the body of a little girl, murdered by her mother; the garbage-strewn backstreet where he saw a colleague stabbed to death; the desolate beach where he and Ruth unearthed the body of another dead girl. There may not have been an actual smell but there was something in the air, heaviness, a sense of secrecy and of things left to fester and rot.

And Nelson had smelt it on that building site. No matter how many years had passed since that little body was buried beneath the floorboards, the smell was still there. It's a murder scene; Nelson is sure of it.

The children's home had closed in 1981; afterwards the building had been used as some sort of council offices. Now Edward Spens is planning to build seventy-five luxury apartments on the site.

'Seventy-five!' Nelson had echoed, when Edward Spens had told him. 'Seventy-five luxury rabbit hutches more like.'

Edward Spens had, of course, been on the phone as soon as Nelson and Clough had got back to the station. He'd been very cordial and full of phrases like 'my duty as a citizen' but had, nevertheless, managed to drop in a few mentions of his very good friend Gerry Whitcliffe and the city's need for new housing, job creation, urban redevelopment la di da di da.

'I appreciate your frustration, sir,' Nelson had said, 'but you must understand that we have a suspected murder enquiry.'

'Murder?' Spens had sounded shocked as Nelson had meant him to be. 'But those bones could be hundreds of years old. That archaeologist chap Ted was telling me that there used to be a medieval churchyard on the site.'

'That's as maybe, sir. I've got Dr Ruth Galloway from the university examining the bones now. I'm hoping that in a few days she'll be able to give me an approximate date.'

'This Ruth Galloway, is she the best person? I know Phil Trent up at the university. He might be able to get us someone more ... senior.'

'Dr Galloway is head of forensic archaeology,' Nelson replied stiffly, 'and an acknowledged expert on bones.' Ruth always claims that this makes her sound like a sniffer dog but, for the present, Spens seemed satisfied.

Spens is losing money, Nelson reflects, not without satisfaction, as he turns off the M25 towards Gatwick. Everyone is talking about the property market caving in. Nelson loathes TV programmes about smug yuppies buying and selling houses but even he has gathered that much. All those smug yuppies will soon be saddled with negative equity and serve them right. His own house is mortgaged up to the hilt, of course, but that doesn't bother him. Nelson was brought up in a council house. For him, a mortgage is a sign of respectability.

But, even so, Spens had better start building quickly or there will be no one left to buy his luxury apartments. Luxury! Nelson snorts as he overtakes a coach loaded with German tourists. Where there was once one, admittedly large, house, now there will be seventy-five soulless shoe-boxes. It's not his definition of luxury. Actually, he's not sure he possesses one.

Father Patrick Hennessey lives in a church-run 'retreat' in West Sussex. He explains on the phone that this is a sort of retirement placing for priests. 'People come here for a week or even just for a few days, to recharge their spiritual batteries. I wander around asking them if they want to talk to a priest and, when they say no, I wander off again.' Nice work if you can get it, thinks Nelson. It is a beautiful May morning, the fields lush and green, the trees heavy with blossom. As he drives past yet another rose-strewn cottage, Nelson reflects how much he prefers this countryside to Norfolk. Everything is contained: a single oak stands in a gated field, flint cottages surround a pond, gentle hills form perfect framing devices for picturesque villages. There is no threatening expanse of sky, none of the windswept des-olation that he so dislikes about his adopted county. Even so, you'd need a ton of money to live here. The villages are heavy on antique shops and low on fast-food outlets. He has to weave his way through a slalom of BMWs, Porsches and shiny Land Rovers. Definitely a cushy retirement billet.

'Can't stand the place,' says Father Patrick Hennessey cheerfully, stomping out over the smooth green lawn to shake Nelson heartily by the hand.

The strength of the handshake does not surprise Nelson. He has met priests like this before; burly, red-faced Irishmen who look more like ex-boxers than clerics. Hennessey is elderly, seventies Nelson reckons, and walks with a stick, but he has a definite physical presence, with shoulders as broad as Nelson's own, a white crew cut and a nose that has clearly been broken several times.

'Why not?' asks Nelson as they walk towards a shady seat overlooking the rose garden. 'Seems a beautiful spot to me.'

'Beautiful,' says Hennessey gloomily, 'yes, I suppose so. But it bores the hell out of me. People talk about seeing God's hand in nature but, in my opinion, when you've seen one tree you've seen them all. Now, when I see a beautiful building and I think of how God has given man the wits to build it, that's worth celebrating. Have you seen the Gherkin in London? Pure poetry.'

'I'm a city boy myself,' says Nelson cautiously, 'but buildings don't make me think about God exactly.'

Hennessey gives him a rather sharp look. His eyes are very light blue in a weather-beaten face. Intelligent eyes, watchful eyes. And, like his handshake, not particularly gentle.

He lowers himself onto the bench and stretches one leg stiffly in front of him. 'So, Detective Chief Inspector Nelson, you said you wanted to talk to me about SHCH.'

Sacred Heart Children's Home, Nelson works out silently. He hates acronyms. Whitcliffe, of course, loves them.

'Yes,' he says brusquely, 'as you may know, the site is being developed. The plan is to build a number of luxury apartments.'

'Dear God.'

'And in the course of the building work a discovery has been made. A body. Skeleton to be precise, buried under the main doorway. It looks to be that of a child.'

Nelson pauses. Silence, as any policemen knows, is the best way to get information.

But Hennessey, it seems, knows the same trick. He fixes Nelson with his cool, light-blue stare. For a few seconds, neither speaks. An elderly couple walk slowly past them and disappear through a rose-smothered archway.

'We're examining the bones now,' says Nelson, admitting defeat. 'It's possible they predate the home, of course.'

'It's an ancient site, I understand,' says Hennessey. 'I had always heard that there was a church there once. I believe it had the reputation of curing lepers.'

A church. That archaeologist bloke had said a churchyard but, of course, it stands to reason that there would be a church there too. Also that, to Hennessey, the church would be the important factor.

'Our forensic archaeology team,' says Nelson, thinking that this is a rather grand way of describing Ruth, Trace and Irish Ted, 'believe that the grave was dug fairly recently. Maybe when the doorway was put in place.'

'The house was old in my time,' says Father Hennessey mildly, 'but I assume that you suspect the body was placed there within living memory.'

'I assume nothing,' says Nelson. 'Just wondered if, during

your years as principal, you ever had a child go missing. Or anything,' he adds after a pause.

Hennessey gets up. 'Let's walk,' he says. 'I get stiff if I sit too long.'

They walk through the archway and between the raised flower beds. Hennessey lets his hand drift amongst the velvety blossoms. 'Stupid things,' he says. 'Could never see the point of flowers.'

Nelson does the silent trick again and this time is successful. After a few hundred yards, Hennessey says, 'Let's get this straight, Detective Chief Inspector, there was never any abuse at SHCH when I was there. You can ask anyone. I'm still in touch with many of our former residents. They've all got good memories of their time with us. I know the fashion is to look for abuse wherever you see a Catholic priest but, in this instance, you will look in vain.' He stops, frowning at a particularly vivid pink rose which is swarming up a low stone wall. 'Nevertheless . . .'

Now we're getting to it, thinks Nelson, careful to keep his face expressionless.

'Nevertheless . . .' Hennessey sighs. 'Two children did go missing when I was principal. A boy and a girl. There was a huge search but we never found them. I've often wondered . . .' His voice drifts off.

'What were their names?' Nelson gets out his notebook.

'Black. Martin and Elizabeth Black.'

'Ages?'

'Martin was twelve and Elizabeth was five.'

Five. Nelson thinks of the little skeleton crouched under the wall.

'When did they go missing?'

'The early seventies. 1973, I think.'

'Have you any idea why they ran away?'

Hennessey starts to walk again. They leave the rose garden and walk down the hill towards an ornamental lake. People sit on benches by the water but no one is speaking. Perhaps they are all praying, thinks Nelson. He is beginning to find the place rather spooky.

'Martin was a bright boy,' says Hennessey, 'a very bright boy. Their mother had died and Martin became obsessed with finding their father, who'd gone back to Ireland. I think we all assumed that's where the children had gone but, when we tracked the father down, he had no idea where they were. He hardly knew what day it was. He was an alcoholic, in a terrible state, but the police didn't suspect him of any wrongdoing.'

'And they dropped the case?'

'Eventually. I paid a private investigator to go on searching but he came up with nothing. And we prayed, of course.' He smiles, rather sadly.

'Did you ever suspect that they'd been . . . abducted?'

Hennessey looks at him angrily. They are almost exactly the same height. 'I suspected that maybe a stranger . . . But if you're implying that someone in SHCH . . . Never! We all adored the children. Little Elizabeth was . . . she was an angel.'

And Martin wasn't, suspects Nelson. Aloud he says, 'We'll investigate further. Thank you, Father, you've been very helpful.'

As they walk back up to the car park, Hennessey says, 'You said it looks like a child's skeleton – do you know how old the child was?'

'No,' says Nelson, 'the bones are still in the ground so we haven't been able to examine them properly. Also, the head is missing.'

'Missing?'

'Yes. We don't know why that it is.'

'The world is a strange and cruel place, Detective Chief Inspector.'

'It certainly is.'

They have reached Nelson's car and the priest holds out his hand. As they exchange vice-like grips, Hennessey says, 'I believe you're a Catholic, Detective Chief Inspector.'

Nelson drops his hand. 'How did you know?'

Hennessey smiles sweetly. 'You called me Father. Just Father. A non-Catholic would have said Father Hennessey, or even Father Patrick if they wanted to be all happy-clappy about it.'

'I haven't been to church for years,' says Nelson.

'Don't give up on God entirely,' says the priest, still smiling. 'There's always the twitch upon the thread. God bless you, my son.'

When he gets back to the station, Nelson laboriously Googles 'the twitch upon the thread' and comes up with a quotation from G.K. Chesterton: 'I caught him, with an unseen hook and an invisible line which is long enough to let him wander to the ends of the world, and still to bring him back with a twitch upon the thread.'

'Bollocks,' says Nelson, switching off the computer.

CHAPTER 8

On the Woolmarket Street site, amongst the bulldozers, Ruth is digging. She works almost in a trance. The sun is warm on her back and, in the distance, she can hear Ted and Trace talking about last night's football. But as far as Ruth is concerned they could be on another planet. Her whole being is concentrated on the skeleton under the doorway. She has levelled off the area above the bones so that the backbone is visible. The body is crouched down, knees curled up, arms around legs. It is now clear that the head is definitely missing although Ruth will have to examine the bones before she can tell if decapitation was the cause of death.

Now, gingerly, she climbs above the trench and photographs the skeleton from another angle. A measuring pole lies beside the bones. The body, bent round as it is, is less than a metre long. A child's body, thinks Ruth, though she has to be careful. Could be an adult of restricted growth – again the bones will contain the answer.

There will have to be a post-mortem; that's standard for any human remains. Ruth will examine the bones at the same time. She is used to the process but she doesn't like it.

She doesn't like the sterile atmosphere, the casual jokes of the pathologists, the smell of formaldehyde and Dettol. She remembers what Erik used to say: 'The earth is kindly. She shelters us, she protects us, to her we must return.' Ruth is taking these bones out of the kindly earth and she feels guilty. Erik was once the person Ruth looked up to most in the world but the Saltmarsh case forced her to see him, and many other things, in a different light. Now Erik is dead, his ashes burnt on a dark Norwegian lake, and Ruth has a job to do. She brushes the earth away from the exposed ribcage. In an adult the pelvis and ribs will give clues about the body's sex. In a pre-pubescent this is almost impossible to judge. Exposed now in the chalky earth, this skeleton looks heart-breakingly small.

'How are you doing?' It is Irish Ted, peering over the lip of the trench like Mr Punch.

'Not bad. Skeleton's almost exposed. Just got a few more drawings to do.'

'We've found something. Want to see?'

Ruth straightens up. Sometimes she feels faint if she gets up too quickly but today she seems miraculously well. Maybe it's the famous second trimester, where, according to the books, you look 'blooming' and have tremendous energy and a renewed sex drive. Sounds fun, thinks Ruth as she follows Ted through the maze of walls and trenches. Something to look forward to at any rate.

At the back of the house some outhouses still remain, their doors hanging crazily, windows smashed. There is also the remains of a conservatory, a skeletal wood frame that still retains a few unbroken panes. As Ruth passes, a workman is systematically smashing the glass. One window obviously contained stained glass, red and blue and yellow. The shards scatter at Ruth's feet like a rainbow.

She follows Ted past the outhouses and into the grounds. Here the new buildings are going up quickly; neat squares of brick and plasterboard. She steps over a cucumber frame, the glass smashed to powder, and passes a tree with a frayed rope hanging from one of its branches. A swing? Broken flagstones form a rudimentary path through the mud. The noise of the cement mixers is deafening.

As directed by Ruth, Ted has dug new trenches along the boundaries of the site, next to the high flint wall. In one of these, Trace is standing, wearing a pink T-shirt emblazoned with the words 'Killer Barbie'.

Ruth looks into the trench. A tiny skeleton lies exposed about a metre below the topsoil. Only this time it is definitely not human.

'What is it?' shouts Ruth, above the noise of the machinery.

'A cat, I think,' says Ted.

'Pet cemetery?'

'Maybe, though I haven't seen any others.'

They haven't found any human bodies either which, given that this was supposed to be a churchyard, is surprising. Disappointing, the county archaeologist would say. Maybe the site was cleared by the Victorians. It wouldn't be the first archaeological site they had ruined. Ruth looks at the bones protruding from the mud. From the shape of the tail, she is pretty sure that it is feline.

'Family pet?' she suggests, thinking of Flint.

'Yes . . .' Ted looks at her sideways. 'Except . . .'

'What?'

'It's headless.'

'What?'

'There's no head. Trace and I are both sure.'

Ruth looks again at the bones. She can see the vertebrae and the tail wrapped neatly around the feet but . . . no head.

'Log it,' she says. 'I'll take the bones back to the lab.'

'Wonder what we'll find next?' says Ted cheerily. 'The Headless Horseman?'

Ted's good humour, thinks Ruth, as she trudges back to her trench, is starting to get her down.

In the afternoon, Clough puts in an appearance. 'The boss has gone down to Sussex to interview some priest who used to run this place,' he explains.

'Pin it on the pervert priest,' says Ted, taking a swig from his flask, 'good idea.'

Ruth feels rather embarrassed that she and the others have been caught on their tea break but Clough joins them readily enough, accepting a Jammy Dodger from Trace and a mug of coffee from Ruth. They are sitting on a low internal wall, still covered with wallpaper, dark red with a faint black pattern.

'Boss turns out to be a left-footer,' says Clough. 'Did you know that?' he turns to Ruth.

'A left . . .? Oh, a Catholic. No. Why should I?' She doesn't want Clough to think she knows Nelson all that well.

'We've found some other people who worked here. Ordinary people, not priests or nuns. Even tracked down some of the residents. It's going to be a hard job taking all the statements.'

'Won't you get overtime?' asks Ruth drily.

'Oh yes,' Clough grins, 'thank God for overtime. Anyway, you find out any more about the skeleton?'

'No,' says Ruth patiently. 'As I explained yesterday, I need to examine it thoroughly in context before we can take the bones away.'

'How long will that take?'

'I'm hoping to finish tomorrow. I've got to bag and record all the bones and take soil samples.'

'That long? Just for a few bones?'

'There are two hundred and six bones in the human body,' says Ruth tartly, 'and about three hundred in a child's.'

'Oh well.' Clough stands up, brushing crumbs from his chinos (like Nelson, he wears plain clothes – very plain in Nelson's case). 'Better get back to the ranch. No peace for the wicked.'

A cliché, like many of Clough's utterances but as Ruth goes back to work in her trench she finds the phrase reverberating in her mind. No peace for the wicked. Were these bones at peace? Is she now disturbing them? Did something wicked happen here, however many years ago? Did somebody kill this child? And what about the cat?

No peace for the wicked. Cathbad would say that places retain memories of evil. This site is spooky enough, with its half-ruined Gothic walls, its grandiose arch, the staircases and doors leading to nowhere. Cathbad would also say that Ruth should be careful, disturbing the dead, meddling with the past. But that is her job. She is a forensic archaeologist. It is her job to excavate the body and discover clues from the bones, from the burial, from the very texture of the earth. It is all very straightforward and there is nothing to get excited about.

Nevertheless, when the light starts to fade and Ted and Trace pack up their tools, Ruth goes with them. Being sensible is one thing; staying on the site after dark is another.

CHAPTER 9

'So you were resident at the Sacred Heart Children's Home for how long?'

'Three years. I came when I was thirteen. I left when I was sixteen. Father Hennessey got me an apprenticeship. I owe him everything really.'

The speaker, a mild-looking man in his forties, looks at Nelson and smiles. Nelson forces himself to smile back. This is the third ex-resident of the children's home who has offered an unsolicited testimonial to the kindness of Father Hennessey. As Clough put it, half an hour ago, 'perhaps the buggers have been brainwashed.'

While Nelson and Clough are interviewing former residents of the children's home, Detective Constable Judy Johnson, another of Nelson's team, is on her way to interview Sister Immaculata, a nun who used to work at the home and is now in a Southport old people's home. As Nelson hates Southport and Clough hates nuns, it was considered that this visit needed 'a woman's touch'.

'Mr Davies,' Nelson leans forward, 'during your time at

the home was there any ill-treatment of inmates ... sorry, residents.'

'No, never,' Davies answers. Too quickly? wonders Nelson.

'No corporal punishment?' asks Clough. 'Quite common in the seventies.'

'No,' says Davies quietly, 'Father Hennessey believed in kindness.'

'What about the nuns? The sisters. Could they be strict?'

Davies considers. 'They could be strict, yes. No physical violence but some of them had sharp tongues. A few were kind. Sister James. Sister Immaculata. But some of the others ... they were good women but not kindly women, if you know what I mean.'

'So what were the punishments for bad behaviour?' persists Nelson.

Davies smiles. 'Well, for really bad behaviour you got sent to Father Hennessey but that usually turned out to be more of a treat than anything else. He'd get you to help clear out his cupboards or weed the kitchen garden. Some of my happiest memories of SHCH are of working on that garden.'

Nelson sighs and changes tack. 'Did you know two children called Black? Martin and Elizabeth Black.'

Davies frowns. He has an anxious, squashed-looking face at the best of times. Now his face is positively pleated in thought. 'Yes,' he says at last, 'they went missing. It was just after I came to SHCH. Martin was about a year younger than me. He was very clever, I remember.'

'Do you remember anything about their disappearance?'

'Well, there was a big to-do at the time. We used to have a free hour at the end of the day and I remember that I'd actually been talking to Martin. There was a craze for collecting football cards and we were filling in our scrapbooks. Elizabeth was there too, playing with some stuffed animal. A dog, I think it was. She took it everywhere with her. After a while she wandered off and Martin went to find her. That was the last I saw of him. Then one of the sisters rang the bell for bedtime and they were nowhere to be seen.'

'What happened next?'

'Father Hennessey went out to search. Then he must have called the police. I remember being interviewed, being asked when I last saw Martin and Elizabeth. The police were around for a few weeks, asking everyone questions. I remember Sister Immaculata being angry because they interrupted us when we were saying the rosary. Then everything went back to normal. We still prayed for Martin and Elizabeth but we didn't really talk about them. We forgot. You know what kids are like.'

'When the police were at SHCH, do you remember them searching the grounds? Digging?'

'No,' says Davies slowly, 'I don't remember them digging.' He looks up suddenly. 'Is that what all this is about? Have you found a body?'

'I'm not at liberty to say,' says Nelson.

'They're knocking it down, aren't they?' says Davies. 'I walked past the site the other day.'

'They're developing it, yes.'

'It's a shame. It was a lovely house. Like a mansion, I always thought.'

'Yes.' Nelson looks at Clough. 'Mr Davies, would you be prepared to come to the site and look around? You might be able to tell us where things were. Which rooms were which, that sort of thing.'

'Yes,' says Davies, 'I'd be happy to.'

He gets up to leave, shaking hands with both policemen. At the door, Clough asks, 'You say Father Hennessey got you an apprenticeship. What trade was that?'

Kevin Davies smiles, the creases in his face turning upwards. 'Oh, I thought you knew. I'm an undertaker.'

Judy Johnson is pushing a wheelchair along Southport seafront. The tide is out and the sand stretches into the far distance, bands of gold and white and silver, dotted with tiny figures carrying nets and buckets. As she watches, three racehorses canter into view, their necks arching as they fight their bits, the sand flying up behind them. Judy stops for a second and Sister Immaculata turns and says, 'Red Rum was trained here. Did you know that?'

'No.'

'I had a bet on him in 1976. That was the year he came second. Typical.'

'Was it each way?' asks Judy, a bookie's daughter.

'No, on the nose. Typical.'

The horses are galloping now, stretching out joyfully across the sand, manes and tails flying. The jockeys hover over their necks, seemingly balanced in mid-air. Judy had wanted to be a jockey once. Before she got interested in boys.

The old people's home turns out to be a convent that looks after aging nuns. The sister in charge suggested that Judy take Sister Immaculata out 'for a walk'.

'That way she'll get fresh air and you can have some

privacy.' A mixture of kindness and absolute authority that Judy remembers from her own (convent) schooldays.

Judy stops by a bench, puts the brakes on the wheelchair and goes to sit beside the elderly nun. She knows from the police records that Sister Immaculata (real name: Orla McKinley) is seventy-five but the veil covering her hair and her high-necked habit serve to mask the most obvious signs of age. Her face is curiously unlined, the blue eyes still sharp. Only the hand, pointing now at Southport Pier, betrays its owner's age. It's a mummy's hand, skeletal and misshapen.

'Sister Immaculata,' begins Judy, 'you worked at the Sacred Heart Children's Home from 1960 to 1980.'

'It wasn't work, it was a vocation,' says the nun sharply.

'I'm sorry. But you were resident at the home?'

'Yes.'

'What sort of a place was it?'

Sister Immaculata is silent, looking out over the miles of pale sand. But Judy notes that her hands are shaking slightly. Age? Infirmity? Or fear?

'It was a beautiful house. Lovely grounds. The sort of place where you can't imagine bad things happening.'

Judy holds her breath. She mustn't mess this up. The boss expects her to get results. That's why she has been sent instead of Clough, who'd probably have accused the nun of satanic abuse by now and be on his way for an early lunch.

'What sort of bad things?' she asks gently.

The nun looks at her sharply, eyes narrowed.

'Two children vanished. Isn't that bad enough for you?'

'Martin and Elizabeth Black?'

'Yes. They disappeared. Vanished. Into thin air.'

Judy shivers. It sounds a little like a fairy tale and she has always found these particularly terrifying. Two children go into the woods and bang! they are eaten by a wolf or enticed into a gingerbread house or given a poisoned apple by a close female relation. Vanished. Into thin air.

She struggles to make her voice sound businesslike. 'How well did you know Martin and Elizabeth?'

Sister Immaculata seems to have recovered her poise. 'I taught Martin,' she says, 'didn't have much to do with the younger children. That was Sister James, God rest her soul. But I remember Martin. Father Hennessey thought the world of him but he was always trouble, in my opinion.'

'In what way?'

'He was clever. Very interested in history. Gladiators, dinosaurs, that sort of thing. Science too. He was always trying some far-fetched experiment. Father Hennessey encouraged him, even made a laboratory for him in the base-ment. Gave him books to read. But he was the sort of boy who used his intelligence to make trouble. Always asking questions in class. Sacrilegious questions about the Holy Ghost and the Blessed Virgin.' She nods her head in pious reflex.

'What did Father Hennessey think about that?'

'He made excuses for him. The children had a tragic start in life. Their mother died. The only other relative was a drunken father in Ireland. Martin was always talking about his father, making him out to be some sort of hero. That's why, when they disappeared, we thought they might have gone to Ireland.'

'Did it come out of the blue, their disappearance?'

'Well, we thought Martin might have been plotting something. He'd been stealing food for weeks. Father Hennessey knew but he didn't want to confront the boy, not until he knew what was in his mind. I think he regretted that later.'

'What did *you* think?' In Judy's experience, everyone likes to be asked their opinion and it seems nuns are no exception to this rule.

'I thought he needed a good hiding. But Father Hennessey wasn't having any of that. No physical punishment, that was the rule. Not even a clip round the ear for cheekiness. Not like it was when I was at school.' She broods for a minute, lower lip stuck out.

'I told Father Hennessey that Martin Black was trouble but he wouldn't have it. Just said the boy needed love and attention. Love and attention! Look where that got him. He ran off, taking his poor innocent sister with him. Probably got themselves killed.'

'Is that what you think happened?' asks Judy.

Sister Immaculata is silent for a moment and Judy sees now that she has a rosary in her hands. She is twisting the beads between her arthritic fingers. 'Yes, I think that's what happened. The world is a dangerous place for children.'

'What did Father Hennessey think?'

Sister Immaculata looks her full in the face, the blue eyes slightly amused. 'Haven't you worked it out yet, girl? Father Hennessey is a saint. And saints cause a lot of trouble for the rest of us.'

CHAPTER 10

Ruth is excavating the bones. The skeleton has been completely exposed, has been drawn and photographed from all angles. Now, it is Ruth's job to remove the bones themselves so that they can go to the post-mortem. She moves calmly, placing each bone in a labelled bag and then checking it against what she calls her 'skeleton sheet', recording the measurement and appearance of each fragment. Respect and care, that's what she tells her pupils. Human bones, however old, should be treated with all the respect that you would give to a body. Excavation should take place over one day so that no fragments are lost or stolen. Every bone should be saved, recorded and preserved. Ruth has worked on sites, like the war graves in Bosnia, where many skeletons are mixed together. Then, the process of trying to separate and record is an arduous one. But this is just one skeleton, one little body. Ruth handles the bones with tenderness, reverence even.

Irish Ted has already bagged the bones of the cat. She will take them to the lab on her way home. Neither cat nor human skull has been found.

'Good day.' The voice is so close that Ruth jumps. She looks up and sees a good-looking man of about her age, immaculately dressed in a cotton shirt and linen trousers. With him is an older man in a panama hat. Ruth straightens up, shielding her eyes with her hand.

The younger man squats down as if he is about to jump into the trench. Ruth is horrified. Like most archaeologists, she likes to keep her trench immaculate. Standing in someone's trench is like walking uninvited into their house.

'Stop!' she says sharply.

The man looks at her quizzically.

'You can't come into the trench,' says Ruth, struggling to keep her voice polite, 'you'll contaminate it.'

The man straightens up. 'We haven't been introduced,' he says, as if the introduction will make all the difference. 'I'm Edward Spens.'

That figures. The famous Edward Spens no doubt considers that Ruth's trench, like the rest of the site, belongs to him.

'Ruth Galloway.' Ruth forces herself to smile up at him. She feels at a disadvantage being so low down.

'So these are the fateful bones.'

Fateful, thinks Ruth. It's a funny way of describing the find but somehow appropriate. She sees Spens' intelligent eyes fixed on her face. She must be careful not to give too much away.

'This is the skeleton, yes.'

'And have you any idea how old it is?'

'Not yet. We might find some clues in the fill.'

'The fill?'

'The grave,' says Ruth, thinking how emotive the word is. But that is what they have found: a grave, where a body is buried. 'We might find bricks or pottery,' she explains. 'I thought I saw a shard from a bottle. That can be dated. And we'll do radiocarbon dating, though that's less useful when dealing with a modern skeleton.'

'What exactly does radiocarbon dating involve?' Edward Spens smiles down charmingly.

'It tests the amount of carbon in the bones. When we're alive, we take in carbon fourteen. When we die, we stop. By estimating when these bones stopped taking in carbon fourteen, we'll be able to estimate the age of the skeleton.'

'Fascinating. How accurate is it?'

'To about plus or minus five per cent.' Then, relenting slightly, 'Other factors affect the carbon dating but we can be accurate to about a hundred years.'

'A hundred years! That's not very accurate.'

'There are other indicators,' says Ruth, slightly irritated. 'Recent bones still contain blood pigment and amino acids, for example. We'll be able to tell if these remains are medieval or relatively modern.'

The older man, who has been looking around him with every appearance of pleasure, now says, 'You know this used to be a church?'

'My father, Sir Roderick Spens,' introduces Edward. 'He's very interested in history.' He says this in a resigned way, as if ferrying his elderly father to sites of archaeological interest is not his preferred way of passing the time.

Roderick Spens doffs his hat with a flourish. 'Delighted to meet you.'

Ruth smiles. She thinks she prefers Sir Roderick's interest to Edward's barely concealed impatience.

'They say that a church used to stand here,' Roderick Spens explains. 'Probably destroyed during the dissolution of the monasteries, gravestones broken up, stained glass smashed, gold and silver melted down.'

Ruth thinks of the workman smashing the windows in the conservatory and the momentary regret she had felt for those coloured pieces of glass, for the destruction of anything that was once prized. 'We found a chalice yesterday,' she says, 'probably 1400s or thereabouts. Some beautiful work on it.'

Sir Roderick's eyes gleam. 'Now that I'd like to see.'

'It's back at the university,' says Ruth, 'but I'm sure we could arrange—'

'Now, Dad,' says Edward warningly, 'we don't want to bother Miss Galloway.'

'Dr Galloway,' corrects Ruth mildly, 'and it's no bother.'

'Strange to think, Dr Galloway,' the older man leans forward, deliberately, it seems, excluding his son, 'that this church was destroyed by Henry the Eighth yet later became a Catholic children's home.'

'Yes.' Ruth is not particularly interested in the age-old struggle between Catholic and Protestant. To her, all religions are as bad as each other. Though at least Catholicism has nicer pictures.

'Do the police think these bones are linked to the home?' asks Edward.

'As far as I know they're keeping an open mind,' says Ruth. 'Now if you'll excuse me . . .'

She turns back to the bones and, after a second or two, Edward Spens takes his father by the arm and leads him away.

Nelson does not arrive until late afternoon, by which time Ruth has finished cataloguing the bones and is helping Trace in one of the trenches at the back of the house. They have found some Roman pottery and what looks like a signet ring. So this site, like the one on the hills, was also once Roman. Hardly surprising, thinks Ruth, and yet the link disturbs her slightly.

Nelson is accompanied by Clough and a sandy-haired man with a furrowed brow under his hard hat. Clough, Ruth is interested to note, peels off immediately to talk to Trace. Nelson and the other man approach Ruth.

'Dr Ruth Galloway,' Nelson's introductions are always brusque, 'Kevin Davies. Mr Davies was once resident at the Sacred Heart Children's Home.'

'I'm afraid there's not much left of the original building,' says Ruth. And there will soon be less, if Edward Spens has his way.

Davies has a misty, far-away look about him. 'This was the conservatory,' he says, 'and over there we had a swing and a tree house. There was a wishing well too. We used to play football on the lawn. Father Hennessey was a really good player. He could have been a professional.'

Nelson rolls his eyes. The last thing he needs is to be told that Father Hennessey, on top of all his other virtues, was Norfolk's answer to Pelé.

'Do you remember a pet cemetery?' ask Ruth. 'Or anywhere where pets might have been buried.'

Davies looks at her with mild blue eyes. 'No. Sister James was allergic to animals so we couldn't even have a cat. We had a canary though. Lovely cheerful little thing.'

'Why don't you have a look round, Mr Davies,' says Nelson. 'Refresh your memory.'

Davies wanders off and Ruth climbs out of the trench. She sees Nelson looking at her strangely and realises that she must, by now, be both sweaty and mud-stained. Well, there's not much she can do about it. Her back is killing her too.

'If I have to hear once more that Father Hennessey is a saint who walks on water in his spare time, I'm going to go mad,' says Nelson as they walk away from the trench.

'Bit of a fan, is he?' asks Ruth, indicating Davies, who is staring at the ruins of the kitchen garden with a rather shell-shocked look on his face.

'A fan! According to him Father Hennessey is a combination of Mother Teresa, Nelson Mandela and Winnie-the-bloody-Pooh.'

Ruth laughs. 'Have you met him, this Father Hennessey?'

'Yes.'

'What's he like?'

Nelson hesitates. 'Seems a nice enough chap. Big, strong man he must have been when he was young. Strong character too, I think. Razor sharp.'

'So, any suspicious deaths at the children's home?' asks Ruth lightly. To her surprise, Nelson answers soberly, 'Yes.'

'Really?'

'Well, a disappearance. Two children. Martin and Elizabeth Black. Vanished without a trace in 1973.'

'How old?'

'Twelve and five.'

They look at each other, thinking of the little skeleton under the door.

'Do you think it's her?' asks Ruth.

'It's possible, isn't it?'

Ruth thinks of the size of the bones. 'Yes. But that would mean . . .'

'That she was killed by someone at the home? Yes.'

'Do you really think that might have happened?'

'Well, we won't know until you've done your dating but . . . I don't know, Ruth. There's something funny about this place. Something's not right. Something smells funny. And what was all that about a pet cemetery?'

'We found the skeleton of a cat buried by the back wall.'

'Probably just the final resting place of some old moggy.'

'Its head was cut off. No sign of the skull.'

Nelson whistles soundlessly. 'Bloody hell. Do you think there's any connection?'

'Probably not but I'll have a look at the bones back at the lab.'

'This case gets wackier and wackier.'

'Well,' says Ruth, not wanting to be drawn, remembering her ridiculous fears yesterday, 'there could be all sorts of explanations for the bones. In fact, considering that there was supposed to be a churchyard somewhere around here, it's surprising we haven't found more.'

'But a decapitated cat,' Nelson raises his eyebrows, 'that doesn't strike you as odd?'

'There's sure to be a logical explanation,' persists Ruth. Nelson is still looking at her oddly. She can feel herself going red. Ruth has always had trouble with blushing and it seems to have got worse during the last few weeks. Feeling the blood pumping into her cheeks, she ducks her head. 'Edward Spens was here earlier,' she says. 'With his dad.'

At least this diverts Nelson's attention away from her. He kicks viciously at an upended paving stone.

'Interfering bastard,' he says. 'What did he want?'

'To interfere, I suspect. His dad was sweet though. Very interested in history. He was talking about the church that was meant to have been here.'

'Father Hennessey mentioned it too. Said it used to cure lepers.'

Ruth thinks of St Hugh's decapitated skull, performing miracles on its own, of St Bridget's cross, holy fires and sacred wells. Fairy tales all of them but, like fairy tales, curiously compelling.

'They're Catholics, you know,' says Nelson suddenly, 'the Spens family. Edward Spens was telling me. His grandfather converted sometime in the fifties.'

'I thought there was something odd about him,' says Ruth.

They are walking back towards the archway, where Kevin Davies is now standing, looking sadly at the devastation all around him. Ruth stops and takes a gulp from her water bottle.

Nelson puts his hand on her arm. 'Are you all right?'

The sudden kindness in his voice makes the blood rush to her head again.

'Fine,' she snaps, 'just hot.'

'Hot?' says Nelson. 'It's never hot in Norfolk.' And he bounds away across the rubble.

11 June
Day sacred to Fortuna Virgo

I suppose I have always known that I am special. Even before all this happened and the curse fell upon us, I always knew that the Gods had something special in store for me. It's not just that I am clever (though my Intelligence Quotient is in excess of 140), it is more that I understand. When I read Pliny or Catullus the gods are not just names to me, they are real. Their power and might overshadows all that comes after – the puny love-feast of Christianity, the ridiculous modern gods of horoscopes and hypnotism and the moving pictures. The Roman gods are logical and that is why I like them. If you kill, you must make amends in blood, a life for a life. Blood can be cancelled out but only by blood. The gods demand their sacrifices but, unlike modern gods, they do not demand more than their due. If you sacrifice correctly, the past is wiped out, made clean.

Soon I will be alone in the house (well, apart from the women and children who do not count) and then maybe I will have the chance to do what must be done. In the meantime I must keep my strength up, eat healthily, more meat and less potato. Caesar himself would not have been able to function on the diet I eat. Must speak to Cook about this.

CHAPTER 11

By the time Ruth gets in her car, her back feels like it is split-
ting in two. She wedges her jumper at the base of her spine
and thinks that it is only a matter of time before she has a
little corduroy lumbar cushion and thus becomes officially
middle-aged.

She drives to the university to drop off the animal bones.
As she gets the box out of the car she wonders whether
lugging bones about is ideal behaviour for a pregnant woman.
Funny but they don't mention that in the books. Ruth esti-
mates that she is now thirteen weeks pregnant. She is having
a scan next week which should, apparently, give a more accurate date. Maybe then, at last, the whole thing will start to
seem real.

She is so deep in thought that she doesn't notice the white-
coated figure coming in the other direction.

'Sorry!'

Thank goodness, she doesn't drop the box but the effort
causes her to fall to her knees. The white-coated man helps
her up.

'Ruth! Are you OK?'

It is Cathbad.

When he is in his full Druid outfit, complete with flowing purple cloak, Cathbad can look impressive, even magnificent. Now, with his greying hair drawn back in a ponytail, white coat, jeans and trainers, he looks like any other ageing hippy who has finally found a nine-to-five job. Ruth is pleased to see him though. Despite everything, she is fond of Cathbad.

'I'm all right.' She gets to her feet rather slowly, annoyed to find herself slightly out of breath.

'Are you taking those to the lab? I'll help you.'

Ruth hands over the box though still keeps hold of her precious rucksack. 'Did you get my email?' asks Cathbad as they walk along the deserted corridor. It is nearly six o'clock and most of the students, and a lot of the lecturers, have gone home.

'About Imbolc? Yes.'

'Are you going to come?'

'Yes. Is it OK if I bring a friend?'

'Of course. The beach belongs to everyone.'

He smiles modestly but Ruth knows that Cathbad regards this particular stretch of beach, where the henge was discovered, as very much his personal property.

'He's an archaeologist. I think you'll like him.'

'Is he the chap from Sussex? I've heard good things about him.'

Impressed by Cathbad's spy system (or sixth sense), Ruth asks, 'What have you heard?'

'Oh, that he's got an open mind. That he's respecting the spirits. That sort of thing.'

Ruth wonders which spirits Cathbad means. Earth spirits, nature spirits, household spirits – there's a wealth of choice for the truly open-minded. She decides not to enquire further. They have reached the lab and Ruth locks the animal bones in the safe. Tomorrow she will clean them and examine them further.

Cathbad is waiting for her outside. 'You look tired,' he says as they walk back towards the car park.

'I've had a long day. Been working on site.'

'Even so,' Cathbad reaches out to take her rucksack, 'you ought to be careful, in your condition.'

Ruth stops dead. The rucksack, which she had not quite relinquished, falls to the floor.

'*What* did you say?'

Cathbad looks back at her innocently. 'Just that you should be careful. Especially in the early months.'

Ruth opens her mouth and then shuts it again. 'How did you know?'

'It's fairly obvious,' says Cathbad, 'to the trained eye.'

'Since when have you had a trained eye?'

'Well, I'm a scientist,' says Cathbad, sounding offended, 'and an observer.'

'And you guessed just from observing me for a few minutes?'

'Well, I saw you the other day on campus and I thought . . . maybe. When I saw you today, I was sure.'

Ruth does not like the implications of this. If Cathbad has noticed, who else has realised? Phil? Her colleagues? Nelson?

'How far on are you?' Cathbad asks chattily, as they push through the swing doors.

'Thirteen weeks.'

'Lovely.' Cathbad is obviously doing the sums. 'A Scorpio baby.'

'If you say so.' Ruth is never sure which star sign is which. She is Cancer, home-loving and caring according to the books, which proves that it's all crap. They have reached Ruth's car and Cathbad hands over the rucksack.

'Thanks.' Ruth slings it into the back seat. 'See you on Friday.'

'Yes,' says Cathbad. 'Tell me, Ruth, does Nelson know?'

'Does Nelson know what?'

'About the baby.'

Ruth looks hard at Cathbad who stares guilelessly back. There is no one on earth who knows about her night with Nelson. Cathbad must surely be fishing in the dark.

'No. Why should he?'

'No reason.' Cathbad raises his hand in a cheery gesture of farewell. 'Take care of yourself, Ruth. See you on Friday.'

After her brush with Cathbad's sixth sense, Ruth is in the mood for solitude as she negotiates the narrow road across the marshes. But even from a distance she can see that she has company. A low-slung sports car is parked by her gate and a flash of brilliant red hair is visible in the driving seat.

Shona. Once Shona was Ruth's closest friend in Norfolk, perhaps her closest ever friend. But then the Saltmarsh case came up and, along with everything else in Ruth's life, her friendship with Shona was thrown into disarray. Ruth discovered things about Shona's past that made her wonder if she had ever really known her friend at all. Worse, she felt betrayed. But somehow they have survived. Shared grief over Erik, a shared sense of regret and a desire to salvage something positive from that terrible time, have drawn them together again. Perhaps they are not quite as open with each other as they once were. Ruth can't forget that Shona lied to her, by omission at least, for almost ten years. Shona feels that Ruth judged her too harshly for those lies. But they need each other. Neither has another close confidante and friends are precious. Ruth's slight sense of irritation at the disruption of her solitude has almost dissipated by the time that she has parked her car behind Shona's.

'Where have you been?' Shona hugs her. She is wearing a witchy green dress that billows in the wind from the sea. Her hair flies out in fiery points. Shona's beauty sometimes makes Ruth feel almost angry; at other times it makes it possible to forgive her anything.

'At the university.'

'You work too hard.'

Shona is also a lecturer at the university, in the English department. Over the past ten years she has embarked on a series of disastrous affairs with married colleagues and is currently involved with Ruth's boss, Phil. Ruth hopes that she is not in for an in-depth analysis of Phil's prowess as a lover and the likelihood of his leaving his wife. The thought of making love to Phil would make her feel sick even if she wasn't pregnant and in her opinion his marriage to Sue, a dull aromatherapist, will endure for ever.

Ruth opens the door and fends off an ecstatic Flint. Shona bends down to stroke the cat. She has often looked after him when Ruth is away.

'Hallo, darling, come to Auntie Shona. Ruth, I'm going to give up men and buy a cat.'

Ruth has heard this many times before. 'Cats aren't so good at mending the Christmas lights. Or checking the oil in cars.'

'No, but they're better listeners.' Shona cuddles Flint who stares hopefully at the floor.

'True. And they don't leave the loo seat up.'

Shona sits on the sofa with her feet curled under her. She looks like someone preparing for a long, cosy chat. Ruth offers tea but Shona says she'd prefer a glass of wine. Ruth puts some crisps in a bowl and stuffs a handful in her mouth before bringing them through to the sitting room.

'Phil says you've found a skeleton,' says Shona.

'Well, the field team found it. It's on a building site in Norwich.'

'The field team. Is that the mad Irishman?'

'Ted. Yes. He's not Irish though, is he? Why's he called Irish Ted?'

Shona's eyes gleam. 'It's a long story. So, the body. Any signs of foul play?'

Ruth hesitates, Shona is always interested in a good story. Maybe that's what comes of being a literature expert. Ruth is less sure about her discretion. The last thing she wants is Shona telling everything to Phil in some steamy pillow-talk session. On the other hand, she badly wants to talk to someone.

The head has been chopped off,' she says.

'No!' Shona is agog. 'Is it a ritual killing then?'

Ruth looks curiously at Shona. Strange that this should

be Shona's first question. Or maybe not strange coming from someone so closely involved with Erik, that expert on ritual, sacrifice and bloodshed. She doesn't think that most people would immediately connect a headless body with ritual.

'Maybe,' she says. 'The Romans sometimes made sacrifices to Janus, the God of doorways. This body is under a door.'

'Is it Roman then?'

'We won't know until we've done the dating. It could be Roman or medieval but I don't think so. The grave cut looked modern.'

'Janus. Was he the guy with two faces?'

'Yes. The God of beginnings and endings. January is named after him.'

Shona shivers. 'Sounds creepy. But, then again, a lot of men are two-faced.'

'How's Phil?'

Shona smiles, rather sadly. 'Pour us a glass of wine and I'll tell you.'

Ruth pours two glasses of wine and hopes that Shona won't notice how slowly she drinks hers. Wine makes her feel sick these days. It's almost as if her taste buds can separate the drink into its component parts: acidic grapes, fermenting alcohol, a hint of vine leaves. She can almost taste the peasants' feet.

Phil, it seems, has been showing his unpleasant face to Shona. He wants her to come away with him to a conference in Geneva but is insisting that they travel separately and that she pays her own fare. Ruth hides a smile. Phil's stinginess is a standing joke in the department. Apparently he says he loves Shona but has taken to referring to his wife's 'fragility', as if it will be Shona's fault if anything happens to upset her.

'I wouldn't mind but she's as strong as a horse. Looks like a horse too. An unattractive horse ... Ruth, why aren't you drinking?'

Ruth looks guiltily at her glass. Shona has emptied hers but Ruth has only managed a few queasy sips.

'Are you OK?'

Everyone seems to be asking her that, thinks Ruth. She suddenly feels a great urge to tell Shona about her pregnancy. People are going to have to know sometime. Cathbad has already guessed. Maybe everyone is talking behind her back. And she'll need an ally when she tells Phil. She takes a deep breath.

'Shona? I've got something to tell you.'

'What?' Shona is instantly alert, her eyes, with their long glittery lashes, fixed onto Ruth's face.

How to put it into words? 'I'm expecting a baby' sounds twee somehow. And she has a hard job thinking of the baby end of things. Better just be as factual as possible.

'I'm pregnant,' she says.

'What?'

Suddenly Ruth is scared of what she might see in Shona's face. She knows that Shona has been pregnant twice and has had two abortions. Will she see envy, hatred, resentment? She forces herself to look at Shona and sees, to her amazement, that there are tears in her eyes.

'I'm pregnant,' Ruth repeats.

Shona reaches over to touch Ruth's arm. 'Oh Ruth ...' she says tearfully. And then, 'Are you sure?'

'Yes. I'm about thirteen weeks.'

'Thirteen weeks. Oh my God.' Shona wipes her eyes and seems to recover some of her equilibrium. Her expression is now straightforwardly curious. And she asks the question that Ruth dreads.

'Who's the father?'

'I'd rather not say.' This doesn't go down any better with Shona than it did with Ruth's parents. Shona flicks her hair impatiently.

'Oh, come on, Ruth. You can tell me. Is it Peter's?'

'I can't say.' Now Ruth feels herself getting tearful. 'Please.'

Shona leans over to give her a proper hug. 'I'm sorry. I'm just . . . gobsmacked. Are you keeping it?'

'Yes.'

'That's brave,' says Shona quietly.

'Not really. I haven't thought it through. The implications, I mean. But I do want it. Very much,' she adds.

'You'll be a great mum! Can I be godmother?'

'In a strictly non-religious sense, yes.'

'I'll be its auntie. Like I'm Flint's auntie.' There is a distinctly brittle edge to Shona's laughter now.

'It'll need all the family it can get,' says Ruth. 'My parents have more or less disowned me.'

'Really? Does that still happen? Everyone has babies now without being married. Even my mother wouldn't mind. And she's a mad Irish Catholic.'

'My parents are . . . old-fashioned.'

'They must be.' Shona fiddles with her wine glass for a second before asking, 'Does Phil know?'

'No, not yet. I'll have to tell him soon, before it becomes

too obvious. I saw Cathbad today and he guessed immediately.'

'Cathbad, really?' Shona knows Cathbad of old. They met on the henge dig all those years ago. Ruth remembers that Shona initially sided with the Druids who wanted to keep the henge in place rather than with the archaeologists who wanted to move it to a museum. She wonders what Phil, an establishment man to the core, thinks about Shona's new-age leanings

'Perhaps the spirits told him?' suggests Shona.

'Perhaps.' Ruth remembers Cathbad saying that Max respected 'the spirits'. She has a sudden vision of a shadowy army hovering around, questioning, commenting and passing judgement. Funnily enough, they all look a bit like her mother.

'He's having a party on Friday,' she says.

'A party?'

'Well, a celebration. In honour of Imbolc, some Celtic thing about the coming of spring. He's organising a party on the beach. Do you want to come?'

Shona brightens up at the prospect of a party. 'Why not? A spot of satanic ritual's just what I need to cheer me up.'

CHAPTER 12

As it turns out, nothing could be less satanic than the Imbolc celebration on Saltmarsh beach. Some of Cathbad's colleagues have even brought their children who play happily on the sand, daring each other to jump over waves. Even the vast bonfire, constructed out of driftwood and old packing cases, seems more like something made by the PTA to raise funds for playground equipment than an offering to the pagan gods of fire.

Ruth and Max walk over the Saltmarsh, carrying offerings of wine and crisps. Though Max does not know it, they are following the path taken by Ruth and Lucy, that wild night in February, when the wind howled from the sea and the marsh shifted treacherously in the darkness. Sometimes it seems to Ruth as if that night was something that happened to someone else; she can think about it quite calmly, as if she is reading about it in a book. At other times, the memory is as sharp as if it happened yesterday: the flight across the marshes in the night, the moment when she knew that she was going to die, the dark wave coming from nowhere.

Now, though, the sky is palest blue and only a light, companionable breeze blows through the coarse grass. Ruth and Max take the path through the dunes and see the beach spread out before them; the silver line of the sea, the deep pools reflecting the evening sky, the miles upon miles of rippling sand.

'It's beautiful,' says Max. 'I'd forgotten how open it is in Norfolk. Nothing but sand, sea and sky.'

'Yes, it is beautiful,' says Ruth, pleased that Max appreciates her beloved Saltmarsh. 'It can be desolate in the winter but on evenings like this I think it's the loveliest place on earth.'

'I like the desolation too,' says Max, looking out towards the retreating tide. The seagulls are swooping low over the waves and the shouts of the children seem thin on the evening air.

Ruth looks at him curiously. She knows what he means. Sometimes the Saltmarsh's sheer loneliness and splendour gives her a thrill of almost sexual pleasure. But she hadn't expected Max to feel the same. Doesn't he come from Brighton, where the beach is more about kiss-me-quick hats than desolate beauty? But he was brought up in Norfolk, she reminds herself.

They walk towards the bonfire, very black against the white sand. Cathbad, wearing Druid's robes and the purple cloak is supervising the stacking of wood but when he sees Ruth he breaks away with arms outstretched.

'Ruth!' They hug and Ruth feels Cathbad's beard tickling her cheek.

'Cathbad, this is my friend Max.'

'Welcome!' Cathbad gives Max a two-handed 'vicar's' handshake. Indeed, in his white robes, he looks not unlike a priest greeting parishioners at the door of his church. Of course, Cathbad would say that this is just what the Saltmarsh is – a church, sacred ground. After all, man has worshipped here for hundreds, thousands, of years; first the Bronze Age people building their henge and then the Iron Agers who buried bodies and treasure at the point where the sea meets the land. It was one of these bodies that Ruth discovered last year.

'Good to meet you,' says Max. 'This is a wonderful spot.'

'Yes,' says Cathbad, looking closely at Max. 'This is a liminal zone, the bridge between life and death.'

'Erik Anderssen 1998,' says Max immediately. 'I love that book. Anderssen was one of my heroes when I was a student.'

Ruth can't stop herself exclaiming. 'Did you know Erik?'

'I never met him but I've read almost everything he ever wrote. No one has ever understood prehistory better.'

'He was a wonderful man,' says Cathbad. 'Ruth here was very close to him.'

'Were you?' Max turns to Ruth.

'Well, I was his student,' Ruth says guardedly. She still finds it hard to talk about Erik.

'His favourite student,' says Cathbad rather aggressively.

'I wouldn't go that far.'

'I wish I'd met him,' says Max lightly.

'We've brought booze,' says Ruth, wishing to turn the subject away from life and death.

'Great,' says Cathbad, 'the gods need their libation. Freya over there is in charge of drinks.'

Freya, a wispy blonde in blue robes, takes their bottles

and stows them away carefully. She then offers them punch from a copper cauldron. Ruth sniffs suspiciously at her plastic cup as they walk away.

'What's in this?' she asks. 'Battery acid?'

'Well, you did say that he works in the chemistry department.'

'He used to be an archaeologist, you know.'

'Is that how he knew Erik?'

'Yes. Erik was his tutor at university. Then they met again on the henge dig. You know, the one I told you about? Cathbad was one of the Druids protesting about us moving the timbers.'

'You can see their point,' says Max slowly, looking out across the expanse of sand, perhaps imagining the henge in place, the circle of wooden posts stark against the sky. As for Ruth, the image is so clear that she is surprised it hasn't materialised in front of her, complete with Erik kneeling in the centre, rhapsodising about the preservation of the wood.

'Erik sympathised,' she says, 'but the sea was getting closer all the time. It would have destroyed the henge in the end.'

Max smiles. 'Destroyed or changed?'

For a second, Ruth thinks about the Latin motto on the archway at Woolmarket Street: *Omnia Mutantur, Nihil Interit*, everything changes, nothing perishes, and she feels a sudden chill, as if a cold hand has touched her shoulder.

'You *are* a fan of Erik's,' is all she says. Erik believed in the cycle of change, decay and rebirth. Has he been reborn? Sometimes it seems impossible that Erik's vibrant spirit can really have died alongside his body. Surely there's some blue-eyed baby somewhere that is Erik having a second go at life.

Or some water spirit maybe, some animal – a seal or a sleek arctic fox.

The bonfire is apparently completed. As the light fades Cathbad and the other Druids join hands and encircle it, chanting and singing. The children join in too, running in and out of the adults, laughing and excited. Max, Ruth and the other non-Druids stand nearby, torn between self-consciousness and interest. There is something magnificent about the spectacle, thinks Ruth, the tiny dark figures silhouetted against the sky, the towering bonfire and the faint crash of the waves in the background.

Cathbad has some trouble lighting his symbolic firebrand. The wind keeps whipping out the flame and, eventually, Freya has to shield him with her cloak. But finally he raises aloft the burning brand. 'Goddess Brigid, accept our offering!'

Flames lick around the base of the bonfire. The children run around, shrieking with excitement. The adults are chanting again but then someone starts to play the guitar and the chanting turns into something cosier, something more like a folk song. There is quite a crowd now. Ruth recognises lots of faces from the university and from the field team, including Ted and Trace. Slightly to Ruth's irritation, Max greets Trace enthusiastically. 'She's been working on the Swaffham site. She's a good archaeologist. Very knowledgeable about the Romans.'

'Mmm.' Ruth's appreciation of Trace's skills is not improved by the fact that she is looking rather stunning in a black T-shirt and black leather trousers. 'Let's go and sit down somewhere,' she says. Her back is killing her.

They sit in the shelter of one of the dunes, eating vegetarian hot dogs. Max has managed to annex one of the better bottles of wine and Ruth is drinking orange juice. Max doesn't comment on her abstemiousness. They talk about the two sites – the Roman excavation and the seventy-five luxury apartments – about the two decapitated bodies, about the Roman gods, particularly Janus, the two-faced God. 'He's also connected to the spring and the harvest,' says Max. 'He's not just the god of doorways but of any time of transition and change, of progression from one condition to another.'

'Is that because he can look backwards and forwards at the same time?'

'Yes, it also helped him pursue women, the nymph Carna, for example.'

'Did he catch her?'

'Yes, and in return for her favours he gave her power over all door hinges.'

Ruth laughs. 'So, instead of WD40 we should pray to Carna?'

'It's worth a try.'

Max pours more wine but Ruth has caught sight of a modern nymph, walking towards them across the sand. Shona, wearing a shawl and a flowing purple dress, accompanied by a very unwelcome acolyte – Phil.

'Ruth! What are you doing skulking here?'

Skulking, thinks Ruth, getting to her feet, is really a very unattractive way of putting it. She had been feeling rather good, lounging on the sand beside a good-looking and intelligent man. Now she feels foolish and somehow rather disreputable.

'Hallo, Ruth,' says Phil, too loudly. This is the first time Ruth has seen him in Shona's company. This evening must represent some sort of 'coming out' as a couple. No wonder Shona looks so triumphant.

'Hallo, Phil,' says Ruth warily. 'You remember Max Grey from Sussex? He's the archaeologist in charge of the Swaffham dig.'

'Yes, of course. How are you? Glad Ruth's looking after you.'

This remark, like Shona's, serves to make the whole evening seem ridiculous. Who is Phil to say that Ruth is 'looking after' Max? Why does he need looking after, anyhow?

'I'm having a wonderful time,' says Max, making things slightly better.

'I've got no time for all this hippie nonsense,' says Phil, 'but Malone is a friend of Shona's.'

'Malone?'

'Catweasel or whatever he calls himself.'

'Cathbad,' says Ruth between gritted teeth.

'I hear he's an ex-archaeologist,' says Max.

'Years ago,' says Phil dismissively. 'He works as a lab assistant now. He's one of the airy-fairy type, believes in the symbolic landscape, ley lines, spirits of the ancestors, all that crap.'

Max says nothing. Ruth is pretty sure that he too believes in some of these things but it is in his interests to stay on the right side of Phil, who is partly funding the Roman dig.

It is nearly dark now. The Druids have planted burning torches in the sand and now the capering figures around the bonfire look monstrous and misshapen, their shadows black against the flames. The scent of wood smoke fills the air with acrid sweetness. Ruth realises that she is suddenly very tired. More than anything she wants to be home, in bed, with Flint flexing his claws against the duvet. But she is sure that Max won't want to leave yet. How many more hours will she have to spend watching Cathbad throwing symbolic objects onto the fire? The last one was a University of North Norfolk sweatshirt; she dreads to think what this signifies.

She realises that Shona is talking to her, lowering her voice so that the men won't hear. 'He's promised to leave his wife. What do you think of that?'

'I've heard that one before,' is what Ruth thinks. Aloud, she says, 'Do you think he will?'

'I don't know,' says Shona, draining her plastic glass. 'I gave him an ultimatum. Her or me. He says I'm the most important thing in his life.'

Hence his presence here, guesses Ruth. A conciliatory gesture, appearing with Shona in front of this significantly insignificant group of people. She is sure that Phil would never accompany Shona to a departmental social or the Dean's lecture. Equally, she is sure he will never leave his wife. Just as Nelson will never leave his.

'Be careful,' is all she says.

'What do you mean?' Shona tosses her hair, which glows as brightly as one of the torches in the darkness.

'I've known Phil a long time. He says what he thinks you want to hear.'

Shona glares at her. Ruth is not sure what she would have said if Max hadn't come over, placing a hand on Ruth's arm. 'Do you want to make a move?' he says. 'It's getting a bit cold out here.'

Ruth agrees gratefully. With the disappearance of the sun, the night has got distinctly chilly. The wind is stronger too. Ruth pulls her jacket tightly around her but the Druids in their thin robes seem impervious to the cold. Their children too. As she and Max walk along the beach she can see them still playing in the near darkness. They have dug a deep hole and are chanting, 'Ding Dong Dell, Pussy's in the well.'

'Some things never change,' she says to Max as they make their way back to the path through the dunes. It is too dangerous to cross the Saltmarsh after dark; they must take the birdwatchers' trail, a raised shingle path that leads back to the car park. Max has left his car there. Ruth hopes he will give her a lift home and won't expect to come in for coffee.

'Interesting rhyme,' says Max in his tutorial voice. 'It's thought that Pussy refers to a prostitute.'

'What are they doing, drowning her?'

'Probably a version of a ducking stool.'

'How does it go? "Who put her in? Little Johnny Green".'

'"Who pulled her out? Little Jimmy Stout". Something like that.'

'Who was Jimmy then? Her pimp?'

Max laughs. 'I like you, Ruth,' he says.

There's no answer to that. 'I like you too' would sound impossibly arch. Changing the subject would sound like a snub. And she does like him. How much, she doesn't really want to consider. It's all so *complicated*, that's the problem. She is pregnant with someone else's baby. That someone else is married and doesn't even know that she is pregnant. He will probably be furious when he finds out. Or will he maybe, just maybe, be pleased? Recently Ruth has been fantasising that the baby is a boy. Perhaps Nelson has always wanted a boy, will be delighted, will leave Michelle . . . Hang on, though, does she even want him to leave Michelle? On balance, she doesn't. She would feel horribly guilty at breaking up the family and she is not sure if she ever wants to live with a man again. Especially a man as large as Nelson.

This is ridiculous anyway. Nelson doesn't love her and never has done. Their night together had been the result of a unique set of circumstances. They had just found the body of a dead child, Nelson had had to break the news to the family. For that one night it seemed as if Ruth and Nelson were alone in the world. Nelson had come to Ruth wanting comfort; the passion had surprised both of them. But Nelson has never, before or since, given any sign that he thinks of Ruth as anything other than a colleague, a fellow professional, perhaps even a friend. Why, then, is she thinking of him now, as Max takes her hand to help her over a stile? Does Max remind her of Nelson? He's a very different person; an academic, soft-spoken and courteous, but, physically, there is something. Like Nelson, Max has presence. It is not just that he is tall. It is more that, if he is in the room, you can't really look at anyone else. Phil faded into insignificance beside him and even Cathbad seemed several shades paler.

'Listen,' says Max suddenly, 'an owl.' They are passing the first hide. These wooden huts for birdwatchers are placed at strategic points on the marsh – this one is on stilts looking out over a freshwater lake. Ruth hears the wind whispering in the reeds and thinks for the hundredth, thousandth, time of that wild night on the Saltmarsh when an owl's call lured a man to his death. Around them lies water, dark and sullen, interspersed with marshy islands. Ruth shivers and Max makes a gesture as if he is going to put his arm round her but thinks better of it. 'Almost there,' is all he says.

The car park is pitch black and deserted apart from Max's Range Rover. Inside it is blessedly warm and Ruth almost cries with happiness at the prospect of sitting down again. Is it normal for a pregnant person's back to ache this much? Perhaps it's because she's overweight.

Max negotiates the turn into the narrow road that leads to the cottages. He's a careful driver. In this respect, at least, he's nothing like Nelson.

'It was quite something, wasn't it?' he says. 'The bonfire and the Druids and everything.'

'Yes,' says Ruth, 'you can't go wrong with a fire for spectacle. I suppose that's why people used to worship it. Fire wards off the dark.'

'Like the cry of the cockerel,' says Max.

Ruth shoots him a curious look. 'Why do you say that?'

For a second Max looks straight ahead, squinting at the dark road. Then he says, 'Something that happened on the dig yesterday. I was just seeing off some sightseers. The Historical Society this time, I think. And I found a dead cockerel in one of the trenches.'

Ruth doesn't know what to say. She is dimly aware that the neighbouring farms might keep hens but she can't think how a bird can have wandered onto Max's site, isolated as it is behind its grassy bank.

'Was it left there deliberately?'

He gives a short laugh. 'I'd say so, yes. Its throat had been cut.'

'What?'

'Slit from side to side. Very neat job.'

For one awful moment Ruth thinks she is going to be sick. She takes a deep breath.

'Why would anyone want to do that?'

They have reached Ruth's cottage. Max turns off the ignition. 'Well a cockerel's a fairly traditional sacrifice. Because they crow in the morning, they're supposed to have power to hold back the darkness. That's what I meant earlier.'

Ruth's head is swimming. 'A sacrifice? Why would anyone leave a sacrifice on an archaeological dig?'

'I don't know. Maybe someone who believes that we're disturbing the dead.'

Briefly Ruth thinks of Cathbad and then shakes her head to clear it. Dead animals are not Cathbad's style.

'Of course,' Max goes on, 'cockerels have a Christian connection too. The cockerel is sometimes used to represent Jesus. It's the whole dawn rebirth thing.'

'Someone killed a bird as a Christian sacrifice?'

Max's voice changes gear slightly. 'Or an offering to Hecate.'

'The goddess of witchcraft?'

'She was the goddess of many things. The Greeks called her the "Queen of the Night" because she could see into the underworld. She's the goddess of the crossroads, the three ways. That's why images of her are often in triplicate. She is meant to haunt crossroads, crossing places, accompanied by her ghost dogs. Another name is Hekate Kourotrophos, Hecate the child-nurse. Women prayed to her in labour.'

'Are cockerels traditionally sacrificed to her?' Ruth tries to keep the disbelief out of her voice.

'Well, it was black and it was traditional to sacrifice black animals to Hecate. Usually dogs or puppies because of her sacred dogs. But birds too occasionally. She's sometimes linked to Athena and is depicted with an owl, the symbol of wisdom.'

'We heard an owl earlier.'

Max smiles, his teeth very white in the darkness. 'Maybe that was Hecate. She appears on marshland sometimes, shining her ghost lights to help you see your way.'

'A will-o'-the-wisp,' says Ruth, remembering another legend of spectral lights.

'Exactly. Marsh lights. Phosphorescence. There are lots of stories about them.'

Ruth shivers. The time on the dashboard says 22:32. 'I'd better be getting in.'

Max does not try to detain her nor does he mention coffee but, when she starts to open the door, he says 'Ruth' and, leaning over, kisses her on the lips.

Ruth goes straight to bed but as she lies cosily under her duvet with Flint purring loudly on her chest she finds that she can't sleep. Instead words and phrases chase themselves crazily around her head. She turns one way and then the other (much to Flint's irritation) but still can't escape them. It's a little like the half-waking dreams that you get when you've drunk too much, which is very annoying considering she only had one sip of punch and drank orange juice for the rest of the evening.

She's the goddess of the crossroads, the three ways

He's promised to leave his wife. What do you think of that?

Does Nelson know?

. . . a liminal zone, the bridge between life and death

. . . everything changes, nothing perishes

Ding Dong Dell, Pussy's in the well

Then, suddenly, the voices vanish and she sees a mild, crushed-looking man who is gazing sadly at a ruined garden.

This was the conservatory, and over there we had a swing and a tree house. There was a wishing well too . . .'

Ding Dong Dell, Pussy's in the well

Ruth sits up, throwing Flint onto the floor. Suddenly she knows, without any shadow of a doubt, where the skulls are hidden.

CHAPTER 13

They find the well at the back of the house, near the tree with the swinging rope. It is half-buried under one of the new walls which Nelson orders to be dismantled, much to the foreman's fury.

All that is left of the wishing well is a ring of bricks pressed into the soil. The hole has been filled with cement but Nelson thinks that this is only a cap, a few inches deep. Sure enough, it takes one of the workmen only a few minutes to break through with his pneumatic drill. Ruth peers into the void. Cold, dank air fills her nose and mouth but she can't see anything but darkness.

'How deep do you think it is?' asks Ted.

'Five or six metres,' says Nelson, 'possibly deeper.'

Nelson has a police diver on hand to climb down into the well. He is wearing a safety harness and is attaching a rope to a grappling hook.

'Why a diver?' asks Ruth. 'There's no water there now.'

'We can't be sure of that,' says Nelson. 'Because he's insured and we don't actually have a police wishing-well division.'

'I'll go down,' offers Ted, 'I'm into extreme archaeology.'

'No, you won't, sunshine,' says Nelson, 'you'll stay where I can see you.'

The diver climbs carefully into the shaft and disappears from view. For a few minutes, there is complete silence apart from a bird singing noisily in the tree.

Then a voice comes from the depths of the well, 'I've found something, sir.'

'What?' Nelson kneels on the edge and shouts downwards.

'A skull.'

'Don't hold it by the eye sockets!' squeaks Ruth, kneeling beside Nelson. 'They're very fragile.'

'I'm coming back up.'

The diver appears a minute later, carrying a skull carefully on the flat of his hand. He looks like an actor playing Hamlet in an experimental production (Shakespeare Meets Beckett perhaps?). Ruth takes the small skull in both her hands.

'Well?' says Nelson.

'It's a child's,' says Ruth quietly.

'There's something else down there, sir.'

'Well, don't hang about here chatting. Back you go.'

This time the diver emerges with what is clearly an animal skull.

'The cat?' asks Ted, leaning over Ruth's shoulder.

'Could be.' Briefly, Ruth thinks of Hecate and wonders about the colour of the cat found buried under the outer wall. The goddess of witchcraft. Hecate the child-nurse.

They all stare at the two skulls, side by side on the tarpaulin. Ruth is thinking about head cults, about St Fremund washing his severed head in a well, about children's bodies buried under the walls of temples. Nelson is thinking about Martin and Elizabeth Black. Did they never, in fact, run away? Does this skull belong to one of the missing children, murdered within the very grounds of the children's home?

Ted breaks the silence. 'Will the coroner want these?'

'The human skull will go to the post-mortem, yes. I'll take the animal skull back to the lab.' Nelson watches as Ruth bags and labels the two skulls. The human skull is then placed in a special container marked, rather grimly, 'Police Pathology'. This she hands to Nelson.

'Will you be at the post-mortem?' she asks.

'Wouldn't miss it for the world.'

'I'll see you there then.'

'I'll walk you to your car.'

Watched curiously by the others, they walk back through the grounds to where Ruth's car is parked on the drive, under the shadow of the oak tree. The Druid's tree, St Bridget's tree, looks green and innocuous in the midday sun. Ruth opens her car boot and carefully places the box containing the cat's skull inside. Nelson walks around the dusty Renault, kicking a loose hubcap into place.

'How long will it take you to do your tests?' he asks.

'A few hours. Samples from the post-mortem will take longer.'

He makes his characteristic horse-pawing-the-ground movement. Nelson, Ruth knows, hates waiting for anything. But, then, still looking at the ground, he says, 'I heard from Cathbad the other day.'

Ruth is instantly alert. 'What did he want?'

'Oh, to invite me to a lunatic beach party to celebrate some pagan feast day.'

'And you didn't go?'

'No, I didn't think it was my sort of thing somehow. Or Michelle's.' He looks at her.

Ruth turns away on the pretext of closing the boot. 'You were probably right.'

'Did you go?'

'Yes.'

'On your own?'

Ruth stares. She can't believe he has asked this. 'No,' she says at last, 'with a friend. Max Grey.'

'Have a good time?'

'OK. There was a bonfire, lots of chanting, horrible food. You know the sort of thing.'

Nelson grins suddenly. 'Sounds like a Masonic meeting.'

'Are you a Mason then?'

'No, Cloughie is though.'

For a second they look at each other in silence and then Nelson says, with what sounds like fake heartiness, 'Well, mustn't stand here all day gossiping. See you at the post-mortem.'

With this cheery salutation he heads off at top speed, almost colliding with Ted and the diver who are clearly off to the pub.

Ruth takes the animal skull back to the lab. The science block is deserted. There is an end-of-term party going on in the grounds, complete with beer tent and live bands. Ruth can hear the bass notes, like a giant heartbeat, and the occasional roar of beery applause. But the lecture rooms and laboratories are silent. No sign of Cathbad or any of the other lab technicians. Cathbad is probably at the party – he enjoys any kind of celebration, pagan or otherwise.

Watched by a poster showing diseases of the eye and by sundry silent bones in glass cases, Ruth gets out the skull and starts to clean it with a soft brush. Going by the shape and size, she is almost certain that it is a cat. The blunt edges of the neck bones show that the head has been removed roughly, probably by an axe. Looking at the cut marks under a microscope Ruth concludes that the head was removed after death. The marks clearly point to cutting from the front. If the animal was still alive this would cause massive bleeding as it would mean sawing through the jugular. It is more likely that the cat was killed first and beheaded later.

Why? She has a million theories, none of them very likely. In so-called Celtic 'head cults' the head was often removed for religious or magical rituals. Placing the heads in the well certainly seems like a ritual act. Are the skulls Celtic then? She doesn't think so somehow.

It is growing darker outside and the party is getting more and more raucous. She can hear doors slamming as students run along corridors looking for deserted rooms where they can have sex or take drugs. Just as long as they don't come in here. The blue 'sterile conditions' light is on outside. That should deter them. She doesn't imagine that any of them are feeling particularly sterile.

Ruth's back is aching so she takes off her gloves and sits down to drink a glass of water. Looking at the little skull on the examination table, she suddenly feels unaccountably sad.

She knows that the dead child is more important than the cat. The cat is simply a clue, an oddity, a slightly macabre detail. But even so, as she looks down on the thin little bones, Ruth feels a surge of pity. She lost her beloved cat, Sparky, earlier in the year and she still misses her. Probably this cat too was loved by someone. She sends a message back in time. 'I'm sorry. I'm sorry for the things that humans do to animals.' She is aware that, in this very university, animals are experimented on every day (once or twice a year there are demonstrations from animal rights protesters and security is tightened) but, by and large, she accepts this as being necessary for the common good. But this – this is different.

Was the cat a sacrifice? Was it practice? Kill an animal first, work up to the ultimate horror of killing a child? What did Max say? 'It was traditional to sacrifice black animals to Hecate.'

On impulse Ruth goes over to the box containing the other evidence bags from the site. Bags of soil and vegetation for analysis, fragments of brick and stone and, yes, there it is ... She gets out the plastic bag containing the Roman signet ring. Carefully she tips the ring onto her hand. A handwritten label says 'Bronze ring with intaglio, probably Roman.' The device is hard to see, three slightly overlapping rings. 'Looks like a shamrock,' Irish Ted had suggested, appropriately enough. But now, looking at it under the microscope, Ruth can see that the three circles are actually three heads.

Hecate. The three-headed goddess.

13th June
Ides

I am Agamemnon. I am the master of the house. Magister mundi sum. *The responsibility is mine and, naturally, as the Master, I have certain duties. Did Agamemnon enjoy making the sacrifice demanded of him? No, but he did it just the same. Sometimes you just have to do what must be done. It is lonely being the master of the house and I wouldn't be human if I didn't wish that it could go back to the way it was. That I didn't have to do this thing. But the gods must be appeased. That's what no one understands. Agamemnon needed a fair wind for Troy. I need our walls to be safe. It comes to the same thing in the end.*

CHAPTER 14

The police pathologist is young and exhaustingly enthusiastic. He is called Chris Stevenson and Ruth knows him only by sight. She knew the previous pathologist better; a charming old-world type who always wore a bow tie and velvet slippers. Stevenson bounds into the autopsy room on puffy American sneakers, his white coat flapping behind him. The old world is obviously gone for ever.

'Dr Galloway! Come to give us your expert opinions?'

'I'll try,' says Ruth tightly.

She knows that today's post-mortem will be a battle. In a normal autopsy, Stevenson would be the expert. He is a flamboyant practitioner who likes, for example, to remove the internal organs in one block rather than in four groups, as is usual. Nelson describes a previous autopsy where Stevenson gestured so theatrically with his scalpel that two police probationers fainted. Stevenson also likes to talk all the time, a constant stream of information, observation and free-association chat in the manner of a Sunday morning DJ – albeit a DJ primarily concerned with blood, guts and medical incisions. Nelson loathes him, Ruth knows.

But, today, there are only bones – dry, academic bones. There is no need for any cutting or sawing or dramatic flourishes. And Ruth will be the expert. Stevenson will conduct the examination but he will be forced to defer to Ruth at every turn. No wonder his flow of humorous commentary has a slightly brittle edge this morning. Ruth says nothing. She is looking at the bones already laid out on the dissection table. Such a small skeleton. Such a little life.

Nelson arrives late, earning him a jokey 'nice of you to join us' from Stevenson.

'Just get on with it,' growls Nelson. He looks unfamiliar in his surgical scrubs, a plastic hat over his dark hair. Probably the most unflattering garments in the world, thinks Ruth, aware that she looks like a large green barrage balloon.

A technologist photographs the bones which have been laid out in an anatomically correct position. Then Stevenson begins his examination, barking his comments into a hand-held recorder. Ruth stands at the opposite side of the stainless steel table, taking each bone from Stevenson as he finishes with it and occasionally adding her own comments. Nelson stands behind Ruth, shifting from foot to foot like a restive horse.

'. . . epiphyses still detached . . . cartilaginous plate not yet ossified . . . size of the long bones indicates a child . . . would you say that it's male or female, Dr Galloway?'

Ruth is looking at the pelvic bones. The female pelvis is shallower and broader than the male but this is not yet obvious in a pre-pubescent skeleton. She examines the sciatic notch, which is shorter and deeper in males. Again, this is barely detectable in a child.

'Female, I'd say.'

'Would you? That's interesting.' From this, Ruth concludes that Stevenson disagrees.

'. . . trauma on sternum and third rib . . . what would you say that was, Dr Galloway?'

'Looks like a knife mark.'

'A knife mark the lady says, we'll see . . .'

Stevenson turns to the skull. 'External trauma to the cervical vertebrae . . .'

An axe, thinks Ruth. The head was cut off with an instrument like an axe and, like the cat, it was done by cutting from the front.

'Cause of death – decapitation?' suggests Stevenson.

'Poena post-mortem,' says Ruth shortly, turning to Nelson. 'Mutilation after death. The head was cut off later. It was cut from the front, death by decapitation is nearly always achieved by cutting from the back.'

Stevenson grunts. 'Interesting theory. What do you think Detective Chief Inspector?'

'Stabbed in the chest, beheaded. One thing's certain; it sure as hell wasn't suicide.'

Stevenson laughs, turning back to the skull. 'No eruption of permanent teeth . . .' Ruth looks round at Nelson. No adult teeth – this means the skull is almost definitely less than six years old. 'Filling on lower left first molar occlusal . . .'

This is interesting. It proves for one thing that the body is relatively modern (although fillings apparently existed in ancient China, it is only in the last hundred years that they have been in common use). Also, fillings are rare in such a young child. The composition will give valuable clues about dating.

Ruth leans forward.

'Thoughts about the filling, Dr Galloway?'

'I'd like a forensic dentistry expert to look at it.'

'Anyone in mind?'

'Yes.'

The examination is almost over. Stevenson takes samples for carbon-14 dating and Ruth fills in her skeleton sheets: post-cranial non-metrics, pathology, conclusions . . . Her back aches from standing up so long but she doesn't want to ask for a seat and risk Stevenson's contempt and Nelson's suspicion. Does he suspect? She can't allow herself to think so.

'Do you want a bet on the dating,' asks Stevenson, 'five years each way?'

'No.'

'Suit yourself. I'll take some samples for DNA testing as well.'

'Will you get any DNA?' asks Nelson sceptically, looking at the dry bones.

'Maybe,' says Ruth, 'but DNA can be damaged by immersion in earth. We may not get a good enough sample.'

'We will,' says Stevenson. 'Well, show's over, folks.'

In the ante-room, Ruth changes out of her scrubs and washes her hands thoroughly. Although there was no blood in this post-mortem she still feels grubby and slightly sordid. Maybe it's just overexposure to Chris Stevenson.

Nelson's head appears round the door. 'Christ, thank God that's over. Bloke's a complete tosser. Fancy a coffee?'

Ruth hesitates. Though the thought of coffee makes her feel sick, she would like, very much to go to a cosy café with Nelson but she has something else she has to do this morning.

'I'm sorry,' she says, 'I've got an appointment.'

CHAPTER 15

'Are you on your own?'

This is a question with so many layers that Ruth is momentarily struck dumb. She is manifestly on her own as she has presented herself at the hospital without anyone accompanying her. But she is doubly on her own as the father of her child does not even know she is pregnant. She thinks of Nelson as she saw him that morning, at the post-mortem, and tries to imagine him at her side, doting and supportive. No, it just doesn't work. Even if Nelson did know, even if they were, in some unimaginable way, together, he would still spend his time looking at his watch and longing to be back at the station. What about her mum? She tries to picture her mother, cosy and smiling, offering advice and encouragement, telling her not to do too much and to eat ginger biscuits if she feels sick. No, even less likely. Shona? She would spend all her time flicking her hair about and making eyes at the doctors. Funnily enough, the only person she can actually imagine at her side is Cathbad. At least he'd be kind, although the purple cloak might prove a trifle embarrassing.

'Yes. I'm on my own.'

The nurse ushers Ruth into a room with a bed and a contraption like a TV screen. Another woman stands by the screen, nonchalantly chewing gum. Ruth is reminded uncomfortably of the autopsy room. Only this time she is the body on the slab. Don't be morbid, she tells herself. This is a perfectly routine procedure. So is an autopsy, persists the voice inside her head.

The nurse tells Ruth to undo her trousers, and rubs gel onto her stomach. Ruth squirms. She hates being touched on her stomach and avoids massages and beauty treatments like the plague. 'Relax!' she remembers a masseuse once saying to her. Eccentric she knows but, for Ruth, having some manicured stranger kneading your shoulder blades whilst chatting about their holidays is the very opposite of relaxing.

The other woman now places something like the end of a stethoscope onto Ruth's stomach, pressing quite hard. Ruth has been told not to go to the loo before the scan and the pressure is really very uncomfortable. For a second she feels like jumping off the bed and heading for the nearest Ladies. But then she sees that the screen is full of what look like wispy grey clouds. In the centre of the clouds something is moving.

Ruth has seen scans before – of bones and other archaeological objects. She knows that the high-frequency sound waves bounce off solid objects. She knows how to look at degrees of light and shade, to assess density and structure. But this – this is something quite different. This collection of dark circles, moving slowly on the screen, this is both completely incomprehensible and suddenly utterly real. This is her baby.

'That's the baby's heart,' says the woman, speaking for the first time and pushing the gum into the corner of her mouth. She points towards four black, pulsating circles.

'That's its spine.' Ruth sees a slender white line moving across the screen. For some inexplicable reason, tears come to her eyes. Then she remembers something.

'Can you tell if it's a boy or a girl?'

'Not at this scan. We'll probably be able to tell at the next one, at about twenty weeks.'

But looking at the screen through swimming eyes, Ruth is convinced that the baby is a boy. There is something masculine, almost jaunty, about the little figure swimming around in her womb. The woman points at another part of the screen. 'Long legs. Has your partner got long legs?'

Has Nelson got long legs? Ruth imagines him striding from place to place, impatient, eager to get to the next job. He is tall, presumably his legs are long. Longer than Ruth's, certainly. Then, suddenly, it hits her for the first time. This baby is half his. Up until this point, she has thought of the baby as entirely hers, has even thought that it is the only thing in the world that is really hers. But it is not hers. For a second she sees the shape on the screen as completely alien – a male, a miniature Nelson. She closes her eyes.

'Are you OK?'

'Yes . . . just a little sick.'

'That's OK. It often happens. We're done anyhow.' She hands Ruth some scratchy paper towels to clean her stomach and Ruth sits up slowly.

'I'll print off an image for you to take home.'

'An image?' Ruth looks at her blankly.

'Of the baby! To show your partner.'

'Oh, yes. Thank you.'

Ruth drives slowly back to the university, aware that she is doing the whole mirror/signal/manoeuvre thing with more care than at any time since her driving test. She keeps to the two-second rule and is so slow passing a bicycle that the car behind her hoots impatiently. She knows that she is driving like an old lady in a hat but she can't help herself. She is filled with the overwhelming realisation that she is carrying another human being inside her. A human being, moreover, with its own personality and its father's long legs. She is its vehicle, carrying it smoothly from A to B, making sure that she gives all the right signals and doesn't crash into an oncoming lorry. How will she keep it up, a journey of nine months, never exceeding the speed limit, no Little Chef to stop at on the way? Perhaps she'll get used to it in time . . .

Term is over for the students. She sees them everywhere: carrying cases into cars, having tearful farewells in doorways, writing loving messages on each other's T-shirts. Get over it, Ruth wants to say. You'll see each other again in September. But she can remember what it's like to have the whole summer stretching ahead of you: working, travelling, lounging around annoying your parents. Four months is an eternity when you're eighteen. By the time the students come back, Ruth will be seven months pregnant. According to the printout in her bag, her baby is due on the first of November.

The students may be on holiday but Ruth isn't. She has dissertations to mark and lectures for next year to prepare.

She climbs the stairs to her office and is touched to find two of her students loitering outside to say goodbye. Ruth teaches postgraduates who are usually on a one-year MA course so this really is the last time she will see them, especially as these two are from the States (she has a lot of overseas students; the university needs the money).

'Goodbye . . . good luck . . . keep in touch . . . come and see us if you're ever in Wisconsin . . .'

Extracting herself, Ruth opens her door and begins collecting papers and books. Seeing her office with its *Indiana Jones* poster, its piles of books and examination scripts, gives her a genuine glow of pleasure. At least here she's Dr Ruth Galloway, Archaeologist, not Ms Ruth Galloway expectant mother (*elderly* expectant mother, she'd been horrified to see on her notes). She is an academic, a professional, a person in her own right. She'll spend a few restful few days at home, reading about bones, decomposition and death.

'Ruth! How are you?' It is Phil.

Phil now knows about her pregnancy and is being supportive. He expresses this by talking in a hushed voice and asking her how she is at every opportunity.

'How was it?' He means the scan (she had to tell him as attending meant she missed the end-of-term lunch) but Ruth chooses to misunderstand.

'The post-mortem? OK. The new pathologist is a bit overkeen, jumps to conclusions too much—'

'I meant . . . the *hospital*.'

'Oh, fine thanks.'

'No *problems*?'

'No.'

Phil stands in the doorway, smiling annoyingly. Ruth longs to get rid of him.

'Going away this summer?' asks Phil.

'No. You?'

'Well . . .' Phil looks embarrassed. 'Sue and I might get away to our place in France for a few days.' Ruth wonders what Shona thinks about this. The latest from Shona is that Phil will leave his wife 'after the final examiners' meeting'. Why this fairly arbitrary date was chosen, Ruth has no idea; she only knows that Shona clings to it like the promise of the second coming. And if Phil does leave Sue, she thinks cynically, Shona's problems are only just beginning.

'Are you planning to drop in on the Swaffham site today?' asks Phil, changing the subject with alacrity. 'I hear they're coming up with some interesting stuff.'

'I might do.' In fact, she is planning to go straight home. Her back aches and she longs to lie down. But Phil is enthusiastic about Max's dig. The Romans are always worth a lottery grant or two, maybe even a TV appearance.

'Great. Could you pick up some soil samples?'

Damn, now she will have to make the detour into Swaffham and spend ages faffing about with sample bags. Why can't Phil do it? Probably off to meet Shona.

'OK,' she says.

It is almost dark by the time she reaches the site. There are no cars parked on the churned-up earth at the bottom of the bank and Ruth is not sure if she feels pleased or disappointed. She hasn't seen Max since the Imbolc night and wonders whether it will be awkward when she does. Did the kiss mean anything to him? Probably not, probably in Brighton they kiss each other at every opportunity. But she knows she has been thinking about it. Not all the time, she has too many other things on her plate, but certainly more than is comfortable. All in all, she is pleased to have the place to herself.

Getting a torch from her car, she climbs the slope to the site. Clearly the students have been working hard. Three new trenches have been dug and small piles of stones indicate that new buildings have been discovered. It looks as if there really was a small settlement here or, at the very least, a villa and surrounding buildings. Intrigued, Ruth moves closer.

She realises that she is in the very trench that Max first showed her but now it has been extended to expose a corner of a wall, plus what look like the remains of under-floor heating. This must mean that this was an important house. She also sees a corner of mosaic. She spares a thought for the people who settled here, on this exposed hillside, two thousand years ago. Were they Romano-British or Romans in exile? No wonder they had wanted heating, thinks Ruth, shivering in the evening air.

She is about to leave when, out of habit, she runs her torch along the foundation level of bricks, looking for anything strange or unusual. And then she sees it. Tiny reddish brown writing, less than an inch high. At first she can't make it out, though the letters look very familiar. Then she realises that the words are written upside down. Craning her head round, she reads: 'Ruth Galloway'.

Afterwards she is not sure quite why this spooked her so

much. In a funny way it was the very size of the words, as if some tiny, evil creature has crept in amongst the stone and rubble and written her name. Why? She has only the most tenuous link to this site. Why would anyone go to the trouble of writing her name, upside down, in letters so small they can hardly be seen, on the wall of some obscure archae-ological site? She doesn't know but she knows she isn't about to hang around and meet the poison dwarf in person. She stands up, heart hammering.

As she does so, she has the strongest sensation that someone is watching her. She swings round, the torch making a wide, panicked arc around her. 'Who's there?'

No answer but footsteps, definite footsteps, coming towards her, walking over the gravel in one of the trenches. Ruth scrambles out of her trench and shines her torch out into the darkness. Now she hears another noise. A slow, steady panting. Someone is breathing, very near her.

Ruth gives up all pretence at courage. Holding the torch out in front of her, she runs headlong down the hill. No longer the careful vehicle for her baby, she is now a terri-fied woman running for cover. The baby will just have to put up with it. She stumbles and almost falls. Oh God, where's her car? But then she sees the comforting lights of the Phoenix and knows she is heading in the right direction. Panting hard, she covers the rest of the distance at a canter. Her car is there. Her lovely trusty, rusty car. Then she stops; her blood freezing.

A dark shape is beside by her car. A man.

Ruth screams.

'Ruth? It's OK. It's me.' It is Max Grey.

Ruth hears someone still screaming and realises, to her embarrassment, that it is her. 'Max,' she gasps. He is by her side, putting an arm round her. He smells of wood-smoke and soap. 'Ruth? What is it?'

'Someone . . . someone up at the site . . . my name . . . on a wall . . .'

'What?'

Ruth takes a deep breath, holding on to Max's arm to steady herself. 'I was up at the site . . . having a look. I saw someone had written . . . written my name on a wall. Then I thought someone was there, watching me. I heard them breathing. Silly, I know.'

She can't see Max's face in the darkness but she feels his arm stiffen. His voice when it comes, though, is calm and reassuring. 'Why don't I go up and have a look? You stay here. Sit in your car, put the heater on. You're shivering. Hang on.'

He turns away and Ruth sees now that the Range Rover is parked beside her Renault. He comes back with a thick jumper and a flask. 'Here, put this on.' She puts on the jumper, it smells comfortingly of musty wool. She opens her car door and climbs inside. Max hands the flask in after her. 'Have a swig. I'll be right back.'

Ruth takes a tentative sip. Black coffee. All drinks taste odd at the moment but this is something different. After a second, she realises it has whisky in it.

Max is back after a few minutes. He leans in through the window.

'Are you OK to drive home? I'll follow you.'

*

For the first time Ruth is relieved to see the security light come on as she opens her gate. Right now, she wants as much light as she can get. She opens the front door, hoping her sitting room is not too untidy.

Max Grey, though, does not seem to notice the papers all over the floor or even the dirty washing on the sofa. He strokes Flint, admires her books and her collection of arrowheads and accepts the offer of tea with every appearance of pleasure. It is only when they're sitting down with their tea (the washing hastily stowed away in the kitchen) that they talk about the events on the site.

'Was anyone there when you first arrived?' asks Max.

'No. It was completely deserted. Phil wanted me to get some soil samples, and I just thought I'd have a look at the trenches – you've done loads of work – and then I saw those . . . those words.'

'You said you thought you heard someone . . .'

'Yes, I heard noises very near me . . . someone breathing. I don't know. I could have imagined it. Did you see anyone?'

Max is silent for a second and then he says, 'I saw a shape, maybe a dog or even a large fox. Nothing else.'

'A dog.' Ruth is so relieved that she laughs. 'That explains the panting then.'

'Yes.' But Max doesn't smile back. He frowns down into his cup.

'Have you any idea who could have done this?' asks Ruth. 'I mean none of your students knows me from Adam. And to go to the trouble of sneaking up to the site with a pot of red paint—'

Max looks up. 'I don't think it was paint.'

'What—' It takes a few seconds for Ruth to realise what he means and then a few more for her to be able to frame the word. 'Blood?'

Max nods, 'I think so, yes. We can check tomorrow.'

'But why . . .' Ruth's voice is rising, 'why would anyone write my name on a wall *in blood*?'

'I don't know,' Max says again. Then, 'Ruth, have you ever read I, *Claudius*?'

Surprised Ruth says, 'Yes, I think so. A long time ago. It's by Robert Graves, isn't it?'

'Yes. You're too young to remember but there was a terrific TV series years ago. Derek Jacobi and Siân Phillips.'

In fact Ruth does remember though she is flattered that Max thinks she is too young. The programme was past her bedtime but she remembers the opening credits: a snake gliding slowly over a Roman mosaic. Her parents used to say that it was disgusting ('a waste of our licence fee. I'm going to write to Mary Whitehouse') but Ruth had a strong suspicion that they used to watch it after she had gone to bed.

'What about it?' she asks.

Max sighs. 'In the book, the child Caligula kills his father, Claudius's brother Germanicus. He does it by, quite literally, scaring him to death.'

Ruth is silent, thinking of the snake moving across the floor. This whole thing has suddenly taken on a surreal tinge, as if she is acting in her own TV drama, quite unreal, the disturbing images existing only to shock the more sensitive viewers.

'He did it,' says Max, 'by exploiting Germanicus's superstitions. He stole his lucky talisman, a green jade figure of

Hecate. He left animal corpses around the house, cocks' feathers smeared in blood, unlucky signs and numbers written on the walls, sometimes high up, sometimes,' he looks at Ruth, 'sometimes very low down, as if a dwarf had written them. Then Germanicus's name appeared on the wall, upside down. Each day, one of the letters disappeared. On the day that only a single G remained, Germanicus died.'

There is a silence. Flint jumps on the sofa, purring loudly. Ruth buries her hand in his soft amber fur.

'Do you really think,' she says at last, 'that someone is trying to scare me, by using an idea they found in I, Claudius?'

Max shrugs. 'I don't know but it was the first thing that came to my head. And when you think about the dead cockerel . . .'

'So we're looking for a deranged Robert Graves fan?'

Max laughs. 'Or someone addicted to classic TV. I don't know, Ruth. What does seem clear is that someone is trying to scare you.'

'To warn me off the Norwich site?'

'Possibly. It's no secret that you're involved. You had quite a high profile in that other case, didn't you? The Lucy Downey case.'

Ruth is silent. She had tried to keep as low a profile as possible (only Nelson knew, for example, that it was she, not the police, who had found Lucy) but she supposes that things always leak out. In any case, it would not be hard to work out that she, as head of Forensic Archaeology, would be involved in both cases.

'They'll have to work harder than that to scare me,' she says at last.

Max smiles. 'Good for you.' There is another silence, a rather different one this time. Then he says, almost shyly, 'Ruth. Will you have dinner with me? One day next week. Not at the Phoenix. Somewhere nicer.'

Ruth looks at him, sitting at ease on her sagging armchair, his long legs folded under him. Beside her, Flint's purrs increase. She shouldn't say yes. She is a pregnant woman. She doesn't need this sort of complication. Max smiles at her. She notices, for the first time, that one of his front teeth is slightly chipped.

'All right,' she says, 'I'd like to.'

When he has gone, Ruth is so tired that she goes straight to bed without even checking that Flint has enough food for the night (he wakes her up later to remind her about this). Lying on her bed, she can still hear Max's Range Rover driving slowly along the narrow road. Ten minutes later, her security light comes on again. But Ruth does not get up.

19th June
Festival for Minerva

I must get organised. I must not act ex abrupto. *So – I have my knife which is honed now to a serviceable edge. I have the axe which will do later for the head. I have been wondering if I need some form of anaesthetic, to prevent the child from crying out. The difficulty is to obtain such things. The dentist might help, he is an intelligent man, at the cutting edge of science. I could easily explain my need for chloroform as a wish to carry out a scientific experiment at school.*

She, as ever, is the problem. She never leaves the child alone. I must ask her – no, order her (I am the Master after all) – to leave the infant alone in the afternoons. Surely she has chores she should be doing about the place.

I have only a week or so in which to act. The trouble is that sometimes I am weak and the gods give me terrible dreams. I wake up sweating and crying – shameful. But I will not be distracted. I have begun to fast in order to purify the flesh. All must be in readiness.

CHAPTER 16

The DNA results show that the body under the doorstep is a girl. The post-mortem confirmed that the child is less than six years old. Father Hennessey, Nelson decides, has some explaining to do.

This time there is no cosy walk in the grounds. Nelson interviews the priest at the local police station. A car is sent to fetch him and when he arrives Nelson is sitting unsmiling behind a desk. Clough is also in the room and as Hennessey enters Nelson says into the tape machine, 'Interview commencing at fourteen hundred hours. Present: Detective Chief Inspector Harry Nelson and Detective Sergeant David Clough.'

Father Hennessey smiles politely and takes a seat opposite Nelson. He shows no surprise at his hostile reception nor does he make any attempt at small talk. He waits calmly for Nelson's first question.

'Father Hennessey,' he's damned if he's going to call him 'Father' again, 'you mentioned two children who went missing in 1973.'

They have looked them up, of course. Nelson was hoping to find Elizabeth Black's dental records to compare them to the skull but there is no record of Elizabeth ever visiting a dentist. And, after 1973, both children vanish completely.

'Yes,' says Father Hennessey, looking intently at Nelson.

'Could you tell us a bit more about their disappearance, please?'

Father Hennessey sighs. 'It was in the evening. The children had some free time before bed and most of them were playing in the grounds. Supervised, of course. Sister Immaculata called them in about six and there was no sign of Martin and Elizabeth. At first we thought they were just hiding. Martin had a ... mischievous sense of humour. But then, after we searched the house and the grounds, we began to get worried.'

He pauses and Nelson says, 'When did you call the police?'

'Almost immediately. They searched the house and grounds too. Some of the staff got quite upset. But nothing was found. Then they switched the search to the wider area.'

'Did *you* search? Personally?'

Father Hennessey's pale blue eyes look past Nelson. 'I searched all night,' he says at last. 'The house, the grounds. Then I rode around Norwich on my motorbike, looking in alleyways, abandoned houses, anywhere I thought they might hide.'

Clough interjects. 'You had a motorbike?'

'It's not against the law, you know,' replies Hennessey mildly.

'And in all this searching,' Nelson cuts in, 'did the police ever dig up the grounds?'

'No.'

Goons, thinks Nelson. They were probably too taken in by

this saintly motorbiking priest. They would never assume that he could have killed the children. Well, Nelson is different.

'Did they look in the well?' he asks.

Now Father Hennessey looks surprised. 'No. It was boarded up, cemented over. No child could have fallen down it.'

Nelson says nothing, playing the silence game. This time he wins.

'Have you found something in the well?'

'We've found a child's skull,' Nelson tells him. 'A child of five. A girl.' 'Under six' is what the autopsy report says but he wants to shock Hennessey into saying something indiscreet.

Father Hennessy certainly looks shocked. His lips move silently, presumably in prayer. He asks, 'Is it Elizabeth?'

'We don't know for certain,' says Nelson, 'yet.' He sees no reason to add that they might never know as they have no DNA of Elizabeth's. But he wants Hennessey to think he will find out. Nelson, the fearless seeker after truth, scourge of wrongdoers.

'How could the skull have got in the well?' asks Hennessey, still sounding shaken. He takes a sip of water. Suddenly he looks an old man.

'You tell me.'

'I have no idea.' Sharper now. Hennessey is pulling himself together.

Silence again. Clough asks, 'Did you get on well with Martin and Elizabeth?' The change of subject, of tone. An old interrogation standby.

But Hennessey is equal to it. He looks directly at Clough.

'Yes. They were lovely children, very bright, very loving. They'd had a traumatic time, with their mother dying and were . . . damaged.'

'Damaged?' says Nelson sharply. 'What do you mean?'

'These things leave scars, Detective Chief Inspector. Martin was angry, angry with his mother for leaving him, angry with the world for letting it happen. Elizabeth was easier. She was very sad, very insecure. She clung to Martin, refused to be separated from her teddy, that sort of thing. But they were getting over it, slowly. Martin was exceptionally bright. I tried to encourage that. I gave him books to read.'

'What sort of books?'

'All sorts. He was interested in science and history. I gave him books about the Greeks and the Romans. He was fascinated by the idea that the house could have been built on a Roman site.'

Nelson remembers Ruth's comments about Roman pottery found on the site. So the priest had known that, even then.

'So you had a close relationship with the children?'

Again the priest meets his eyes squarely, almost defiantly. 'Yes.'

'And the other staff members?'

'Everyone loved Elizabeth. She was a very lovable child. Martin was . . . Martin was more difficult.'

'We've spoken to Sister Immaculata —'

'Have you?' Hennessey leans forward eagerly. 'How is she?'

'In reasonable health,' Nelson replies coldly, 'mentally unimpaired,' he adds.

Hennessey nods. 'Good. She's had a hard life, poor woman.'

Nelson ignores this. 'She says that Martin was a trouble-maker.'

'As I say, he was angry.'

'Did he have uncontrollable rages?' asks Clough sympathetically.

For the first time, Father Hennessey looks angry. 'No, he did not have "uncontrollable rages".' His voice puts irritable quotes around the words. 'Nor did he kill his sister in a fit of demonic temper, as I imagine you're implying. He loved her. They were exceptionally close.'

'Unnaturally close?'

'No, naturally close. They were a brother and sister with no one else in the world. Don't you think they would be close?'

'I assume nothing,' says Nelson. 'You knew them. I didn't. I just want to find out who would kill a child and throw its head down a well. Now whoever did that, they were unnatural.'

Father Hennessey looks at him. 'Unnatural maybe,' he says in his quietest voice, 'evil certainly.'

The drive home is silent apart from Clough chomping his way through two packets of Hula Hoops. Nelson is conscious that they haven't really got much further. Father Hennessey had seemed shocked at the discovery of the skull but he had also seemed genuinely surprised. Not surprised enough though to blurt out any confessions. Not that Nelson ever really thought he would; Father Hennessey is a cool customer. Controlled, hard almost, despite the surface warmth. Does this make him a murderer?

'Do you think he did it?' Nelson asks Clough as they speed

through several picturesque villages ('Kill your speed, not a child!').

'The priest? Maybe. Easy enough to kill them, hide the bodies and bury them later. The cops didn't even dig up the grounds.'

'Bloody muppets.' Nelson grinds his teeth. 'Do you think there's anyone still around from those days?'

'Maybe Tom Henty. You know, the desk sergeant at Lynn. He's been around for donkeys' years.'

'Good idea. I'll talk to him.'

'Do *you* think Hennessey did it?' Clough looks curiously at his boss

'I think he's hiding something,' says Nelson slowly. 'Something to do with the children. Maybe he's covering up for someone.'

'What about that nun? Judy said she was a nutter.'

'No she didn't. She said she was as sharp as a needle.'

'Same thing. The nun could have killed them.'

'Why?'

'Maybe she abused the little girl and the boy found out.'

'Your mind's like a tabloid.'

'Thank you.'

'It's not a compliment. Pretty hard to dispose of the body of a twelve-year-old.'

'If they're not dead, where are they then?'

'That's the question. We'll widen the search. Try to find some relatives in Ireland. Talk to other people from the home. Nine times out of ten, missing people turn up right back where they started. It's almost as if they can't keep away.'

'Do you think they're alive?'

'The boy maybe. He was old enough to look after himself. The girl . . . I think the girl might be our skeleton.'

'Well, it would be a bit of a coincidence if she isn't,' says Clough, probing his empty Hula Hoops packet with a moistened finger, 'two dead children on one site.'

'Yes,' says Nelson thoughtfully. He is thinking about the site – it has held a children's home, a churchyard and maybe even a Roman villa. Who knows how many other incarnations it has had, how many deaths it has witnessed? He shakes himself mentally. What's the matter with him? He's starting to think like Cathbad.

'You know what was funny?' says Clough, finally abandoning his search in the packet. 'How much he talked about love.'

'Priests do that.'

'No. It was creepy. He said the girl was "lovable". I think that's a bit weird.'

Nelson considers. Was it weird? He had dismissed Hennessey's remarks ('Everyone loved Elizabeth') as standard priest-speak but what if Clough is right? Is something more sinister at work here? Is 'lovable' an odd word to use about a five-year-old girl? Does he mean, in fact, that he was in some perverted way in love with her?

'That's what the nun said. It was in Judy's report. She said Hennessey believed the boy needed "love and attention".'

Nelson is rather impressed that Clough has remembered this. But then again, it's a sad world if no one is allowed to love children.

'Maybe he did love them,' he suggests, 'in a non-sexual, fatherly way.'

'Jesus,' scoffs Clough, 'you're sounding like a right God-squadder.'

'Rubbish,' says Nelson angrily, pulling out onto the motorway with the minimum of care. 'I'm just not jumping to conclusions. Never assume, that's what my first boss used to say.'

'I know. It makes an ass out of you and me.' Clough looks out of the window. Nelson wonders if he's getting a bit above himself. A good spell in the archives tomorrow will take him down a peg or two.

'Tomorrow,' he says coldly, 'you can start the search for the kids' family. And look up the Land Registry for the house. I want a list of everyone who's ever owned the site.'

'Jesus,' mutters Clough, in a distinctly non-religious tone.

CHAPTER 17

Max has suggested that they meet at Reedham which strikes
Ruth as extremely inconvenient. Reedham is on the Broads,
on the opposite side of Norwich. Getting there will involve
a long and boring drive through the seven circles of hell, or
the Norwich bypass. Why on earth couldn't they meet somewhere in King's Lynn, thinks Ruth crossly as she gets into
her car. King's Lynn is not exactly short of restaurants. Maybe
Max is a food freak who is going to take her to one of those
experimental places that offer sausage-flavoured ice cream
or deep-fried hedgehog. Well, if anyone gives her deep-fried
hedgehog, she will be sick all over them and serve them
right. She is beginning to wish that she had stayed in with
The Wire and an M&S lasagne.

They are meeting by the Ship, a well-known Norfolk pub
popular with river trippers. Surely she hasn't come all this
way to have a pub meal surrounded by braying Londoners?

Max is sitting at a table overlooking the river. He jumps
up when he sees Ruth and when she gets near enough kisses
her awkwardly on the cheek. Is this a date then?

'Ruth! You look great.'

Ruth is wearing a smock top over cotton trousers. She hated this style when it first came in because it makes everyone look pregnant. Now, of course, this is an advantage.

'Are we eating here?' Ruth gestures at the pub, which certainly looks inviting in the evening light. The tables are starting to fill up and swans are venturing up from the river in search of snacks.

'Here? No. A bit further along.'

To Ruth's surprise he leads the way to his car.

'Where are we going?' she asks suspiciously.

'You'll see.'

They drive past houses set on the hill with smooth gardens stretching down to the river. Has Max got a house here? He must be earning more than most archaeologists if so. But Max drives past the residential area and along an unmade-up road. Ships' masts rise up in front of them.

He parks at the end of the road where there are several other cars as well as a low building marked 'Showers'. In front of them is a small marina, crammed with shiny boats. Some of the owners are having a barbecue and there are children and dogs running around. It all looks very jolly but Max doesn't give the boat owners a second look. He strides along the pontoon, making it wobble alarmingly. Ruth follows more carefully. The last thing she wants is to fall in the water and to be pulled out by a drunken holidaymaker. They are at the end of the marina now and Max pauses by a small wooden gate. 'Not far now.'

Through the gate is another pontoon, far more rickety than those in the marina. As they walk along in single file,

Ruth sees the river flowing swiftly past them, smooth as silk. Fields rise up on either side, the corn as tall as they are. It is getting dark and the birds are flying low over the reeds. Ahead of them the river divides into two, like an illustration in a storybook. Which path will you take?

'Here she is!' shouts Max suddenly.

Bemused, Ruth looks round for the 'she'. Maybe Max has brought her all the way here to meet his wife? Then she sees that Max is gesturing to a boat moored at the end of the pontoon. It is small and compact, blue and white with a striped awning.

'This is yours?'

'Welcome aboard the *Lady Annabelle*.'

'Is this where you're living?'

'Yes.' Max leaps lightly on board and holds out a hand to Ruth. 'It's great. I can moor at a different place every day but I keep her here mostly. Bit of a drive to Swaffham but it's worth it. It's just magical at night, sleeping out under the stars and listening to the river.'

On deck a small table has been laid for two, with candles and wine in a silver bucket. Ruth looks around her. Although they are still fairly near the marina, there is not a sound apart from the water slapping against the sides of the boat. Swallows swoop over the water and, on the opposite bank, she can see cows, knee deep in the wet grass.

Max is looking at her, rather anxiously. 'Is this OK? I thought it would be nicer than a restaurant. And I don't often have a chance to cook for anyone.'

'It's perfect,' says Ruth. Now that the initial surprise has worn off, she finds that she is relaxing for the first time that day, allowing the beauty of the evening to sweep over her. Max pours them both a glass of white wine (Ruth doesn't like to refuse) and offers to show her round the boat. 'She's very small so it should only take a minute.'

'Is it . . . she . . . yours?'

'No, she belongs to a friend who lives near here. When he heard I was coming to Norfolk for the summer, he offered me the boat as my base. It's an ex-hire boat, a bathtub they call them round here. Very handy for getting through low bridges.'

The boat is very small but Ruth is fascinated by the evidence of Max's life on board. Below deck is a stove with something delicious-smelling simmering in a saucepan, and ropes of herbs and garlic hang from the ceiling. Opposite is a bench seat and a narrow table. At the pointed end (the prow?) there is a bed piled high with cushions. Ruth notices a dry-looking classical book on the bedside table and, more surprisingly, a stuffed toy on the pillow. Perhaps Max is not as assured and grown-up as he seems. Over the bed are windows which must open out onto the front of the boat. There is also a shower and a tiny loo which, to Ruth's embarrassment, she has to use.

They sit on deck drinking wine (in Ruth's case very slowly) and talking about Max's dig.

'I think it's going to be important. It's a significant site. Several buildings grouped around a temple. Could be a vicus.'

'Vicus?' Ruth feels she should know this word.

'A small settlement, usually near a military site. A garrison town, really.'

'Have you found any more skeletons?' asks Ruth.

'No. Some more pottery. A few coins. Some other metal pieces, possibly from a game. A signet ring with seal.'

'That reminds me.' Ruth tells him about the ring found on the Norwich site. Max is silent for a minute, pouring more wine. 'Sounds like Hecate. Were they human heads?'

'I think so.'

'Because sometimes Hecate is depicted with three animal faces; a snake, a horse and a boar.'

'They looked human to me.'

'Is there any other evidence of a Roman settlement on the site?'

'Not yet but we found some pottery. Samian ware.'

'Really?' Max looks genuinely interested.

'Why don't you come and have a look one day?'

'I will.' He disappears below to check on the food which, when it appears, is absolutely delicious – chicken in red wine, saffron rice, green salad.

'You really can cook,' says Ruth, smiling.

'I like to cook but . . . living on my own . . .' There is a small, charged silence.

'Have you always lived on your own?' asks Ruth, aware that it is a rather personal question.

But Max answers easily. 'I lived with a girlfriend for a while but we split up, amicably enough. Now I think it would be hard to go back to living with someone. You get used to your own space. What about you?'

'I lived with a boyfriend for a few years. When we split up I remember being quite relieved to have the house to myself. I guess I'm just not cut out for living with someone.'

'Do you have a boyfriend now?'

'No.' Ruth knows that now is the time to tell Max that while she doesn't have a boyfriend, she does have another, rather permanent, commitment. She hesitates, trying to find the words.

'Ruth,' Max reaches out to touch her hand.

'I'm pregnant,' Ruth blurts out.

'What?' Max sits back. It is dark now and Ruth can't see the expression on his face. She takes a deep breath.

'I'm pregnant. I'm not with the father. It's complicated.'

'Wow, Ruth . . .' Max seems completely at a loss. Ruth eats a last piece of chicken and instantly feels ashamed to be thinking about food in the middle of such an important declaration. It's very good though.

'I don't know what to say,' says Max at last.

'It's OK,' says Ruth through chicken. 'You don't have to say anything. I just thought you ought to know, that's all.'

'When's the baby due?'

'November.'

'I've got cheese for afterwards,' Max says suddenly, 'soft cheese. You'd better not have any. It's not good when you're pregnant is it?'

Ruth laughs, touched that he is thinking of her welfare, relieved to have got the announcement over with. 'I'm full up anyhow.'

'I've made chocolate brownies.'

'Although I do have a space for chocolate brownies.'

Over the brownies, Max tells Ruth that one of the reasons he split up with his girlfriend was that he wanted children and she didn't.

'I never wanted children,' Ruth says, 'or I thought I didn't.

I was quite happy with my cats. But then, when I got pregnant, accidentally, I was surprised how delighted I felt. Suddenly I wanted this baby more than anything.'

'It must feel amazing,' Max laughs, rather embarrassed. 'Sounds weird I know but I've always envied women for being able to get pregnant. Must be incredible to have all that going on inside you.'

'Yes and you can eat without worrying about getting fat.'

'Another brownie?'

'Thanks.'

'It's scary though too,' Ruth continues, after a pause. 'I don't know enough about babies or anything. I'm ... estranged from my mother. None of my friends have babies.'

This isn't quite true. Some of Ruth's friends from school and university have had babies, most of whom are children or even teenagers now. It's just that, as soon as they had children, an invisible wall seemed to appear between them and their childless friends. Ruth could turn up at the hospital with flowers and balloons ('It's a girl!'), she could remember birthdays and Christmas, but she was forever outside that charmed circle of motherhood. Gradually, those friendships faded and died.

'And the father ...?'

'He doesn't know.'

'Oh.' Ruth hears disapproval in the monosyllable. Of course, Max wants children. He would identify with the unknown father, will accuse her of abusing father's rights and other newly invented crimes. In fact he's probably about to jump on the roof dressed as Superman.

'I will tell him,' she says, 'it's just ... he's married.'

'Oh.' A different sound, more understanding, perhaps even sympathetic. 'You can talk to me,' he says, 'I don't know anything about babies, but you can talk to me.'

'Thank you.'

The silence, a companionable one this time, is broken by Ruth's mobile ringing. She snatches it up, meaning to turn it off, but then she sees the caller display. 'Debbie Lewis.'

'Excuse me,' she says, 'I'd better take this call.'

Nelson is at home, reading through some of the results of Clough's sulky trawl through the files. Nelson doesn't usually bring work home (at the outset of their marriage he promised Michelle he wouldn't and, by and large, he has kept his word). But he is keen to point the case in a new direction. If Clough has found any useful leads on the children . . . but it seems that he hasn't.

He has birth certificates for Martin and Elizabeth: mother Louise Black, née Maxwell; father Daniel Black. He has a death certificate for Louise Black dated 1970 and, in 1998, a death certificate for Daniel Black. If, as Nelson suspects, Daniel Black knew more about his children's disappearance than he admitted, it is too late to talk to him.

He also has statements from other employees at the Sacred Heart Children's Home – cleaners, gardeners, health visitors, someone calling themselves a Play Specialist. All these statements, without exception, attest to the saintliness of Father Hennessey and the high standard of care in the home. One of the gardeners describes Martin Black as 'trouble' but this could have been linked to his habit of digging holes in the lawn. The Health Visitor says Elizabeth was prone to colds and sore throats but was otherwise healthy; Martin was 'as strong as a horse'.

Clough has also tracked down a distant cousin living in Ireland but, as she hasn't seen Martin since 1963 and has never set eyes on Elizabeth, this contact is of little use.

Nelson also talked to Tom Henty, the grizzled Desk Sergeant, who remembered the Black case very well. 'Massive manhunt, all leave cancelled. We couldn't work out how two children could just vanish like that. I was a PC then and I was one of the first to go into the house. Great big place, it was. Like a stately home almost, high ceilings, chandeliers and all that but with kids' stuff all over the place, toys and little tables and gym equipment in the dining room. Strange place.'

'Why do you say that?' asked Nelson.

'I don't know. The priest in charge, he was a good bloke, you could see that, and the kids were happy but the house was strange. I searched the bedrooms, they were up in the attics, lots of little beds under the eaves and, I don't know, something about it gave me the creeps. I kept expecting to see a dead body in one of the beds.'

'But you didn't find anything.'

'No.' Seeing Nelson's look, Henty added, rather defensively, 'We did a proper search but there was nothing. We searched the grounds, had frogmen in the river, did a house-to-house, nothing.'

'Did you look in the well?'

Henty looked confused. 'It was boarded up. Hadn't been tampered with, you could see that.' He stared at Nelson with sudden fearfulness in his eyes. 'Is that what this is about?

Have you found a body in the well?'

Now Nelson sits in his 'study' (also called 'the snug' by Michelle and 'the playroom' by Laura and Rebecca), reading through the print-outs and photocopies and wondering where the hell he's going to go from here. It can't be long before the press gets hold of the story and if he hasn't got a credible suspect by then he'll be hanged, drawn and quartered. A child's body buried under a former children's home – the tabloids will love it. And it's getting close to summer when other news will be thin on the ground. If he isn't careful, Inspector Plod of the Norfolk flatfoots will be on the front page of every paper for months.

He sighs. He can hear the *Sex and the City* music coming from the sitting room which means, at least, that he's not tempted to go in. His wife and daughters are addicted to the programme which is on every night on Sky. To him it seems sheer unadulterated filth combined with the most bizarre-looking women he has ever seen. 'It's fashion Dad,' Rebecca had explained. But, if it's fashion, how come he's never sees anyone else dressed like that? Maybe it's American fashion. Apart from a trip to Disneyland, which hardly counts, Nelson has never been to America and has no desire to go. Unlike some cops, he does not have a secret FBI fantasy which involves guns, fast cars and improbably glamorous settings. Life as a cop in America, he is sure, is much the same as anywhere – ten per cent excitement, ninety per cent mind-numbing boredom.

'Dad!' A shout from the sitting room. 'Your phone's ringing.' Grumbling Nelson goes into the hall, where his phone is ringing from his jacket pocket. Of course, it stops as soon as he lays hands on it. 'One missed call from Ruth.' Nelson presses call back.

'Ruth? What is it?'

She sounds very distant but he knows, from her voice, that she has made some sort of breakthrough.

'I've had a call from Debbie Lewis. She's the forensic dentistry expert I mentioned.'

'Bloody hell. That sounds a fun job.'

'It's fascinating. Anyway she's come back with some interesting results. Apparently there are traces of stannous fluoride on the teeth.'

'So?'

'Well stannous fluoride was first introduced by Crest toothpaste as a trial in 1949. But they found that it stained the teeth so, in 1955, they switched to sodium monofluorophosphate.'

'So what?' Nelson's head is starting to swim.

'So the skull must be from a child who was alive before 1955. When was the girl born? The girl in the children's home?'

'Elizabeth Black?' Nelson rifles through the papers on his desk but he thinks he already knows the answer.

'1968,' he says.

CHAPTER 18

Nelson calls a special team meeting in the morning. Working on Saturday means overtime, which won't please Whitcliffe, but he knows it is imperative that they make some headway on the case before the press get hold of it. Nelson arrives at the station in a mood of manic efficiency. He bounds upstairs, crashes open the door to the incident room, rips the picture of Father Patrick Hennessey off the pinboard and barks, 'Right, the priest's in the clear. Any other ideas?'

The effect is rather ruined because Judy and Clough are the only people in the incident room. Clough is eating a McDonald's breakfast burger and Judy is reading the *Mail*.

'What did you say?' asks Clough, screwing up greaseproof paper and throwing it in the bin.

'The priest.' Nelson puts the picture on the table. Father Hennessey's blue eyes stare blandly up at him. 'He's innocent. Ruth Galloway has identified traces of fluoride on the skull that could only have come from before 1955. Elizabeth Black was born in 1968.'

'Fluoride?' Clough still looks blank.

'In the teeth. Apparently there's some special sort of flu-

oride that was only used between 1949 and 1955. So that's
our range.'

'Don't they put fluoride in the water anyway?' asks
Clough.

'Not in Norfolk,' offers Judy, folding away the paper.
'Fluoride occurs naturally in our water. There's no need to
add it to the supply.'

'Anyway, this is different stuff. Stannous fluoride, it's
called. Apparently they don't use it any more because it stains
your teeth. Or rather they do but only in one specialised
brand.'

'So Holy Joe didn't do it?' Clough sounds disappointed.

'No.'

'I never thought he did,' says Judy.

'Well, you're another one of them.'

'What?'

'Catholics.'

'They're everywhere, Cloughie,' says Nelson, 'except in the
Masons. Now, come on, we've got work to do.'

Ruth also wakes in an optimistic frame of mind. It is Saturday
so she can have a lie-in. Light filters in through the curtains
and onto the bed where Flint sleeps stretched out, his claws
twitching. Ruth stretches too, touching the cat with her toes.
It had been a good night last night. The meal on the boat,
getting the pregnancy thing off her chest, the breakthrough
in the case. The perfect evening in fact. After the call from
Debbie and Ruth's call to Nelson, she and Max had chatted
some more and then he had driven her back to her car.
Drinkers were still sitting outside the pub and the moon

was high above the treetops. He had kissed her cheek and told her to take care. 'See you soon,' Ruth had said. 'I hope so,' Max had replied.

There was something in his tone, and in the kiss, which makes Ruth's heart beat a little faster as she remembers it. He can't possibly fancy her, especially now he knows she is pregnant but, nevertheless, there is something, a hint that they might be more than just friends. Does she fancy him? A little, she admits. He is very much her type, tall and dark and intelligent, a little distant. But all those usual women's magaziney feelings have been submerged by the over-whelming fact that she is expecting a baby. She can't really think of anything else. Even now, lying here luxuriating in the warm bed, she is thinking about the creature inside her. She even fantasises that she can feel him move, although the nurse at the hospital said it was too early. There is something though. A heaviness, a presence, a sense of space filled. She has even thought of a name for him. She has begun to call him Toby. She doesn't know why, she doesn't even par-ticularly like the name, but she just has a feeling that this baby is called Toby.

Damn, she needs to go to the loo again. She might as well make a cup of tea now she's up. Downstairs, the early morning view over the Saltmarsh is spectacular, seagulls wheeling against the pale blue sky. The news is on the radio but soon there will be that blissful listening hour between nine and ten: feel-good stories, inheritance tracks, bizarre facts about people who collect matchboxes or who have unknowingly married close blood relations. Perfection.

Ruth pads upstairs with her tea. She'll listen to the radio

and then she'll think about getting up. She might even go for a swim, do something healthy. It'll be good for Toby. Humming tunelessly, she gets back into bed.

Nelson faces his team across the now more crowded incident room. 'So,' he is saying forcefully, 'whilst the evidence needs to be verified, it does seem that we are looking at an earlier timescale for this crime. Elizabeth Black was born in 1968. If the expert evidence is correct, the skull can't possibly be hers.'

'Are we sure the skull and body are the same child, sir?' Nelson cranes his head to see who has asked this excellent question. A new recruit, Tanya Fuller.

'Good question, Tanya. Yes, the DNA results confirm this. So, we're looking at earlier events in the house. Cloughie, what does the title deed registration tell us?'

Clough, who has been glaring resentfully at Tanya, jumps to his feet. He flicks importantly through his file.

'Prior to 1960, the house was owned by . . . Bloody hell!'

After breakfast, Ruth contemplates her day. There is always work, of course, but the sun is shining in the dust motes by her window and she doesn't feel like working. Exercise would be good but she no longer fancies the swimming pool with its smell of chlorine and other peoples' feet. A walk, that's what she'd like. A brisk walk with a pub lunch at the end of it.

She almost phones Shona, who is sometimes amenable to walking if compensated by alcohol, but then she hesitates, wondering if she's up to further bulletins on the state of Phil's marriage. Anyway, Shona would want to eat in King's

Lynn, somewhere where she can be sure of extra virgin olive oil and ciabatta. Ruth fancies something a little more rustic. Suddenly, a vision of the Phoenix comes into her head – the smell of chicken cooking on the outdoor grill, the view over the hills, the clink of glasses and the hum of conversation.

Didn't Max say something about discovering some more finds on the site? If Ruth drives out to Swaffham, she won't be going to see Max, she'll be going to see the pottery and the coins and the pieces from the Roman board game. That's all right then.

Ruth fetches her jacket.

'Prior to 1960,' Clough looks portentously around the room, 'the house was owned by Christopher Spens.'

'Christopher . . .' Nelson echoes, 'not the same family . . .?'

'One and the same.' Clough sounds like he is enjoying himself though, in retrospect, this is an oversight of fairly epic proportions. 'Father of Roderick Spens, grandfather of Edward Spens.'

'Explains why he still owns the site really,' says Tanya brightly. Clough scowls at her.

'Did the Spens family actually live in the house?' asks Judy.

'Looks like it – I've got the census here. Yep, census of 1951. Christopher Spens, Rosemary Spens, children Roderick and Annabelle.'

'Right.' Nelson gets to his feet. 'Cloughie, you find out all you can about the Spens family. Judy and Tanya, you get on to the lab for the test results. I'm going to have a little chat with Edward Spens.'

*

The weather stays bright all the way to Swaffham but as Ruth pulls off the A47 (carefully mirror-signal-manoeuvring) dark clouds are scudding across the sky. As she parks on the grass at the foot of the hill, fat raindrops are beginning to fall. She watches as the students run laughing down the slope, holding coats and tarpaulins over their heads. Most disappear into the pub, some bundle into dilapidated cars and drive off in a blur of exhaust smoke. Soon Ruth's is the only vehicle parked at the bottom of the mound.

'Is it important, Harry? Otherwise one does rather like leave weekends free for the family.'

'Oh it's important, Mr Spens,' says Nelson grimly. He decides to do away with any introductory niceties. 'Why didn't you tell me that your family used to live on Woolmarket Street?'

A slight pause. 'I assumed you knew.'

'Never assume, Mr Spens. So, even when a body was discovered on the site, you didn't think it was worth mentioning that the house was once your family home?'

'I never lived there. The house and land was leased to the diocese in 1960.'

'But you still owned it?'

'Yes. But you were interested in the years when it was a children's home. The Spens family had nothing to do with the house then.'

'And now we're interested in the Spens years,' says Nelson smoothly.

'What do you mean?'

'We've got evidence that the body was that of a child born in the early to mid-fifties. When would be a good time for me to pop over?'

The rain seems to be slowing down. Ruth, who feels slightly sick after the car journey, decides to take a short walk after all. Just up to the site and back. She gets out of the car, pulling on her yellow sou'wester.

The climb up the hill is hard going and she finds herself staring down at the grass, willing her feet to keep moving. When she gets to the top and looks around her, she realises that the sky is now completely black. Far off, she hears the first faint rumble of thunder.

As she heads towards the main trench she thinks she sees something out of the corner of her eye. She whirls round but there is nothing, just the wind blowing across the coarse grass. But Ruth is sure she saw something – a black shape skirting around the edge of the site. An animal maybe but, for some reason, Ruth feels shaken. She hears Max's voice. *She is meant to haunt crossroads, crossing places, accompanied by her ghost dogs.*

Don't be ridiculous, she tells herself. Hecate's hounds are hardly going to be lying in wait for you. It was probably a fox or a cat. But, nevertheless, she has a strong urge to go back to her car and drive as far away from the site as she can. It is only the thought of climbing all the way up the hill for nothing that stops her. She'll just have a quick look in the main trench and go back. Just to say that she's done something.

The sky murmurs again. Pulling her hood further over her head, Ruth lowers herself into the trench.

Ruth stumbles slightly and almost falls onto the packed earth. Suddenly lightning splits open the sky. Ruth shuts her eyes. When she opens them again, there is a dead baby at her feet.

20th June
Festival for Summanus

Last night I had a terrible dream – a snake-faced woman, a man with two faces, a child thrown into the furnace, its flesh melting off, like a plastic doll that has fallen in the fire. I woke drenched in sweat but I was too scared to go back to sleep. I stayed awake, reading Pliny and waiting for dawn to break. Why am I troubled in this way? I have made all the right sacrifices yet it is almost as if the gods are angry.

The weather has got warmer. Yesterday Susan was working in the garden with her sleeves rolled up. I could see her arms, speckled like hens' eggs, covered with surprisingly thick blonde hairs. I had to reprimand her, of course. I am the Master.

I am tired. Sometimes I just want to lie down and sleep and forget everything. By a sleep to say we end the heartache . . . Hamlet Act 3, scene 1. To die, to sleep. To sleep, perchance to dream.

Ay, there's the rub.

CHAPTER 19

Ruth is floating in a dark sea. Toby is somewhere near but she can't see or touch him. It's funny, but suddenly she feels she knows him inside out, his hopes and fears, his loves and hates, as if he were an old friend, not a three-month-old foetus. She even knows what his voice sounds like. It sounds like he's saying goodbye.

She is on the beach and a tide of bones is washing up against the shore. She hears Erik's voice. He is talking to Toby, 'It's the cycle of life. You're born, you live and then you die. Flesh to wood to stone.' 'But he's not even born yet,' she wants to scream but somehow her head is underwater and she can't speak or hear or breathe.

The tide brings her back again but now she's in the trench and it's too dark to see. She knows there's someone there with her. Someone evil. She sees a woman with two black dogs, a crossroads, the yellow eyes of an owl.

Now it is Max's voice she hears in her head. 'She was the goddess of many things. The Greeks called her the "Queen of the Night" because she could see into the underworld ... She's the goddess of the crossroads, the three ways ...

Another name is Hekate Kourotrophos, Hecate the child-nurse.'

'Hecate!' she says, forcing the breath out of her lungs, 'save me!'

Then another wave washes over her and everything is black.

Nelson is on his way to interview Edward Spens when he gets the call. He listens intently and then performs a screeching U-turn in the middle of the dual carriageway. Then he switches on the siren.

She is in the sea again and the tide is pulling her backwards and forwards, dragging her body against the stones, engulfing her in darkness. Now and again she sees lights, very far away, darting to and fro in the black water. She hears voices too, sometimes louder, sometimes softer. She hears her mother, Phil, Shona, Irish Ted and the nurse at the hospital. *Are you on your own?*

Once she hears Nelson's voice, very loudly. 'Wake up, Ruth!' he is saying. But *he* has to wake up, he has to leave, get back home before his wife finds out. They can never be together again. *Thanks. What for? Being there.*

Two children are digging a well on the beach. They are singing, 'Ding Dong Dell, Pussy's in the well.' Flint appears, very large, licking his whiskers. Then Sparky wearing a necklace of blood. A headless bird singing in a cage. The light glinting on coins thrown into a wishing well. A penny for your thoughts. *Ding Dong Dell, Pussy's in the well.*

Erik is rowing her to shore. He is talking about a Viking funeral. 'The ship, its sails full in the evening light. The dead man, his sword at his side and his shield on his breast.' The tide rocks the boat up and down. 'Do not be afraid,' Erik tells her, 'it is not your time.' Time and tide wait for no man. The sea carries her back through her life – Eltham, school, University College, Southampton, Norfolk, the Saltmarsh, the child's body buried in the henge circle. Cathbad, torch upraised. *Goddess Brigid, accept our offering.*

Another wave takes her right out of the water and leaves her stranded in daylight, gasping and shaking. She opens her eyes and sees Max, Nelson and Cathbad looking down at her.

She closes her eyes again.

Nelson drives like a maniac towards the hospital. 'Ruth's hurt,' Cathbad had said. 'I think she might be losing the baby.'

The baby. He does not stop to wonder how Cathbad knows or what Cathbad knows. He does not even wonder why Cathbad is the one who is ringing him, why he is with Ruth at all. All he can think about is that Ruth's pregnancy, which was hitherto only a suspicion, has become reality. And that the baby she is losing may be his. He presses his foot harder on the accelerator.

At the hospital he finds not only Cathbad, complete with cloak, but the know-all from Sussex University, Max Whatshisname. They are standing in the waiting area, by the rows of nailed-down chairs and ancient copies of *Hello!*, looking helpless.

'What's going on?' barks Nelson, going straight into policeman mode.

'They're examining her now,' says Cathbad, putting a calming hand on Nelson's arm. He shakes it off irritably.

'Let me speak to the doctor.'

'In a second. The doctor's busy with Ruth now.'

Thwarted, Nelson turns on Max who is looking awkward and embarrassed.

'What happened?'

'I found her at the site.' If Nelson sounds like a policeman, Max sounds like a suspect. 'I went to check on the dig after the rain and she was there, in a trench, unconscious.'

'Was anyone else there?'

'Not at first but while I was . . . looking at her . . . Cathbad appeared.'

'Just appeared?' growls Nelson, looking at Cathbad. 'Got magic powers now, have you?'

Cathbad looks modest. 'I just happened to be at the site. I wanted to have a look round. As you know, I'm interested in archaeology.'

'And you just happened to be there when Ruth collapsed?'

'I must have arrived a few minutes after Max. I saw his car at the foot of the hill.'

'And what happened to Ruth? How come she collapsed?'

In reply, Cathbad holds something out. Nelson recoils.

'What the hell's that?'

It is Max who answers. 'It's a model of a newborn baby. When I saw it, I thought . . .'

'So did I,' says Cathbad, sounding rather shamefaced. 'That's why I sent you the message.'

Nelson looks at the model. It is an anatomically perfect plastic replica of a full-term foetus. Its face is blank, its eyes sightless. Turning it over, he sees a name stamped at the base of the spine. 'It's from the museum,' he says. 'I went to some ridiculous party there and I remember it. They've got these models of foetuses at all stages of development.'

Max looks as if he is about to speak but at that moment the doctor (a disconcertingly youthful Chinese woman) appears in front of them.

'Are you with Miss Galloway?'

'Yes,' answers Nelson immediately.

'How is she?' asks Cathbad.

'Still unconscious but her vital signs are good. She should come round soon. I understand she's pregnant?'

'About sixteen weeks,' says Cathbad, 'I told the ambulance crew.'

The doctor nods soothingly. 'There's no sign of a miscarriage but we'll do a scan later. Go in and talk to her. It might help her come round.'

The invitation seems to be addressed to Cathbad alone but all three men follow the doctor into a side ward, where Ruth is lying in a curtained cubicle. Her name is already at the end of her bed. This efficiency strikes Nelson as ominous. Aren't people meant to wait for ages in Casualty, lying on a stretcher in the corridor?

Ruth is lying on her side with one arm flung over her head. She seems to be muttering under her breath. Cathbad sits beside her and takes her hand in his. Nelson stands awkwardly behind him. Max hovers by the curtain, seemingly uncertain about whether he should stay or go.

'What's she saying?' asks Nelson.

'Sounds like Tony,' says Cathbad.

'Toby?' suggests Max from the background.

Suddenly Nelson steps forward. 'Wake up, Ruth!' Ruth's eyes flicker under her lashes.

'Don't shout at her,' says Max. 'That's not going to help.'

Nelson turns on him furiously. 'What's it got to do with you?'

But Cathbad is looking at Ruth.

'She has come back to us,' he says.

'What's happened?' Ruth's voice is faint, but accusatory, as if somehow this is all their fault.

'You fainted,' says Cathbad. His voice is soothing. 'You'll be fine.'

Ruth looks, rather desperately, from one face to another. 'The baby?' she whispers.

'Fine,' says Cathbad bracingly. 'They'll do a scan but there's no sign that anything's wrong.'

'The baby in the trench?'

'It was a model,' says Nelson, 'some nutter must have put it there for a joke.'

He holds out the plastic baby. Ruth turns her head away and tears slide down her cheeks.

'Your baby's OK,' says Nelson in a softer voice. Ruth looks up at him and somehow it seems as if they can't look away. The seconds turn into minutes. Max fiddles with a hand sanitiser on the wall. Cathbad, of course, is incapable of embarrassment.

'I think,' he says brightly, 'that we should all give thanks to the goddess Brigid for Ruth's safe recovery.'

Luckily, at that minute a nurse pushes aside the curtains

and says that they are transferring Ruth to another ward. They will keep her in for the night, she says, just for observation. 'And in the morning,' she says cheerfully, 'one of your friends can drive you home.' She looks at the three men, from Cathbad's purple cloak to Max's mud-stained jeans and Nelson's police jacket, and her smile fades slightly.

In the morning, Ruth is only too keen to leave hospital. At first it had been wonderful to lie between the cool, starched sheets and have kind nurses bring her tea and toast. They had wheeled her down for the scan and there was Toby, floating happily in his clouds. To Ruth's embarrassment she had cried slightly, sniffling into the pink tissues handed to her by a nurse. Jesus, they're so *nice* in here. It's a wonder they don't go mad.

But as the night drew on she had started to worry about Flint (Cathbad had offered to feed him but who knows whether he'd remember), about her baby (how on earth is she going to cope on her own?) and, finally, about herself. It seems that someone is trying to scare her to death. Her name written in blood (Max has confirmed this) and now the final gruesome discovery of the plastic baby. Did whoever put it there know she is pregnant or was it just another grisly classical allusion? And who could it be? It must be someone close enough to put the objects in place the split second these sites are deserted. And why? This is the question that chased itself around in her head all through the long night, full of nurses padding to and fro and white figures hobbling to the loo and back. The woman next to her snored continually, but unevenly, so Ruth was unable even to fit the noise into a soothing background rhythm. She had nothing to read and eventually this need became so pressing that she asked the nurse for something, anything, with words on. The nurse came back with *Hello!* magazine so Ruth spent the rest of the night reading about footballers' weddings and obscure Spanish royalty to the accompaniment of jagged grunts from the bed next door.

Morning starts early with a tepid cup of tea at seven and Ruth is already asking when she can go. She must let the doctor see her first, say the nurses soothingly. By eight she is sitting, fully dressed, on the bed. She had not thought to ask any of her visitors yesterday to bring her a change of clothes and, in any case, she would have been too embarrassed. But there is something sordid about putting the same clothes back on. She hasn't even got a toothbrush but a nurse brings her toothpaste and she rubs it vigorously round her mouth. The woman next door (very pleasant when she isn't snoring) offers her deodorant and some rather violent-smelling body spray. Ruth sits on the bed, smelling of roses, rereading an account of how some actress she has never heard of overcame tragedy to marry some sportsman she has never heard of. It's all very inspiring.

Eventually a teenage boy masquerading as a doctor appears, examines her head and tells her she can go home. 'Come back at once if you have any dizziness or blackouts,' he says sternly. He's wearing baseball boots. Baseball boots! How can Ruth possibly take anything he says seriously?

She has nothing to pack so she asks the nurse if she can call a taxi. 'No need,' says the nurse, smiling sweetly (though, to Ruth's knowledge, she has been on duty for the last twelve hours). 'A friend of yours rang and said he'd come to collect you. Wasn't that nice of him?'

The nurse doesn't say which friend but as she emerges from the main doors Ruth is not really surprised to see Nelson's Mercedes parked in the space reserved for minicabs. She gets into the front seat and for a few minutes they sit in silence.

'Why didn't you tell me?' asks Nelson at last.

'I was going to.'

'Oh, that's all right then.'

'It was difficult,' retorts Ruth, 'you're married. I didn't want to rock the boat.'

'Didn't you think I had a right to know? If it is mine, that is.'

'Of course it's yours,' flares Ruth, 'whose did you think it was?'

'I thought maybe your ex-boyfriend . . . Peter.'

'I haven't slept with him for ten years.'

'It's not his then,' says Nelson with a slight smile.

'No, it's definitely yours.' There is another silence broken only by the minicabs behind starting a strident chorus of hooting. Nelson swears and puts the car in gear. They drive in silence through the Norwich backstreets. It's Sunday morning and everything is quiet, people are emerging from newsagents with giant Sunday papers under their arms and café owners are putting tables out on the pavements. As they pass through the centre of the city, they can hear church bells ringing.

'What are you going to do?' asks Nelson, breaking sharply at a zebra crossing.

'Have the baby,' says Ruth determinedly, 'bring it up on my own.'

'I want to help.'

'Help? What do you mean "help"?'

'You know . . . financially. And other things. I want to be involved.'

'How involved? Are you going to tell Michelle?'

Nelson says nothing but Ruth sees his eyes narrow. Eventually, he says, 'Look, Ruth. This isn't easy. I'm married. I don't want to break up my family. The girls—'

'Don't think for one second that I want to marry you. That's the last thing I want.'

She thinks Nelson relaxes slightly and when he speaks again his tone is gentler. 'What do you want from me then?'

'I don't know.' She doesn't. Of course, on one level she does want a totally committed partner who will come with her to the birth and bring up the baby with her. But that isn't on offer. 'I just want someone to talk to, I suppose,' she says.

'Well, you can talk to me. Have you had a scan yet?'

'Yes, he's got long legs apparently.'

'He?'

'I think it's a boy. I'm calling him Toby.'

'Toby!' The car swerves. 'Toby! You can't call him Toby.'

'Why not?'

Nelson hesitates. Ruth waits for him to say 'because it's a poof's name' but supposes that, even for Nelson, this is a step too far.

'I suppose you think I should call him Harry,' says Ruth.

'Harry? No. Ever since Harry bloody Potter that's been a nightmare. But couldn't you name him after . . . What's your dad's name?'

'Ernest.'

'Well, maybe not.'

'I could ask Cathbad.'

'Jesus. He'll want to call him Jupiter Moon Grumbleweed or something. Why not just give the poor kid a normal name. Like Tom.'

'Or Dick. Or Harry.'

She and Nelson are never together very long without arguing, reflects Ruth. But all the same she is happy, almost exhilarated. Talking about the baby, discussing names, has made her pregnancy seem more real than at any time since the first scan. No, it's not the pregnancy that seems real, it's the baby. Or rather, it's the idea that the baby will grow up to be a child, a *person*, someone who will eat Marmite sandwiches, make finger paintings, play football, jump in puddles. She realises that she is grinning.

They are on the ring road now. Nelson is driving too fast as usual. Ruth sometimes thinks he only became a policeman to avoid speeding fines.

But it seems that he also has been thinking. 'It's odd, isn't it,' he says, overtaking a lorry, 'we don't know each other that well, but we're having a baby together.'

'We're not "having a baby together",' says Ruth.

'Yes we are,'

'But we're not "together". You're not going to come to parent-teacher evenings, are you?'

'That's a bit of a way off, Ruth.'

'I just mean, I'm having the baby on my own but you're the father. That's all.'

'Thanks.'

'You should be pleased I'm not making all sorts of demands.'

'You should be pleased I'm not running for the hills.'

The ridiculousness of this exchange makes them both laugh.

'What about your parents?' asks Nelson. 'Are they supportive?' He says this as if he is proud to have thought of such a PC term.

'Not exactly,' says Ruth, 'they're Born Again Christians. They think I'm going to burn in hell.'

'Nice. They might come round when the baby's born though.'

'They might, I suppose.'

'Have you got brothers or sisters?'

Nelson is right, thinks Ruth, it *is* odd that they can be having a baby together when they know nothing about each other's lives. She has no idea if Nelson has brothers or sisters either.

'I've got a brother. He's OK but we're not close. He lives in London.'

'Has he got children?'

'Yes. Two.'

Toby will have cousins. That has never occurred to her before either.

'Are you going to carry on working?' asks Nelson.

'Of course. I've got to support the baby, haven't I?'

'I told you, I want to help.'

'I know, but realistically, if you don't tell Michelle, you're not going to be able to do very much. That's OK though. I don't want help. You can buy him a bicycle or something.'

'His first football.'

'You're not going to insist he supports some ridiculous northern team are you?'

'Blackpool. Of course.'

'What if I want him to support . . .' She wracks her brain for the most annoying choice. 'Arsenal?'

'Then I'll apply for custody.' After a short silence, Nelson says, 'What will you tell about me? I don't want him growing up not knowing who his father is.'

'I don't know,' says Ruth. 'I'll cross that bridge when I come to it.' But the bridge looks more like a rickety plank across the Niagara Falls. If Michelle doesn't know, how can she possibly tell her baby that Nelson is his father?

They are on the Saltmarsh road now. The tide is in, forming sparkling blue pools between the islands of long grass. Ruth opens her window and breathes in the salty sea smell.

Nelson watches her. 'You love this place, don't you?'

'Yes.'

'Then there's no point in me saying it's an isolated spot to bring up a baby?'

'No.'

Nelson parks outside Ruth's cottage. 'Do you want to come in?' she asks.

He looks awkward. 'I ought to get back. I said I'd take Michelle to the garden centre.'

'Oh, all right.'

Ruth gets out and scrabbles in her bag for her key. Nelson

watches her from the car. For some reason, the sight of her standing there on her doorstep in her crumpled shirt, a bandage over her left eye, makes his throat constrict.

'Ruth!' he calls.

She turns.

'Take care.'

She waves and smiles and then, finding her key, disappears into the house.

24th June
Fors Fortuna

It's very hot. Too hot. Last night I slept with only a sheet over me and I was covered in sweat by the morning. She came to me again and I was weak. Perhaps my weakness is why this house is cursed, why nothing grows here but dust and ashes. In the morning I sacrificed again and the entrails were rotten, stinking and putrid. I buried them behind the greenhouse where the grass grows long. The time is near. We cannot escape.

CHAPTER 20

Edward Spens lives in Newmarket Road, a busy thorough-
fare on the outskirts of Norwich. This is the land of the seriously rich. The houses are huge, set back from the road and
surrounded by trees. So many trees, in fact, that the houses
themselves are almost hidden until you come to the end of
the driveway and they suddenly appear in all their smug,
landscaped glory. Nelson drives slowly up to Edward Spens'
house, past a covered swimming pool and a child's play house
that looks as if it must have needed planning permission.
Sprinklers play on the perfectly manicured lawn, and as he
comes to a halt a gardener hurries past carrying emergency
plant supplies. Nelson is pleased to see that his dirty
Mercedes distinctly lowers the tone.

He is still feeling shell shocked after yesterday's revelation. Well, not exactly revelation, more confirmation. How
unlucky can a man be? He has a one-night stand and, hey
presto, he's going to be a father again. Other men (he knows
this from Cloughie) sleep around all the time with never a
whisper of consequences. Why the hell hadn't he used con-

traception? Why hadn't Ruth? His feelings towards Ruth veer crazily between anger, admiration and a sort of heart-clenching compassion. He admires her for her determination to have the baby and is grateful that she doesn't seem to want anything from him. But he is slightly irritated too. Ruth seems to think that she can just have this baby and bring it up on her own, with the occasional birthday present from him. But he knows, as she doesn't, that parenthood can be a lonely business. He knows that Michelle struggled sometimes, especially when they moved down south, when he was working long hours and she was alone all day with the kids. Ruth will have no one to turn to, except her Jesus-freak parents and that flaky girlfriend of hers. Maybe Cathbad will offer to babysit. That's no life for a son of his.

His son. Contrary to popular belief, Nelson has never been desperate for a son. He has always been delighted with his daughters. He likes their otherness, their ability to disappear behind secret feminine rites, he even likes being out-numbered at home; it's restful somehow ('It's a girl thing, Dad. You wouldn't understand'). A son – now a son brings all sorts of buried emotions to the surface. Nelson was never that close to his father. He was the only boy in the family (he has two older sisters, a pattern that he now sees is going to be repeated) and he realised, early on, that there were expectations attached to the role. Unlike his sisters he wasn't expected to be good; he was expected to be tough, athletic, embarrassed about emotions, passionate about football. And, by and large, Nelson achieved this. He suppressed an early interest in ponies (which had deeply worried his father) and became a football fanatic, playing for the school, and later the county teams. His father had always been there to watch him, yelling incomprehensible advice from the touchline despite the fact that he, Nelson's father, had never actually played the game. He had a withered foot, the result of childhood polio, and walked with a stick. How had this affliction affected his vision of manliness? Was this the reason why he wanted his son to be a sportsman above everything? Nelson never asked him and now it is impossible. His father died when he was fifteen. Archie Nelson never saw his son become a policeman, a career choice which would have delighted him.

Nelson's mother, Maureen, was a much bigger influence. She is a forceful Irishwoman who shouted at her children and sometimes even clouted them. Archie never raised his hand or his voice (except on the touchline). Yet, despite this, Nelson was closer to his mother. They had some epic rows during his teenage years but he also knew that, deep down, Maureen loved him fiercely. Perhaps that's why, even now, he actually prefers the company of women. Oh, he can do the lad stuff all right, he wouldn't be able to survive in the force otherwise. He still plays football and golf, likes a night in the pub, enjoys the camaraderie of police work. But he also likes the company of strong, intelligent women. Which is why he was drawn to Ruth Galloway, which is why he is in this mess today.

Nelson sighs as he parks his car outside the Spens mansion. Having spent Sunday being the perfect husband, he now feels emotionally exhausted. He not only took Michelle to the garden centre but out for a pub lunch afterwards. He has even agreed to go to see some God-awful play with her tonight.

Now it's a relief to be able to turn back to business. And Edward Spens won't be able to hide behind his perfect house and double garage. Nelson wants some answers. Why didn't Spens mention from the beginning that his family used to own the house on Woolmarket Street? And is there a dead child that he also forgot to mention? Not in Edward Spens' lifetime perhaps but, sometime during the years that the Spens family lived in the house, a child was killed and buried under the wall, its head thrown into the disused well. That's quite some family secret.

Edward Spens greets Nelson as if he is a long-lost friend. 'Harry! Nice to see you. Come in.' Nelson silently curses Whitcliffe and the circumstances which have led Spens to believe they are on first name terms. All he can do is reply, in his stiffest manner, 'Good morning, Mr Spens.'

'Edward, please.' Spens ushers him through to the kitchen, which is at the back of the house with windows opening onto the garden. Michelle would die of envy if she saw this kitchen, thinks Nelson. Everything is perfect; from the gleaming surfaces, to the yellow roses on the table, to the blue cushions on the wicker sofa (sofas in the kitchen – that would never happen in Blackpool), to the expensive Italian coffee machine chugging away in the corner.

'Coffee?' asks Spens, pulling out a chair for Nelson. 'This machine does a tolerable cappuccino.'

'Just black will be grand, thanks.'

To complete the picture, as Spens busies himself with the coffee, the perfect woman walks in from the garden. A gleam of honey-blonde hair, a flash of blue eyes, a general impression of suntan and scent and expensive clothes and the vision is holding out its hand to Nelson.

'My wife Marion,' says Spens shortly.

Marion wasn't at the medieval party (Nelson doesn't blame her) so this is Nelson's first meeting with Mrs Spens. His first thought is – never trust a man with a beautiful wife. He should know; he has one himself.

'Pleased to meet you,' says Marion Spens. Close up, her face is almost too perfect, the contours too smooth, everything too symmetrical. She looks nervous too, glancing at Edward before she speaks.

'Harry is just here to ask questions about Woolmarket Street,' says Spens heartily.

'They've found a body haven't they?' says Marion with a quick flicker of eyes towards her husband. 'Roddy told me.'

'Roddy?' As far as Nelson knows, the Spens children are called Sebastian and Flora. Typical Newmarket Road names.

'My father, Roderick. Mad keen on history.'

'He said the body could be medieval,' offers Marion.

'I'm afraid it's far more recent than that,' says Nelson. 'I'd like to ask a few questions about your family's ownership of the house.' He is perfectly happy to talk in front of Marion. He has a feeling that she will give more away than her husband. Edward, it seems, has other ideas.

'No problem. Bring your coffee and we'll go through into the study. Excuse us, darling.'

The study is, of course, decorated in leather and dark wood. The bookcase displays pristine hardbacks and well-thumbed paperbacks. The walls are the colour of underdone roast beef.

Spens sits himself behind the desk, Nelson takes what is obviously the visitor's chair. Family photographs grin up at him, on the wall is a picture of a rugby team. Nelson is willing to bet that Spens is in the middle, holding the trophy.

'Well, Harry, this is all very mysterious.'

'Not at all, Mr Spens. Just following a line of enquiry. Your family lived at the house in Woolmarket Street from . . .'

'From 1850. It was built by my great-great-grandfather Walter Spens.'

'I'm interested in the years between 1949 and 1955. Who would have been living in the house at that time?'

'My grandfather, Christopher Spens, his wife Rosemary and their children Roderick and Annabelle.'

'And Roderick is your father?'

'Sir Roderick. Yes.'

'I'd like to talk to him. Does he live locally?'

Edward pauses, fiddling with an executive toy on the desk. 'Well, actually he lives with us.'

'He does?' Wondering why on earth Spens didn't mention this before, Nelson asks, 'Is he in?'

'I believe so.'

'Could I speak to him?'

'Of course.' But Spens doesn't move. Finally he says, 'My father is in the first stages of senile dementia. He can seem lucid, very lucid, but he gets confused very easily. And when he gets confused he gets . . . upset.'

'I understand,' says Nelson, though he doesn't really. He has never met anyone with dementia and can't imagine what it would be like living with someone who is slowly losing their sense of themselves. It makes him see Edward and Marion in a rather different light. 'Must be hard,' he offers.

'Yes,' Spens agrees. 'Hardest on Marion because she's at

home more. Sometimes, what with my father and the children . . . though we have an au pair, Croatian girl, very good. And Dad keeps himself busy, has the Conservative Association, the Historical Society, still plays bowls. He's a silver surfer too. Better with new technology than I am. He's not an invalid yet.'

The 'yet' hangs on the air because the one thing Nelson does know about dementia is that it is irreversible.

'I'll get him for you,' says Edward. He smiles slightly. 'He'll probably be pleased. He loves talking about the old days.'

This is certainly true though Edward Spens hadn't mentioned that the old days included Ancient Rome, the Counter Reformation and the Crimean War. When he can get a word in, Nelson asks, 'Sir Roderick, do you remember your years at Woolmarket Street?'

'Remember them?' Roderick looks at him sharply from under bushy white eyebrows. 'Of course I do. I remember everything, don't I, Edward?' Edward agrees that he does.

'You would have been, how old?'

'I was born in 1938. I lived at the house until I left for Cambridge, when I was eighteen.'

That makes him seventy, Nelson calculates. No great age these days. His own mother has recently taken up line-dancing at seventy-three. Roderick Spens could be a decade older.

'You lived with your parents?'

'Yes, my father was the Headmaster of St Saviours on Waterloo Road. He taught classics as well.'

'The school's not there any more, is it?'

'No, it closed sometime in the sixties. Great shame. It was an excellent school.'

'Did you go there?'

'Yes, it was my father's school, y'see.' He looks beadily at Nelson as if suspecting a trap. 'My mother wanted me to go to Eton but m'father insisted. His word was law in our house.'

Nelson tries, and fails, to imagine one of his daughters saying the same about him. 'And your sister . . . Annabelle. Did she go there too?'

Roderick looks confused. 'Annabelle?'

Edward Spens cuts in. 'It's all right, Dad.' He turns to Nelson. 'My father still gets upset when he talks about her. She died young, you see.'

'How young?' asks Nelson, his antenna up.

'Five or six, I believe.'

CHAPTER 21

Ruth is at Woolmarket Street. The builders are starting work again tomorrow and she wants to collect the rest of the finds. Not that the other trenches have turned up anything very exciting – some more pottery, some glass, a few coins. But there might be something interesting there and she needs to check that the site is tidy. That's her job as lead archaeologist. It's another warm day and it's surprising how innocuous the site looks in the sunlight. Nevertheless, Ruth finds herself looking over her shoulder every few minutes and jumping when a squirrel runs across the wall in front of her.

Although she still has a plaster stuck rather rakishly over one eye, Ruth feels remarkably well after Saturday's trauma. The boy doctor had told her not to be alone in the night, 'in case you fall into a coma' he explained cheerfully, but Ruth had been so exhausted that she went to bed at nine and slept beautifully with only Flint for company. She's sure that it was the conversation with Nelson that caused her to sleep so peacefully. He knows. He may be agonised and conflicted and all the rest of it, he may now drive her mad by interfering at every stage in the pregnancy, but at least he knows. She is no longer entirely on her own. And this morning she had a civil, if stilted, conversation with her mother. Ruth didn't mention any of the events of the last few weeks but assured her mother that she was no longer feeling sick, had more energy, was not doing so much awful digging. 'I sailed through both my pregnancies,' said her mother smugly and Ruth is only too happy to allow her this victory.

The site is still deserted. Ruth had half expected to see Irish Ted and Trace. There is still some work to do back-filling trenches, though maybe they have decided not to bother in view of the fact that the house is shortly to be razed to the ground. Ruth collects the finds from the foreman's hut. No sign of him either, thank goodness. She looks across at the arch silhouetted against the blue sky. *Omnia Mutantur, Nihil Interit.* She must remember to ask Nelson to check when the arch was built. It seems a strange, grandiose thing to find in a private house. Ruth is reminded of Roman generals being granted triumphal arches when they achieved great victories. She thinks of a trip she and Shona took to Rome a few years ago. The arch of Titus in the Roman forum, decorated with reliefs illustrating Titus's victory against the rebellious Jews. She remembers reading that it is meant to be impossible for a Jew to pass through the arch. 'I can do it,' Shona had exclaimed, running laughing underneath. 'You're not Jewish,' Ruth had objected. But Shona had been in the midst of an affair with a Jewish law lecturer and considered that this counted.

She should have another look at the trench where the cat was found but something makes her wary about going into the grounds, so far away from the main road. There is something heavy, something watchful, about the silence. Don't be silly, she tells herself, it's broad daylight. What can possibly hurt you? She shoulders her backpack and picks her way through the rubble, past the outhouses and into what was once the back garden. Was this ever the happy place that Kevin Davies remembers? Ruth tries to imagine children running laughing through the garden, swinging on the tree, throwing pennies in the wishing well. No, the well was covered up by then. She approaches the well now and looks inside. A dank, unpleasant smell meets her and she straightens up hastily. When was the well covered? That's another question for Nelson. The skulls must have been put in the well before the concrete cap was put in place. Skulls in a well. The words have a crazy, topsy-turvy sound, like a nightmare nursery rhyme. She thinks of the children on the beach. Ding Dong Dell.

The cat's trench is by the outer wall, bulging now with age. This is the boundary. Terminus, the God of boundaries. 'I pray to him whenever I go to Heathrow,' Nelson had said when he heard the name. She can't imagine Nelson on holiday somehow. She is sure that Michelle insists on somewhere sun-kissed and glamorous whereas Nelson is more suited to wilder, colder places – the Yorkshire moors, perhaps, or the Scottish Highlands. She can just picture him up to his waist in some freezing loch.

Ruth stands up, easing her back. It is really hot now and the air is still. She climbs out of the trench and walks along by the outer wall. The new buildings are obviously going to come up right to the edge of the boundary. So much for spa-

cious apartments. The modern walls look brash and confi-
dent against the crumbling flint of the originals. There are
still some apple trees here though, and, in the far corner of
the site, Ruth finds gooseberry and redcurrant bushes
choked with thistles and dusty with builder's dirt.
Blackberries too, the brambles reaching out like tiny, spiteful
fingers. The flowers haven't set yet and, by the time they are
berries, these bushes will have been ripped out to make room
for 'spacious landscaped gardens with water features'.

'Blackberry and apple pie,' says a voice, 'now there's a dish
fit for a king.'

Ruth wheels round. An elderly man in a dark suit is
standing smiling at her. He has an unripe apple in his hand
and, for one mad moment, Ruth thinks of Adam in the
Garden of Eden. An older, sadder Adam come to mourn the
devastation of paradise. Then she sees the clerical collar and
her brain clicks into gear.

'Father Hennessey?'

'Yes.' The man holds out his hand. 'You have the advantage of me, I'm afraid.'

'Ruth Galloway. I'm an archaeologist.'

'An archaeologist?'

'I specialise in forensics.'

'Ah,' says Hennessey, understanding. 'You're involved in
this sorry affair then.'

'Yes.'

Father Hennessey sighs. From Nelson's description, Ruth
imagined that he would be a more aggressive presence, like
one of the fire and brimstone preachers she remembers from
her childhood. This man just looks sad.

'The building work's more advanced than I thought it would be,' he says. 'How on earth have they managed to cram so much onto one site?'

'By making everything extremely small,' says Ruth drily. 'The whole of one of these flats could probably fit into the drawing room of the original house.'

'You're right there,' says Hennessey, 'this was a grand house once.'

They walk back through the garden. Hennessey stops once to look at a fallen tree, patting its stump sadly. It is hotter than ever. Thunder weather, Ruth thinks. Her shirt is sticking to her back and her feet seem to have melted and are spilling over the sides of her shoes. She longs to be lying down.

When they reach the front of the house, Hennessey looks up at the stone archway.

'*Omnia Mutantur, Nihil Interit*. Everything changes, nothing is destroyed.'

'The arch was there in your time then?'

'Yes. It's a folly, of course, but a rather magnificent one. And I always thought the words quite appropriate. After all, if you're a Christian, you believe that death itself is just a change, not destruction.'

Ruth says nothing. Death is death as far as she is concerned. There is no way of cheating death except, perhaps, by having a child. But Hennessey's words remind her of something. Max, on the beach with the Imbolc bonfire behind him, talking about Janus. 'He's not just the god of doorways but of any time of transition and change, of progression from one condition to another.' The ultimate transition, from life to death.

'Miss Galloway,' Hennessey's soft Irish voice cuts into her thoughts, 'I wonder if you can show me . . . where you found the body.'

'All right. And it's Ruth.' She hates to be called 'Miss' and Dr Galloway seems too formal somehow.

Part of the front wall still stands, the steps and the stone portico. Was this from the same period as the arch? It has a similar grandiose feel. A folly, the priest had said. The words reverberate uneasily in Ruth's head.

'Careful here,' she says as they go through the doorway. On the other side, the ledge of black and white tiles is still there. It will be the last thing to go, thinks Ruth. The last link to the old house.

'This way.' She leads Hennessey along the ledge. As they climb down into the trench, he stumbles and almost falls.

'Are you all right?'

'Fine.' But he is breathing heavily. He must be in his late seventies or even eighties, Ruth thinks.

Ruth points to the pile of earth in front of her. 'The body was buried directly under the doorstep. We've removed that. We tried to leave everything else undisturbed.' She looks at Hennessey's face. 'We're very careful,' she finds herself explaining, 'very respectful.'

Hennessey's lips move silently for a second. Is he praying? Then he says, 'Buried under the doorstep, you say?'

'Yes.' She doesn't mention the foetal position.

'And the skull was in the well?'

'That's right.'

Hennessey is silent for a few minutes and then he says, 'Would you mind if I said a prayer?'

'Go ahead.' Ruth backs away. She finds public prayer embarrassing at the best of times but to be trapped in a trench with someone chanting in Latin and waving incense – it's her worst nightmare.

However Hennessey's prayer turns out to be mercifully short, the words muttered and not (as far as Ruth can tell) in Latin. At the end he takes a small bottle from his pocket and sprinkles water onto the earth.

'Holy water,' he explains. He looks at Ruth's face. 'You're not a Catholic?' He sounds amused.

'No. My parents are Christians but I'm not ... anything.'

'Oh, you're something, Ruth Galloway,' says Father Hennessey. He looks at her for a second and Ruth has the strangest feeling that he knows her very well, almost better than she knows herself. But then the moment passes and Hennessey says briskly, 'I'm parched. Do you fancy a cup of coffee?'

Nelson is leaving the museum when he gets a call from Judy. 'I've got Annabelle Spens' death certificate, boss.'

'Good. Anything interesting?'

He hears her rustling paper and he thinks of his father's death certificate, those few stilted words encompassing all the pain and grief. His father's cause of death had been 'myocardial infarction'. At the time he had no idea what that meant.

'Date and place of death,' reads Judy. '24 May 1952, Woolmarket House, Woolmarket Street, Norwich. Cause of death: Scarlet fever. Children don't get that any more do they?'

'They get it,' says Nelson, 'they just don't die of it.' He stops as a party of schoolchildren stream past him, holding photocopied worksheets and trying to trip each other up.

'She died at home,' Judy is saying. 'How come she wasn't in hospital?'

'I don't know. Perhaps it was more usual to nurse children at home in those days.'

'But they had money, they could afford health care. This was before the NHS, wasn't it?'

'Early days of the NHS.'

The children push through the glass doors of the museum. He can hear their teacher telling them that they're going to be divided into groups. 'You're in my group, Ryan.' That's your day ruined, Ryan, you poor sod.

'What about the certificate of interment?' he asks.

'Tanya's getting it,' says Judy, sounding slightly pissed off. 'Boss, do you really think that Annabelle was buried in the house and not in a grave?'

'I don't know,' says Nelson. 'But there's something odd about that house. There's something odd about this whole case.'

He had been to see the curator, to ask how the foetus model could have escaped from the museum and ended up at Ruth's feet in the trench in Swaffham. The curator had been perfectly pleasant but unable to offer any answers. The stages of development model had been taken down from display a few weeks ago (they had had some complaints from parents) and the components placed in the store room. Who had access? Well, any of the museum staff. The more valuable exhibits were kept in a safe but who would steal a plastic model of a baby? Who indeed?

Nelson stands on the steps, looking about over the Norwich rooftops and wondering what his next move should be. Should he go back and question Edward Spens again? He is sure that the man is holding something back. Should he get back to the station and bully Tanya about the interment certificate? They need to get hold of the dental records too. He sighs. It's a hot, muggy day and more than anything else he fancies diving into a pub for a cold beer. That's what Clough would do, he's sure of it.

'Hi, Detective Chief Inspector.'

Nelson whirls round. A young woman with lurid purple hair is smiling cheekily up at him. Who is she? One of his daughters' friends? A trendy acquaintance of Michelle's?

'I'm Trace,' says the apparition. 'From the dig.'

Oh yes. The skinny girl who was on the site the first day. The one they all think Cloughie fancies. Rather him than me, thinks Nelson, looking at the metalwork gleaming on Trace's ears and lip. But she seems friendly enough.

'What are you doing here?' she asks.

'Routine enquiries,' he answers. 'What about you?'

'I work here, Mondays and Fridays. There's not enough field archaeology to keep me busy all year round so I do some curatorial work, processing finds and that.'

Nelson has no idea what 'processing finds' means but he knows one thing: Trace could be an important contact within the museum. She might well know if anyone has been waltzing off with the exhibits. 'Fancy a drink?' he says.

Ruth tries to steer towards one of the picturesque cafés around Woolmarket Street but Father Patrick Hennessey heads like a bloodhound towards the shopping centre and Starbucks, a place Ruth loathes. 'You can get a grand coffee in here,' says Hennessey, rubbing his hands together. The air-conditioning is so strong that Ruth is shivering.

She notices some odd glances as they enter the café – the overweight woman with mud-stained trousers and a plaster over one eye, and the priest, red-faced in his black clothes. Ruth orders mineral water but Hennessey goes for the full skinny-latte-with-an-extra-shot-of-espresso palaver.

'It's impossible to get a decent coffee where I live,' he explains.

'Where do you live?'

'In a godforsaken corner of the Sussex countryside.' He says 'godforsaken' like he really means it.

'Nelson, DCI Nelson, said it was very pretty.'

'It's pretty enough if you like trees. No, I'm a city boy. Born and brought up in Dublin. I've always lived in towns – Rome, London, Norwich.'

It sounds a bit like Del Boy's van – New York, Paris, Peckham. Ruth suppresses a smile. 'Norwich isn't exactly cosmopolitan.'

'Sure and it's a fine town. I miss it. I miss my work, my parishioners, everything.'

'You ran the children's home, didn't you?'

'I started it and ran it, yes. I'd seen an orphanage in the East End of London, a place where the children lived together almost like a family. I tried to create something similar. Recruited all the staff myself. I chose young religious people, people who still had some ideals left.'

'I met one of your ex . . . residents. He remembered the place with great affection.'

Hennessey looks interested. 'Who did you meet?'

'Davies, I think his name was.'

'Oh, Kevin Davies. He was a nice boy. He's an undertaker now I believe. He always had a serious way about him.'

Ruth thinks of the worried, crumpled-looking Davies. She can't imagine him as a child. She is sure that he always looked forty.

Hennessey is looking at her. He has very blue eyes, with white smile-lines etched against his weather-beaten face.

'Must be a difficult job,' he says, 'uncovering the past.'

Ruth is struck by this description. Most people see archaeology as 'digging up bones' but 'uncovering the past' is really what it is. She looks at the priest with new respect.

'It is hard,' she says carefully, 'especially in cases like this where you're dealing with the fairly recent past and especially when there's a child involved.' She stops, feeling that she has said too much.

But Hennessey is nodding. 'As a priest I've often come across things that are best kept hidden. But the truth has a way of coming to the surface.'

Like the bones under the doorway, thinks Ruth. If Spens hadn't been so keen to develop the site, if Ted and Trace hadn't dug in that exact spot, would they have remained hidden for ever? Or would the long-forgotten crime have risen to the surface, crying out for vengeance?

'Sometimes it's hard to know what's true and what isn't,' she says.

'Pontius Pilate would agree with you. "Truth" he said, "what is that?" And he was a wise man, Pilate. A coward but a wise man.'

Ruth is slightly confused by the way he is talking about Pontius Pilate as if he might, at any moment, walk into Starbucks. 'DCI Nelson will find the truth,' she says, with more confidence than she feels, 'if anyone can.'

'Ah, DCI Nelson. He's a fine man, I think. A man with morals.'

Ruth is furious to find herself blushing. 'He's a good detective,' she says.

'And a good man,' says Hennessey softly, 'which may prove more difficult for him.'

Rather reluctantly, Nelson settles for a coke but Trace asks for a pint of bitter.

'I thought all archaeologists drank cider,' says Nelson.

Trace pulls a face. 'Cider's for wimps.'

I could get to like this girl, thinks Nelson.

'How long have you been an archaeologist?' he asks.

'I left uni five years ago. I did an MA in London and worked in Australia for a bit. I didn't really want to come back to Norwich but my mum and dad live here and it's cheaper to live with them. There's lots of archaeology here too.'

'Lots of prehistoric stuff,' says Nelson. He knows this from Ruth.

Trace nods. 'Bronze Age and Iron Age. And Roman. That's my favourite period. The Romans.'

'Did you see *Gladiator*? Great film.'

Trace snorts. 'Films get everything wrong. All that decadent stuff, lying about eating grapes. The Romans brought law and order and infrastructure. We were nothing but a band of disparate warring tribes until they came along.'

Identifying 'we' as the British, Nelson says, slightly aggrieved, 'They were invaders, occupiers, weren't they?'

'They were here for four hundred years. That's more than fifteen generations. And, when they left, we forgot everything they taught us – all the stone building and engineering works, glass-making, pottery. We slipped into the Dark Ages.'

Nelson feels rather proud of this. They may have been here four hundred years, he thinks, but to us they were still foreigners, occupiers, with their fancy, glass-making ways. He does not say this to Trace though.

'Have you been to the site in Swaffham?' he asks. 'Max Grey's site?'

Trace's face lights up. 'Yes. I've done quite a bit of work there. He's great, Max. He really knows his stuff. He did this great tour the other week for the Scouts. Made it all come alive.'

'Do you get lots of visitors on the site?'

Trace shrugs. 'A few. It's become quite well-known since they mentioned it on Time Team. We've had some coach parties.'

'Has Edward Spens paid a visit?'

Trace's face, so open and animated when talking about the superiority of the Romans, becomes closed again. 'I think he came once. I wasn't there though.'

'Do you know him?'

'Everyone in Norwich knows him.'

*

'The Spens family,' Nelson tells his team, 'have lived in Norwich for generations. Walter Spens built the house on Woolmarket Road. He was, by all accounts, rather an eccentric. Had a collection of stuffed animals and liked to dress as an African chieftain.'

Clough, scoffing peanuts at the back of the room, coughs and almost chokes. Nelson glares at him.

'His grandson, Christopher Spens, was headmaster of St Saviours, the public school that used to be on the Waterloo Road. According to his son, Roderick Spens, he was a bit of a tartar, made his children call him sir and forced them to speak in Latin at mealtimes.'

Nelson stops. Sir Roderick had not described his father as a tartar, in fact he had sounded almost admiring, but Nelson had the strong impression of a cold, controlling man. He wonders if he is betraying his own prejudice against public schools, Latin and posh people in general.

Nelson looks at his team. Clough is still spitting out peanut crumbs. Tanya Fuller has her notebook open. Judy Johnson has her eyes fixed on Nelson's face, frowning slightly.

'Sir Roderick Spens is in the first stages of senile dementia,' continues Nelson, 'so his impressions are rather confused. He remembers his father very clearly but it upsets him to talk about his sister. According to the death certificate Annabelle Spens died of scarlet fever aged six. She died at home and is buried in the churchyard at St Peter and St Paul.'

He looks at the team, wondering if they realise the implications of this. Judy does, obviously, but Clough can sometimes be a bit slow on the uptake. Sure enough, it is Tanya who speaks, 'Could it be Annabelle who was buried under the door?'

'I don't know but I think we have to consider the possibility.'

'But they buried her.' This is Clough, sounding almost aggrieved.

'Yes but it might have been fairly easy, if they had the coffin at home on the night before the funeral, to remove the body and then screw the lid on again.'

'Why would anyone do that?'

'I don't know,' says Nelson impatiently, 'but I intend to find out.'

'Dental records?' asks Tanya.

'Yes. You can get on to that, Tanya. The skull we found in the well had a filling in one of the teeth. That's unusual in such a young child. Should be fairly easy to match. I'm also going to find out if there's a DNA link between the dead child and Sir Roderick.'

'What if there aren't any dental records?' asks Judy.

'Then I'll dig up the grave,' says Nelson grimly.

CHAPTER 22

All in all, Nelson does not feel in the right frame of mind to attend an experimental production at the Little Theatre that evening. But, then again, when would he ever be in this particular frame of mind? However, he has promised Michelle and even the news that the play has been written by the ridiculous Leo from the medieval evening does not dent his determination to be a good husband.

'What's it about?' he asks, as they edge through the streets looking for a parking space. The Little Theatre is in the new Arts Centre by the docks, a place so trendy that everything is in lower case, making it extremely difficult to read the signs.

Michelle is reading from a flyer which this Leo type has had the nerve to post to her.

'*The Two-Faced God.* Narrated by Janus, the Roman God of beginnings and endings, this is a play about openings, about doorways and fissures and sexual orifices. The action stretches from Roman times, through the industrial and sexual revolutions and ends in a space station set in the distant future.'

'Jesus wept,' says Nelson. 'Sexual orifices?'

'Harry, you're such a prude,' says Michelle, examining her reflection in the passenger mirror. 'All modern plays are about sex.'

Is he a prude? Nelson considers this accusation as he parks Michelle's Golf in a space vacated by a moped. It's true that he seldom finds Cloughie's jokes funny and that he thinks that *Sex and the City* is borderline pornographic (and that's just the shoes). But he's a man of the world, sex is all very well in its place (he doesn't allow himself to dwell very long on where that place is), it's just that he doesn't want to watch some weedy drama student going on and on about bodily functions. That's not unreasonable, surely?

'I'm not a prude,' he says at last, 'it's just that there's a time and a place.'

Michelle looks at him under her lashes. 'You didn't always think that way. Remember the ghost train on Blackpool pier?'

Nelson grunts. 'We were young and stupid then.' But he takes her arm as they walk towards the theatre.

A motley collection of individuals are gathered in the foyer, drinking overpriced cocktails and squinting at the lower case programme. Michelle's employers Tony and Juan are there, surrounded by a group Nelson privately categorises as 'exotic'. There are a few older couples, looking worriedly at the photographs posted around the walls showing actors in Greek masks and very little else. There are lots of young people too, probably from the university.

'She's attractive,' says Michelle.

'Who?' Nelson is fighting his way back from the bar carrying a half of lager and a glass of white wine.

'There. With the red hair.'

Nelson looks and sees a striking-looking woman in black who seems strangely familiar. With her is . . . Jesus Christ.

'Come this way.' He tries desperately to steer Michelle in the opposite direction. 'There's a seat.'

'I don't want a seat. Who's that with her? It's Ruth! Harry, look, it's Ruth.'

Michelle is off through the crowd. Nelson watches as she taps Ruth on the shoulder and is introduced to the redhead, whom he now recognises as the nutcase Shona who was involved in the Saltmarsh case. Ruth greets Michelle with every appearance of pleasure. She looks pale, he thinks, but otherwise well, wearing a loose red top over black trousers. Thank God for loose clothing. With any luck Michelle will thinks it's just fashion.

'Harry!' Michelle is beckoning imperiously.

Nelson stumps over and Ruth gives him a slightly mischievous smile.

'I wouldn't have thought this was your sort of thing, Nelson.'

'It was Michelle's idea.'

'Ruth took a bit of persuading too.' This is Shona, tossing back her hair and twinkling at Nelson. He stares impassively back.

'We met Leo at Edwards Spens' party,' explains Michelle. 'I thought he was very interesting.'

'He's taken some fascinating ideas from Greek and Roman theatre,' says Shona, wearing an intense, twitchy look which makes Nelson fear that an intellectual conversation is on its way.

'Are you looking forward to the play?' Ruth asks him. She is drinking orange juice and looks happier than he has seen her for weeks. He feels his lips moving into a grudging smile.

'No. You know how thick I am. I don't even eat yoghurt because it's got culture in it.'

Ruth laughs. 'I can't say I'm looking forward to it either but Shona thought a night out would do me good.'

Nelson lowers his voice. 'How are you feeling?'

'Fine. No ill-effects at all. I was at the Woolmarket Street site today.'

Nelson bristles. 'On your own?'

'I met Father Hennessey.'

'Hennessey? What was he doing snooping around?'

'I think he just came to have a look round. Don't you always say that people come back to the scene of a crime?'

'Yes, but whose crime is it?' answers Nelson soberly. 'That's what we need to find out.'

The play is as bad as Nelson fears. A man in a mask appears in front of a black curtain and drones on about January. Then he puts on another mask and drones on about the lottery and choices and whatnot. At least this reminds Nelson that he hasn't bought his ticket for Wednesday's draw yet. Then the curtain goes up and there are these people in togas having an orgy, only they can't have much of one because the production obviously can't stretch to more than four actors. Then the curtain comes down and the man in the mask drones on about women's rights, puts on his other mask and starts on about rape. The curtain goes up and there are two people in Victorian dress having breakfast. Turns out the man is seeing a prostitute and the woman kills herself. Up pops Chummy in the mask again and goes on about terminations and oral sex and the pill. Cue a blast of sixties music and the four actors at another orgy, only this time with LSD rather than grapes. Somebody dies of a drug overdose and the others sing 'Yellow Submarine' as a kind of funeral dirge. The man in the mask appears to say it's all the fault of the planets and the jolly foursome appear in space suits to say that the Earth has finally disappeared into its own orifice. Cue applause and calls for 'Author, Author'.

'Jesus,' says Nelson as they file out of the doors, 'what a load of crap.'

'Shh.' Michelle looks round. 'Leo's just over there.'

Nelson looks and sees the bearded playwright surrounded by admiring friends. He thinks he sees Shona's red hair in the crowd but there's no sign of Ruth.

'I'll arrest him under the Public Decency Act,' Nelson mutters.

'Shh.'

In the car, Michelle admits that the play was dire and she even agrees to stop off for a Chinese. Cheered, Nelson hums under his breath as he negotiates the Norwich suburbs, the car flying merrily over the speed bumps.

'So,' says Michelle chattily, 'what did you think of Ruth?'

Nelson stops humming. 'What do you mean?'

Michelle laughs. 'Oh Harry, you're hopeless. Didn't you notice?'

'Notice what?' Be careful, he tells himself.

But Michelle is still laughing. 'She's pregnant.'

Nelson counts to ten, keeping his eyes on the road.

'Hadn't you noticed?'

'You know me,' he says, 'I never notice anything.'

'A fine detective you make,' teases Michelle.

'You don't know for sure that she's pregnant,' counters Nelson.

'Yes, I do. I asked her when we went to the loo together.'

Nelson curses women's inability to go to the loo on their own. And why do they have to chat? Catch men chatting in the bog. No wonder women always take so long in there.

'She didn't say who the father is,' Michelle continues, leaning forward and fiddling with the car's radio.

'Didn't she?'

'No. I bet it's her ex-boyfriend. You know he went back to his wife?'

'Did he?'

Michelle changes stations until she finds some music she likes. A woman's voice fills the car, telling him that girls just want to have fun. 'You know, Harry,' says Michelle slowly. 'I'd like to help Ruth a bit.'

Careful, Harry, he tells himself again. Careful.

'Why?'

'Because she's going to have a baby and she's on her own and she's not with the father. I'm sure she's got lots of friends at the university, people like that weird warlock who gave us the dreamcatchers, but we're probably the only *normal* family she knows. So I'd like to help her. Take her shopping for baby stuff, that sort of thing.'

In all the years he's known her, Michelle has never wanted to take another woman under her wing. Why, thinks Nelson despairingly, does she have to start with Ruth? He glances at his wife. She is smiling to herself, twisting the ends of her blonde ponytail like a little girl.

'All right,' he says at last, 'anything you say.'

Ruth is in a good mood as she drives home. She has survived a social event without being sick or rushing to the loo a million times. Even though the play was terrible it was nice to go out for the evening, to see well-dressed people and to talk about something other than bones and decapitation and death. It was nice too to spend time with Shona. Maybe they will be able to stay friends even after Ruth has passed into the shadowy Mother World. Even seeing Nelson and Michelle hadn't been too bad. It had been a bit of a shock when Michelle had asked her about the baby but she supposes that everyone will know soon. And, the funny thing is, she *would* like to go shopping for baby clothes with Michelle. Ruth is dreadful at shopping. It is a female ritual that she has never mastered. Other women can disappear into a shop for half an hour and come out with piles of tasteful clothes in the right size, artfully matching accessories and the perfect pair of shoes. Ruth can shop all day and still only have a T-shirt two sizes too small to show for it.

And she needs a woman friend. Someone who is not jealous or disapproving but who has had children herself and is ready to give advice and encouragement. It's just a pity that the only woman who fits the bill is the wife of her baby's father who, if she knew the truth, would certainly never speak to Ruth again.

She sighs as she turns onto the Saltmarsh road. The light

and noise and colour of the Little Theatre seem a million miles away. Here everything is dark and still. Far off she can hear the roar of the sea. Strange how loud it is at night. The tide must be coming in. At high tide water covers the salt marshes completely, stopping at the freshwater marsh only a few hundred yards from Ruth's front door. Sometimes, on nights like this, it is hard to believe that the waters won't engulf her altogether, leaving her little house bobbing on the waves like Noah's ark. As Ruth knows to her cost, one should never underestimate the sea.

An animal runs out into the road, its eyes glassy in her headlights. A cat, maybe, or a fox. She hopes it isn't Flint. When she parks outside her house, the security light comes on, bathing everything in theatrical brightness. Maybe she should leap out and start declaiming a speech about Janus. But, unlike Shona for instance, Ruth has never wanted to be an actress. Giving lectures is one thing, emoting on stage quite another. She gets out her bag and starts scrabbling for her key. Since her mother bought her an organiser handbag she has never been able to find anything. Christ, her back hurts. She is longing to sit down with a cup of tea and a giant ham sandwich.

There it is. Ruth hauls out her house key attached to a black cat key ring (a present from her nephews). Then she stops. The light is still on and the sea is still thundering away in the distance. But there is now another sound too. Very faint but unmistakably there. The sound of breathing.

Frantically, Ruth fits the key into the lock and throws herself into her house. Once inside, she puts on the lights and double locks the door. The security light goes off and outside there is complete darkness. Trembling, Ruth turns off her own lights in order to see outside. But, even though she presses her face to the glass, there is nothing. Blackness.

Flint rubs against her leg and she jumps. Stroking him calms her down. Relax, she tells herself, it's nothing. Just a fox or some other animal. But Ruth knows that the breathing, heavy and regular, was that of a human. A human, moreover, who is still outside, still waiting for her. Is it the person who left the baby for her to find, who killed the cockerel and wrote her name in blood on the wall? If she opens the door, what will she see? Will it be the Goddess Hecate herself, flanked by two spectral hounds, the moonlight white on her skeletal face? Or will it be only too human, the killer who murdered a child and threw her head down a well? The killer who has now, inexorably, come back for Ruth.

She doesn't know how long she stands there, stroking Flint and looking out into the night. It is as if, as long as she doesn't move, she will be safe. As soon as she moves, *he* will move. The unknown person outside. He will move and he will come for her. Tears come to her eyes.

A tiny movement in her stomach brings her back to herself. She has to protect her baby. The creature outside can't move through solid walls after all. Gathering Flint in her arms, she turns away from the window and stumbles upstairs to bed.

She is woken by Flint meowing outside the front door. He often declines to use the cat flap, preferring the personal touch. Groggy with sleep, Ruth descends the narrow staircase and opens the door. A dawn mist billows in from the marshes. Flint is halfway down the path, his mouth open in outrage. On Ruth's doorstep is a dead calf. A black calf. A calf with two heads.

CHAPTER 23

'What *is* it?'

'It's an exhibit,' says Nelson, 'from the museum. Just like the baby.'

Ruth had called Nelson immediately and he was with her in ten minutes. He is wearing a tracksuit and his hair is wet. 'I was at the gym,' he says, seeing her questioning glance.

'I thought you hated the gym.'

'It was Michelle's idea. We go before work. Not bad when you get used to it. I like the pool. A swim sets you up for the day.'

'If you say so.'

Nelson is kneeling in her front garden, examining the calf which, she now sees, is stuffed. Close up, it looks less sinister and more pathetic, its fur threadbare in places, its four eyes glassy. The second head is really just a protrusion from the neck with rudimentary ears and muzzle. The eyes have obviously been added by the taxidermist to contribute to the freak effect. Ruth feels sorry for it but she still wishes that it hadn't turned up on her doorstep. Is it an offering from whoever was lurking outside her house last night?

'The Two-Headed Calf of Aylsham,' says Nelson, straightening up.

'What?'

'Like I said, it's from the museum. They've got a collection of stuffed animals. Apparently this little chap was quite famous in Victorian times. Used to travel round with one of these fairs exhibiting freaks and suchlike.'

'But how did the Two-Headed Calf of Aylsham end up on my doorstep?' asks Ruth, aware that she sounds both petulant and terrified.

Nelson shrugs but his face is sombre. 'I don't know. I'll get back on to the museum today. I was only there yesterday.'

'Were you? Why?'

'Asking about the model baby. Seems that someone likes leaving these things for you to find.'

But why, thinks Ruth. And why does she get the feeling that the person, whoever it is, is getting nearer and nearer, is becoming angrier and angrier. Aloud she says, 'Would you like breakfast? A cup of coffee?'

'No thanks. I'd better be getting on. I'll take Chummy with me.' And, pulling on plastic gloves, he staggers off down the path, carrying the two-headed calf.

Ruth watches him go. The sight is made more surreal by the fact that the mist is still clinging to the ground, obliterating everything up to waist height. Nelson's torso, with the weird two-headed shape beside it, seems to be floating on a white cloud. Ruth shivers. The morning air is cold and she is wearing only a jumper pulled on hastily over her pyjamas. She is sure that her hair is standing up wildly and her face feels puffy from sleep. She must have presented a nice contrast to Michelle, whom Nelson would have left at the gym, her toned body encased in a designer tracksuit. Oh well. She pads over the wet grass towards the cottage. She'll have a shower and get dressed. She is due at the hospital at ten. It's time for her next scan.

But, before she can get to the bathroom, her phone rings. It's Nelson ringing from his car. 'I'm thinking it's not safe for you to be alone in the house with this nutter out there. Have you got anywhere you can go?'

'No,' says Ruth flatly. Once, under similar circumstances, she stayed with Shona. Never again.

Nelson sighs. 'Then I'll send someone to sleep at the cottage.'

'No!'

'I have to, Ruth. You're in danger.'

'All right. As long as it's not Clough.'

He laughs. 'I'll send my best WPC.'

Ruth puts down the phone feeling both irritated and obscurely comforted. She stumps back upstairs and goes into the bathroom. She feels exhausted already and it's not nine o'clock yet. Just as she steps into the shower, the phone rings again. Bloody Nelson. Probably just ringing to tell her not to slip on the soap. She considers leaving it but the fear that the call might be bad news (something happening to one of her parents) makes her descend the stairs again.

It's Max. 'Hi, Ruth. Hope I'm not ringing too early. Just wondered how you were feeling, you know, after Saturday.'

Was it only Saturday night that she was in hospital? It seems weeks ago. 'I'm fine,' she says.

'I was wondering . . . about your Norwich site . . .'

'Yes?'

'Well, could I come over and have a look? You mentioned that you'd found some Roman pottery . . .'

Ruth is silent for a moment. She knows that she invited Max to visit the Woolmarket Street site but she hardly expected him to take her up on the offer. The Roman finds have hardly been significant and the building work is starting again today. Why does Max suddenly want to see the site? Could it possibly be because he wants to see her again?

'I've got an appointment at ten,' she says, 'but I could meet you on the site at eleven thirty.'

'Perfect. I'll see you then.'

This time she runs back upstairs and sings in the shower.

The Two-Headed Calf of Aylsham causes quite a stir at the station.

'See you've got a new pet, boss.' This is Clough.

'How disgusting.' Leah.

'What's it doing here?' Judy.

'Is it from the museum?' Tanya, bright-eyed and eager.

Nelson puts the calf in the incident room. He doesn't want it in his office; the glassy stare is beginning to freak him out.

'Cloughie! I want you to take this thing back to the museum and find out how it got out.'

'Maybe it just fancied a walk?'

Nelson ignores this. 'Find out who had access to the exhibits. Tanya!'

'Yes?'

'I need you to look after Sir Roderick Spens. He's coming in today for a DNA test.'

'Yes, sir.'

'Judy, I need you to stay with Ruth Galloway for a few days.'

Judy looks put out for some reason. He hopes she isn't going moody on him. 'Why?' she asks.

'Because I think someone is going to try to kill her.'

This scan seems very different from the first. Ruth knows what to expect and, having had a scan after her accident, she feels pretty sure that the baby is all right. She can even feel him moving now, little butterfly motions rippling across her stomach, quite unlike any other sensation she has ever experienced. 'It feels as if something's moving about inside me,' she had said in answer to Shona's query. 'But that's what it *is*,' Shona had replied.

She is ushered into the room with the ultrasound. They are running late as usual and she begins to worry that she won't get to the site for eleven thirty. The technician rubs gel onto her stomach and, miraculously soon, there are the grey, cloudy insides of her womb. Ruth leans forward.

'There's the baby's legs. Long legs.' The technician presses some buttons. 'There's a good one of the face.' Ruth looks and sees only overlapping shapes, like a Cubist painting. The technician points, 'There's the nose.' And then Ruth sees an actual profile: forehead, tiny nose, lips, chin. She even thinks she can discern an expression, stern and serious.

'Do you want to know the sex?' asks the technician.

Ruth is surprised quite how much she does want to know. Somehow her relationship with this creature, this *person*, has become such that she can't not know.

'Oh . . . yes please.'

The technician points. 'We can never be one hundred per cent certain but I'm pretty sure it's a girl.'

Ruth stares. 'A girl?'

'Well, sometimes the tackle's hidden, if you know what I mean, but we're getting a pretty good full-frontal here. I think you've got a girl.'

A girl. A daughter.

Nelson is having a trying morning. Clough seems to be taking a hell of a long time at the museum. Probably stuffing his face at the café. Or maybe he's met up with Trace and they're having a cosy chat about the Romans. Then Roderick Spens arrives, all confused charm and long stories, and has to be coaxed through the testing routine. Judy would have handled it better, thinks Nelson, watching as Tanya tries to shepherd the old man out of the office. Firm but polite, that's what you need to be. But he's never been that good at the touchy-feely stuff himself.

Then, to cap it all, Whitcliffe pays him a visit.

'Morning, Harry. Just popped in to see how the Woolmarket Street case was progressing. Had a call from Edward Spens. Seems he's a bit worried about his old dad being involved.'

Typical, thinks Nelson. Edward Spens is just the sort of man to complain to the boss. The warmer feelings engendered by Spens' kindness to his father are quickly dispelled.

'Sir Roderick's here now,' he says. He has a feeling Whitcliffe already knows this. 'We're seeing if there's a DNA match with the body. One of my WPCs is looking after him.'

'Is it likely there'll be a match?'

Nelson explains about Annabelle Spens but Whitcliffe still looks dubious. 'Clutching at straws a bit, aren't you, Harry?'

'Perhaps.' Whitcliffe calls Nelson Harry but there is no way that Nelson can call him Gerry. He's not about to call him 'sir' though.

Whitcliffe is about to say something but Nelson's phone suddenly buzzes with a text message. Nelson picks it up. 'Excuse me.'

The message is from Ruth. Three words. 'It's a girl!'

Nelson stares. In the background Whitcliffe is droning on. 'Important local businessman ... relations with the wider public ... care and respect for the elderly ...' But Nelson can only think about Ruth's text. A girl. Another daughter. He can hardly believe it. Ruth had been so sure she was having a boy and, somehow, he had believed it too. Michelle is so ultra-feminine it had always seemed impossible that she could give birth to a male. But Ruth, tough and independent, he had been sure that she would have a son. Another daughter. Well, he needs no practice in loving a daughter.

'Harry?'

'Yes. Yes. Of course. Consider it done.'

Whitcliffe looks at him curiously and Nelson wonders what he is agreeing to. But the answer seems to please his boss who swaggers out of the office in high good humour.

As soon as the door has closed behind him, Nelson rings Ruth. 'Ruth! Is this true?'

She laughs. 'Apparently so. We're having a girl.'

'But you were so sure it was a boy.'

To Nelson's irritation, he sees that Sir Roderick Spens has wandered in, closely followed by Tanya. Nelson waves a hand for them to leave.

'I know but the radiographer was pretty certain.'

'Another girl. My God.'

'Are you pleased?'

He laughs. Of course he isn't pleased, Ruth's pregnancy could be about to blow his marriage sky-high but, on another level, of course he is pleased. He is delighted.

'Where are you?' he asks.

'On my way to the Woolmarket Street site.'

'I'll meet you there.' He looks at his watch, it is twenty past eleven. 'I'll be there in fifteen minutes.'

And he rings off before Ruth has a chance to say that she is meeting Max.

The site is busy again. Diggers trundle to and fro and a large skip is blocking the entrance. Max, wearing a hard hat, is standing by the foreman's hut looking glum.

'I didn't think the building work would be so advanced.'

'I think they're making up for lost time,' says Ruth. 'Nelson says that Edward Spens is desperate to get the work finished.'

'Typical.'

Ruth looks curiously at Max. 'Do you know him then?'

'We were at university together.'

'Really?'

'Yes, we both read history at Sussex.'

Ruth thinks about the suave figure she met on the site.

It's hard to connect him to Max but, come to think of it, they must be about the same age.

'How come he ended up running a building firm?' she asks.

'It's the family business. He always said his dad would insist on it.'

'Are you still in touch with him?'

Max looks slightly sheepish. 'Just Friends Reunited, that sort of thing.'

Ruth loathes Friends Reunited. She has kept in touch with the few people she liked at school and university. As far as she is concerned, the less the rest know about her the better.

'Come on,' she says, 'I'll show you round.'

The foreman is obviously irritated to find archaeologists under his feet again but he agrees to let Ruth show Max over the site 'as long as they keep out of the way'. But, when Ruth goes to find the grave under the door, it has disappeared. The black and white tiles have been broken up and the ground is a seething mass of mud. No walls or divisions can be seen, just a level stretch of ploughed-up earth.

The well is still intact. The diggers haven't got this far but they are looming. Ruth can see their mechanical claws churning up the garden, the vegetable patch, the tree with the swing, the cucumber frame. Soil and rubble pour into the skips. Who knows how many artefacts are there – medieval, Roman, Victorian? All destroyed to make room for seventy-five luxury apartments, each with en-suite bathroom.

Max kneels and looks into the well. 'Design looks Roman.'

'That's what I thought.'

'Heads have been found in Roman wells haven't they?' asks Ruth.

'Sometimes,' Max replies cautiously. 'At Odell in Bedfordshire they found a Roman skull deliberately inserted into the lining of a well. Head cults are more Celtic though. And holy wells were common in medieval times. St Thomas's well at Windleshaw was said to have sprung up where a priest was beheaded.'

The noise of the diggers is making it hard to speak. Ruth is about to suggest they leave the site when she sees Nelson coming towards them, frowning as he strides through the rubble. She had forgotten about Nelson.

'Does he follow you everywhere?' mutters Max.

Nelson, too, seems less than pleased to find that Ruth has company. 'Long time no see,' he says drily to Max.

Ruth can't stand much more of this. 'Come on,' she says, 'let's get out of here.'

They stop, as if by mutual consent, by the stone archway, still standing although the rest of the front wall has disappeared. Towers, archways, crenellations – all crumbled into dust.

'Are they leaving the arch?' asks Max.

'Yes,' says Ruth, 'it's classy apparently.'

They stand for a minute looking up at the words inscribed in the stone and Ruth sees another figure approaching. A man dressed in clerical black, walking slowly along the boards laid down over the churned-up earth. Father Hennessey. The foreman will have a fit, thinks Ruth.

Father Hennessey approaches and, suddenly, his face is filled with such recognition and delight that Ruth is stunned.

Why on earth is he so pleased to see her? Or is it Nelson he is looking at?

But the priest looks straight past Ruth and Nelson. His blue eyes are full of tears.

'Martin,' he says, 'how good to see you again.'

25 June
Ludi Taurii begin

An opportunity presented itself today. The mother had gone out, leaving the child asleep in its bed. It no longer sleeps in a cot but in a bed with bars at the side to stop it falling out. She was worried about leaving the child alone in the house with me but she was in pain from an infected tooth and needed to see the dentist urgently. I assured her smoothly that the child was safe with me, as indeed she will be. As soon as the mother had gone I got my knife and went straight into the room.

She was asleep, her mouth slightly open. She is not an attractive child, whatever the mother says. I turned her over so the neck was exposed. I could see a little pulse there. The perfect place.

To tell you the truth, dear diary, I had slightly been dreading this moment. Would I be struck by Pity, that emasculating emotion? Would I lack the requisite manliness to do the deed? But I am pleased to report that, as I stood above the infant like an avenging angel, I felt no pity at all. Rather a great joy swept over me, a feel of immense power and righteousness. Yes, that was it. I knew beyond any doubt that I was doing the right thing. My arm felt like steel, strong yet flexible. My eyes burned in my skull. I lifted the knife.

Then – oh banality! – the phone rang. Oh, evil modern influence, obtruding on the ancient rituals! Of course, the moment was ruined and I went to answer the infernal machine. It was Them. We chatted quite civilly but they will be back next week. So little time.

Still very hot. The house waits.

CHAPTER 24

At first Ruth does not understand what is happening. She looks from Hennessey to Max and back again, wondering as she does so why Nelson also looks so shell shocked. And it is Nelson who speaks first.

'Martin,' he says, '*you're* Martin Black?'

Max laughs. A laugh Ruth has never heard before, harsh and slightly wild. 'Black, Grey,' he says, 'what's the difference?'

And then Ruth remembers. Martin and Elizabeth Black. The two children who had lived at the home and had vanished so mysteriously. Can it really be true? Can Max, who claimed to know nothing about the Woolmarket Street site, actually have lived here once? Is this why he has come back to Norfolk? And if he has kept this secret from her, says another, darker, voice in her ear, what else has he been hiding?

Father Hennessey now comes closer to Max, who has turned deadly white. 'Martin,' he says, in a voice choked with emotion, 'I never thought I'd see you again. My dear boy.'

Max reaches out a hand and touches the priest's arm. His eyes, too, are full of tears.

'Father Hennessey,' he says, 'I never forgot you.'

'And Elizabeth?' It is barely a whisper.

'She died.' Max turns his face away.

Nelson's voice is like a rush of cold air. 'I think you need to answer a few questions, Mr Grey. Or is it Mr Black?'

'I've done nothing wrong,' says Max defiantly.

'I'll be the judge of that,' says Nelson. 'Now, if you'd accompany me to the station.'

Max looks as if he is about to refuse but then he gives a little shrug and follows Nelson out through the archway. No wonder he knew what the inscription meant, thinks Ruth.

Father Hennessey hesitates and then, with an apologetic glance at Ruth, he hurries after the other men. Ruth is left on her own amongst the diggers.

Late afternoon and Ruth is at home. For the first few hours after the revelation at the building site she had been certain that either Max or Nelson was about to call at any minute. Surely someone was going to tell her what was going on? But as time passed and she fed Flint, made herself a light lunch (and heavy pudding), tidied the sitting room, put the washing on, answered emails and finally settled down to read a dissertation on 'The Archaeology of Disease', she had to face the fact that no one was going to think it worth updating her. She is peripheral to this case, the bones expert, the slightly eccentric academic. She is outside the main action. Max had lied to her, probably used her to get news of the Woolmarket Street site. Nelson forgets her the instant that he gets the scent of a breakthrough. The only person who thinks she is central to the case, she thinks bitterly, is the madman who keeps leaving museum exhibits for her to find.

But then, as the birds start gathering over the Saltmarsh for their evening spectacular, thousands of little black dots like iron filings dividing and converging against the sky, Ruth sees a black Range Rover draw up beside her gate. Max.

She goes to the door, uncertain how she feels. On one hand she just wants to know what the hell is going on, on the other she has decidedly mixed feelings about Max Grey. Martin Black, of course, she doesn't know at all.

He looks desperately tired, chalk white with dark rings under his eyes. Five hours of questioning by Nelson can't be fun for anyone, of course, but Ruth now realises that he has been looking strained for some time, probably ever since the news of the body under the doorway. No, before that, from the moment he realised that Ruth's site was the old children's home, when she asked him about the words cut into the archway. Despite herself, Ruth feels sorry for him.

'How are you?' she asks.

'I've felt better.'

'Do you want a cup of tea?'

'A drink would be good.'

She gets him a glass of wine and makes herself a herbal tea (so disgusting that it must be good for her).

They sit for a minute in silence then Max says, 'I'm sorry.'

'What for?'

'For lying to you.'

'You didn't exactly lie, you just didn't tell me.'

He smiles. 'Father Hennessey would say that was the same thing.'

'It's incredible that he recognised you after all that time.'

'He said it was partly the setting. Seeing me standing by the archway. Jesus – when you asked me what those words meant! They're burned into my heart.'

He takes a gulp of wine. His hands are shaking.

'What happened at the police station?' Ruth asks.

'Oh, Nelson took a statement. Went on for hours. They took fingerprints and everything. Talked to Father Hennessey too but they wouldn't let him stay when they questioned me.'

'What did they question you about?'

'My disappearance. After all, I've been a missing person for over thirty years. And about Elizabeth.'

His voice breaks when he says her name. He rubs his eyes.

Ruth says gently, 'You said she died?'

Max looks up and now his eyes are hard. He stares at Ruth as if he doesn't see her.

'She died,' he says. And he is not talking to Ruth but to someone else, himself perhaps, and she knows, somehow, that it is twelve-year-old Martin Black who is speaking.

'We wanted to get to our dad. I'd had it all planned. I'd got his address from Father Hennessey's records. He always let me go into his office. I stole enough food to last us. I'd even got a tent from the storehouse – Father Hennessey used to take us camping sometimes. It was all fixed but Elizabeth . . . she didn't really want to go. She liked it at the home. She loved Sister James, the nun who taught the little ones. She felt safe there. But she loved me more.' For a second he sounds almost triumphant. 'She loved me so she went with me. Only thing she wanted to take was her blasted stuffed dog.'

And Ruth sees Max's bed on the boat: the classical text open on the side table and the stuffed toy on the pillow. Elizabeth's dog.

'At first it was OK. We stayed in an abandoned warehouse the first night and then we headed for London. I'd brought our old school uniforms. I knew they wouldn't be looking for children in uniform and I was lucky. There was a school trip to London that day so we tagged along behind them. No one noticed us. But when we got to London, that's when it started.'

'What started?'

'Elizabeth got sick. She'd always had lots of sore throats and colds so at first I thought it was that. I stole some throat stuff for her and she seemed better for a while. We were staying outside Swindon in an empty school. We had to head west, you see, to Holyhead. Jesus – that school. It had big snakes and ladders painted on the playground, on the tarmac. Elizabeth was scared of them. At night she thought they were coming to get her. We were sleeping in the staffroom. They had sofas in there. But she had a fever, she used to scream. It was like she didn't know me. She used to scream for our mum.'

His voice has all but died away. He is sitting slumped forward, head in hands. Flint has abandoned him. Ruth doesn't want to hear any more. The thought that the five-year-old Elizabeth might have died in that empty school, with only her twelve-year-old brother to care for her, is almost too awful to contemplate. And, if she can't contemplate it, what about Max, who has kept this secret all these years? But Ruth also feels that, having started telling his story, it would be good for him to finish it. So she prompts gently, 'What happened?'

Max looks at her, his gaze anguished. 'She died. Just like that. I woke up one morning and she was dead. Lying on the sofa with a rug over her and she was dead. Her little face was cold . . .' He turns away and, after a few seconds, continues in a harder voice. 'I buried her in the school grounds. They had a little vegetable patch where the earth was soft and I buried her there. I was going to bury Wolfie, her dog, with her but, when it came to it, I couldn't bear to. It smelt of her, you see. I buried her and I went on. I suppose Nelson will dig her up now. Bit of a shock for some poor primary school.' He laughs harshly.

'What happened to you?'

'Oh, I got to Ireland but when I saw my dad, he was drunk as a lord, didn't know me from Adam, so I didn't hang around. I lived rough for a while and got taken in by some travellers, gypsies. They were kind to me. I used to help with the horses, they went to lots of horse fairs and they had ponies that just roamed free, even in the cities. The children went to local schools sometimes. I went with them and got interested in history again. Met a teacher in one school who liked me and he encouraged me to stay and take some exams. I lived with him and his family. They were kind too. I called myself Max Grey by then. I took O Levels and A Levels and, eventually, got into Sussex. End of story.'

'Why did you come back here?' asks Ruth.

'Well, mostly it was the Roman dig. I am an archaeologist after all. But I suppose I wanted to see the home again. I wanted to but I was scared. DCI Nelson said that runaways almost always go back to the place that they ran away from. Well, I suppose I was no exception. Then, when you were excavating the site, I couldn't believe it. I wanted to tell you, Ruth, I really did.'

He is looking at her earnestly. Martin Black has vanished and he is Max Grey again, soft-spoken and unthreatening.

'That's OK,' she says, 'it must have been . . . awful for you.' She is aware how inadequate this sounds.

'I couldn't face going to the site at first, but then I couldn't resist it. I suppose I just wanted to see it one last time. Then, seeing Father Hennessey like that . . .'

'I think he was very fond of you.'

'He was really good to me. I was a delinquent in those days. Got into fights, swore, stole, but he never gave up on me. He always thought I'd make something of myself.'

'He was right,' says Ruth.

'Was he?' They look at each other and suddenly the moment is charged, by sadness, understanding and, unexpectedly, by something else, something that makes Ruth blush and turn away.

'Ruth?'

But the spell is broken by the doorbell. Judy Johnson is on the doorstep, an overnight bag in her hand.

'Hi, Ruth. I've come to stay for a few nights.'

CHAPTER 25

The DNA results are waiting on Nelson's desk when he gets into work in the morning. He studies them, black coffee in hand. They prove, without a shadow of a doubt, that Roderick Spens is related to the body found under the doorway. More than that, they show that Roderick and the dead child share a common male ancestor. Nelson frowns down at the print-out in his hand, thinking hard.

Finding Martin Black had been a bolt from the blue. Despite his theory about offenders returning to the scene of the crime, Nelson never honestly expected to find Martin Black wandering around the ruins of the former children's home. And never in a million years did he connect the smug archaeologist who seems to dog Ruth's footsteps with the twelve-year-old boy who went missing. 'People grow up,' he always tells his team, 'you're not looking for a little boy, you're looking for a man in his forties.' But, even so, the distance between Dr Max Grey and desperate runaway Martin Black seemed too vast to be straddled by one person.

And his story – his story had been heart-rending. The little girl dying in the empty school (possibly of meningitis, Nelson suspects), the grief-stricken brother burying the body. It is just outlandish enough to be true. Well, they'll know when they find the school and dig up their vegetable patch. The press will love that.

Briefing is at nine. Tanya has her notebook open in front of her, Clough enters the room still chewing, Judy is drinking tea.

'Everything all right at Ruth's?' Nelson asks her.

'Not a sound all night.'

'Is Ruth OK?'

Judy looks at him curiously. 'She seems fine. She had a friend there when I turned up.'

'Who?'

'That archaeologist chap. The one who was here yesterday.'

'We need to talk about him,' says Nelson. He tells the team about the unexpected appearance of Martin Black.

'Bloody hell,' says Clough, still chasing stray bits of breakfast around his mouth, 'was it really him?'

'Father Hennessey verifies it. According to Black, he and his sister ran away, hoping to get to Ireland. Elizabeth became ill and died in a deserted school outside Swindon.'

'Do you believe him?" asks Clough.

'I never believe anyone without checking first. But, in any case, we've established that the body at Woolmarket Street can't be Elizabeth Black. We've had the DNA results,' he pauses impressively, 'and they show that Sir Roderick Spens and the dead child share a common male ancestor.'

'So it could be Annabelle Spens?' gasps Judy.

'It's possible. Tanya, how are you getting on with tracing Annabelle's dental records?'

'It's difficult,' says Tanya, rather defensively Nelson thinks. 'I've been through all the dentists operating in Norwich in the forties and fifties. None of them are still practising and their records have vanished.'

'Keep trying,' says Nelson. 'According to our expert there was some pretty fancy dental work done on that little girl.'

'If the child is Annabelle Spens,' says Judy slowly, 'who could have killed her? It was a really brutal death, stabbed and then beheaded.'

'I don't know,' says Nelson, 'but I do know that in cases where a child has been murdered the killer is almost always one of the family.'

'Christopher Spens?'

'It's possible. He sounds a nutcase to me. All that stuff about Latin. Roderick Spens said his father kept a shrine to the Roman Gods in his garden. The well too. That was built by him, to an authentic Roman design apparently.'

'What about the mother?' asks Tanya. 'What was she like?'

'Sir Roderick says she was "like an angel" but I get the impression that he didn't really know her that well. Probably brought up by a nanny. The mother died quite young, in 1957.'

'Only a few years after her daughter,' says Judy, 'probably died of grief.'

'This isn't a woman's magazine,' says Nelson, 'she died of pneumonia. Quite common in those days.'

'All the same,' says Clough, 'they were an unlucky family, weren't they?'

Ruth is having trouble working. Having Judy in the house

forced her to get up early, offer to make tea, etc. But Judy said that she would get something at the station. She left at eight, looking far more together than Ruth ever manages before ten a.m., or indeed ever.

It had been unexpectedly pleasant to have company last night. Max had left almost as soon as Judy arrived and that had been a bit of a relief too. She feels that she needs time to absorb Max's story, to come to terms that Max Grey is, in fact, Martin Black. How could anyone go through all that and emerge the other side apparently normal and well-adjusted? If she had ever thought about Max's childhood she would have imagined a middle-class home, public or maybe grammar school, a smooth transition to university, the usual relationships and friendships along the way. Never a children's home, a dead sister, living rough, adopted by gypsies. Jesus – it's like *Wuthering Heights*. And there is, she admits, something slightly Heathcliffy about Max.

Ruth sits down at her table by the window. It is a dull morning, the grey marsh merging seamlessly with the grey sky. She opens her computer but, after staring at her lectures notes for a minute, closes it again. She opens a drawer and gets out a beautiful clean piece of paper. One of the few things she and Nelson have in common is a liking for lists. At the top of her list Ruth writes: <u>Woolmarket Street</u>. Then she lists everyone she knows who is connected to the site.

<u>Children's Home</u>
Father Hennessey
Max Grey (she stares at this name for a second before crossing it out and writing Martin Black)
Kevin Davies, undertaker

Other former residents

Staff (Max had mentioned a Sister James and she knows that Judy went to Southport to interview another nun)

<u>Building Site</u>

Edward Spens

Foreman and other building workers

Ted

Trace

She looks at the list for so long that Flint becomes bored and tries to sit on it. Ruth pushes him off. Anyone on the list could have put the two-headed calf on her doorstep, could have put the baby in the trench and written her name on the Roman wall. Of all the names, she has to face the fact that Max is the most likely. He knows about Roman ritual, he was the one who told her all that *I, Claudius* stuff in the first place; he has had the means and the opportunity. He was there when she found the writing on the wall. He was the one who found her in the trench after she had fainted. What if he had been there all along? What if he was the one who put the baby there (it was only the night before, after all, that she told him that she was pregnant)? As an archaeologist, he would have access to the museum; he could easily have got hold of the two-headed calf and the model baby too.

But why? Why would Max want to scare her, scare her to death, as he himself put it? To warn her away from the Woolmarket Street site? To prevent her from discovering his identity as Martin Black? Or is there some other mystery concerned with the old children's home?

She looks at the list again. If the body under the door was

killed over fifty years ago, there is only one person who was alive at the time. Father Patrick Hennessey. Well maybe there are still some nuns or other staff members alive but Father Hennessey is the only one she knows. If there is a secret, he will be the one who knows it. Don't priests always know secrets? Isn't that the whole point of the Catholic confessional?

When they met at the site, Father Hennessey had given her his card. At the time, she had thought it amusing that a priest would possess something as worldly as a business card. Father Patrick Hennessey SJ it says, in discreet grey capitals. She has no idea what SJ stands for and she doesn't want to know. On the other hand, it wouldn't hurt to meet him again and ask him a few questions of her own.

Her hand hovers by the phone.

Judy is sitting at her desk, fuming. Bastard! How *dare* he sneer at her. 'This isn't a woman's magazine.' And in front of Tanya Fuller too. Judy likes Tanya. She's fun on a night out and she certainly provides a welcome antidote to Clough and the rest of the lads. But Judy also knows that Tanya is competition.

Judy has been in the police force for three years. She's a graduate (something she doesn't often mention to Nelson) and, as such, on the so-called 'fast track' to success. When, after eighteen months, she'd been given the transfer to CID she felt that she really was on the way up. She loves detective work and she gets on well with Nelson whose bark is definitely worse than his bite. He may sound like an unreconstructed male chauvinist but, in practice, he is fair to the women in his team and (unlike some DCIs) does not view them as useful only in cases of rape or domestic violence. But somehow Judy feels that her career has stalled. She is a Detective Constable, by now she should be a Detective Sergeant, like Clough. She knows that Nelson has the funding for another sergeant so why hasn't he given her the stripes? At least until Tanya Fuller turned up she could be sure that she was the best candidate for the job. But now Tanya breezes in from another force with her intelligent questions and her eyes fixed adoringly on Nelson's face. What if Nelson promotes Tanya over Judy? She couldn't bear it. She'd jack it all in and become a bookie like her dad.

Judy is meant to be helping Tanya with the dentist search but instead she is going over the notes from the case. She is sure they are all missing something. And, if she spots it, that will mean one in the eye for Nelson, Tanya, all of them.

Idly she sketches a Spens family tree. She met Edward Spens once at a police do and found him rather attractive. This doesn't affect her deep-seated belief that his family have something to hide.

Sir Christopher Spens (d 1981) = Rosemary Spens (d 1957)
|
Roderick (b 1938) + Annabelle (b 1946, d 1952)
|
Charlotte + Edward
|
Tracy + Luke
Sebastian + Flora

She looks hard at the name Rosemary Spens. She hears Nelson's voice, speaking in the flat tone he uses for briefings: 'Sir Roderick says she was "like an angel" but I get the impression that he didn't really know her that well. Probably brought up by a nanny.' That's it. Judy goes back to the file and rifles through until she comes to the census of 1951. She remembers Clough reading it out to them: 'Christopher Spens, Rosemary Spens, children Roderick and Annabelle.' But, typically, Clough has overlooked something and Nelson's casual words have brought it back to her. There would have been other people in the house – servants, a cook and almost certainly a nanny. And, sure enough, there are four other names on the list:

Lily Wright – cook general
Susan Baker – domestic
Edna Dawes – domestic
Orla McKinley – nanny

Judy looks at the last name for a long time.

Clough, swallowing the last of a chunky doughnut-to-go, is in a stonemason's studio. The air is thick with dust and out of the fog loom disembodied shapes – columns, fireplaces, the occasional half-finished statue, horses and angels and Greek goddesses. Clough walks carefully through the stone figures thinking that it's like a book he read as a child where a witch turned her enemies into stone and then decorated her house with them. Either that or a graveyard.

They have had a bit of luck with the stonemason. The firm who made Christopher Spens' archway in 1956 are still in business. The actual mason has retired but his son is now in charge and has volunteered to bring his old dad into the studio to talk to the police. Clough now wends his way slowly towards the back of the vast room where the comforting sounds of Radio 1 are mingling with the smell of reheated coffee and calor gas. Clough sniffs appreciatively.

An old man is sitting in an armchair in from of the gas stove. A younger man, presumably the son, is chipping away at a small block of marble. Duffy is begging for mercy in the background.

'Mr Wilson?' Clough extends a hand. 'Detective Sergeant Clough.'

The old man holds out a thin hand in a fingerless glove. 'Mr Wilson senior. Reginald Wilson. I assume it's me you wanted?'

'Well, yes, sir. As I explained to your son on the phone, we're interested in an archway you built in 1956, on Woolmarket Street. For Christopher Spens.'

Reginald Wilson gestures towards a cloth-bound book on his lap marked, in black ink, 1954–1958. 'It's all in the book. I always say to Stephen here, put it in the book. You never know when you might want to refer to it. But it's all computers these days. Not as safe as a book.' The younger man rolls his eyes good-naturedly.

Clough follows the shaking finger to an entry marked in pencil. 'Stone archway and portico. Portico with Roman-style columns. Archway, stand-alone, granite. Eight foot by four. Inscription to read: Omnia Mutantur, Nihil Interit.'

'Latin,' says Clough. 'Gobbledegook, eh?'

'I studied Latin at school,' says Reginald Wilson mildly. 'It's a fairly well-known saying. It was important to Mr Spens,

I think, because of his daughter dying. He said that the arch was a memorial to her, a sign that nothing was ever really lost.'

Feeling snubbed, Clough says, 'What sort of a man was Christopher Spens?'

Wilson is silent for a moment, holding his hands out towards the fire. Then he says, 'He was always very courteous to me. Treated me as a craftsman. That's important in our line of work. But he was distant, if you know what I mean. Of course, he'd lost a child and that changes you. But he was a difficult man to know, that was my impression.'

'What about his wife, Rosemary?'

'I hardly saw her. I understood she was a bit of an invalid. We saw the son though, nice lad, he helped us dig.'

'Roderick?'

'Yes. He runs the business now, doesn't he?'

'His son, Edward.'

'Ah, fathers and sons.' Reginald Wilson glances at his son, working industriously on the marble, its sides shining in the light from the fire. 'That's what it's all about, isn't it? Passing the business on to your son. That's the only reason why any of us do it.'

On the way out, moving through the stone menagerie, Clough remembers the name of the book. *The Lion, the Witch and the Wardrobe.* He must remember to tell Judy. She's always saying that he never reads anything.

27th June
Festival of Jupiter Stator

This morning a black dog appeared on the front lawn. Clearly a messenger from the goddess. As it paused on the lawn, it turned and looked at me (I was reading Suetonius in the drawing room). I looked back, sending a message, 'Is it soon, lady?' And she answered, 'It is soon.'

CHAPTER 26

'How charming,' says Father Hennessey politely, although the café chosen at random by Ruth is, in truth, anything but charming. Determined to avoid Starbucks she'd Googled 'cafés Norwich' and come up with Bobby's Bagels, an old-fashioned greasy spoon with Formica tables and dirty net curtains. The owner (Bobby himself?) has at least three days' worth of food spattered on his apron and is either talking on a hands-free phone or is in the grip of severe schizophrenia.

The café is, at least, fairly near to Woolmarket Street and Ruth was able to look in at the site as she went past. Apart from the archway, the old house has now vanished completely: reception rooms, kitchens, bedrooms, wishing well, outhouses all subsumed in a smooth sea of mud. At the back of the site, the new apartments are rising stealthily, now at first-floor height complete with flimsy-looking balconies. Edward Spens is obviously going all out to beat the property crash.

Ruth orders tea because she doesn't trust the coffee. Father Hennessey orders coffee and, rashly, a bagel. This he eats with every appearance of relish despite the fact that the plate seems to have traces of egg on it. The priest looks completely calm and relaxed. It is Ruth who fiddles nervously with the sugar bowl and twice spills her (disgusting) tea.

'You must have been delighted to see Martin again,' she says.

Father Hennessey smiles. 'Indeed I was. It was a great gift from God. I had feared I would die without knowing what had happened to Martin and Elizabeth.'

This is, presumably, more than a manner of speaking. Father Hennessey, Ruth knows from Max, is over eighty; death is no longer a metaphor. What must it be like, wonders Ruth, to know that you are going to die and to be sure that eternal life awaits?

'Max . . . Martin . . . said that you were very good to him.'

Father Hennessey looks meditatively into his coffee cup. 'Ah, I tried to be but we never know how much harder we could have tried. If I had been more understanding, maybe he wouldn't have run away. Maybe Elizabeth wouldn't have died.'

'Maybe she would have,' says Ruth gently. 'Max says she was often ill as a child.'

Hennessey smiles but says nothing. There is a silence broken only by Bobby in the background having a fierce row with someone called Maggie. Eventually Ruth says, 'You're probably wondering why I asked to see you.'

'I assumed you'd tell me,' says Father Hennessey mildly.

So Ruth tells him about the baby and the two-headed calf, about the writing in blood and the presence lurking outside her house. She probably tells him more than she means to and she attributes this to some innate spooky priest power. Certainly Hennessey's pale blue eyes never leave her face.

'So,' she concludes, 'someone is trying to scare me. Someone linked to the house. And I wondered if you had any idea who that could be.'

She forces herself to confront that blue stare. Father Hennessey looks steadily back at her. 'Do you have any ideas yourself?' he asks.

'No,' says Ruth though, in truth, she does.

'Have you ever met anyone else from the children's home?' asks Hennessey.

'Only Kevin Davies.'

'None of the nuns?'

'No.'

Is he really, as Ted would say, going to pin it on the nuns? But the only person Ruth knows from the Sacred Heart Children's Home is Father Hennessey himself.

'Why do you ask?' says Ruth.

For the first time, Hennessey does not meet her eyes. He looks down at the murky grey liquid in his coffee cup.

'There are other secrets,' he says at last. 'The evil in that house began long before I ever saw it.'

Nelson is actually at Judy's desk when she calls him. He has been looking for the transcript of her interview with Sister Immaculata and is, therefore, surprised and a little spooked to hear that Judy is actually on her way to Southport to see the nun again.

'What are you playing at, Johnson?'

'I think I've discovered something about Sister Immaculata. I think it's important.'

Nelson starts to counts to ten and gives up on five. 'When will you be back?'

'Later tonight.'

He sighs. Judy is a good officer. He trusts her instincts and, God knows, they could do with a breakthrough.

'No. Stay the night if you have to. I'll get Tanya to stay at Ruth's tonight.'

Some routine surveillance will do Tanya good, he thinks. She's been a bit too pleased with herself lately. He hopes she hasn't got her eyes on Judy's job. Tanya is obviously intelligent but she still has a lot to learn. Besides he would never promote a newcomer over a long-standing officer. Nelson believes in precedence; it comes of being the youngest of three.

He continues rifling through Judy's (incredibly neat) papers and comes across the sheet of paper on which she has jotted down the Spens family tree.

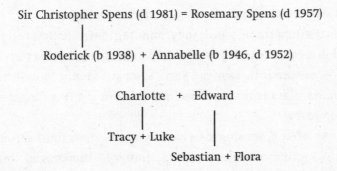

Sir Christopher Spens (d 1981) = Rosemary Spens (d 1957)

Roderick (b 1938) + Annabelle (b 1946, d 1952)

Charlotte + Edward

Tracy + Luke

Sebastian + Flora

He stares at the scribbled names, sure he is missing something. He is so deep in thought that he doesn't hear his name being called. It is not until Cathbad is actually in the room with him that he registers his presence, purple cloak and all. Tom, the desk sergeant, hovers in the background looking embarrassed.

Since the Saltmarsh case, Nelson and Cathbad have almost become friends. There is an understanding between them, despite Nelson's contempt for new age philosophy and Cathbad's dislike for authority. Cathbad has even visited Nelson's house, bearing dreamcatchers for the girls and Nelson has once or twice met him for a drink in dodgy pubs where the beers all have names and, unless you are careful, people play folk music at you.

'I'm sorry, sir,' says Tom. 'He said it was important.'

Nelson notices that, cloak notwithstanding, Cathbad does look unusually serious, even worried.

'What it about?' he asks.

'Max Grey,' Cathbad answers.

Judy arrives at Southport at just after four to be told that Sister Immaculata is 'unwell' and can't see anyone.

'It's important,' pleads Judy, standing in the spotless reception area surrounded by tropical plants and pictures of saints.

'I'm sure it is,' says the Sister sympathetically, 'but Sister Immaculata is having a bad day. Perhaps she'll be brighter tomorrow.'

So, after promising to be back tomorrow, Judy finds herself on Southport seafront, tired, hungry, discouraged and slightly scared. What if Nelson is furious with her for disappearing like that? What if Ruth gets murdered tonight and it's all her fault? What if Tanya finds the dental records, solves the case and gets promoted? She sighs and starts to walk towards the nearest B and B.

Ruth had not been pleased to open her door expecting Judy but finding Tanya Fuller, designer glasses flashing, on the doorstep. She likes Judy and had been looking forward to seeing her again. The morning's conversation with Father Hennessey has left her rather more unsettled than before. What did he mean, 'The evil in that house began long before I ever saw it.'? 'Surely you don't mean the place is haunted?' Ruth had answered lightly.

'Maybe I do,' the priest had replied.

'But priests don't believe in ghosts.'

'Sure we do,' Hennessey had smiled. 'What about the Holy Ghost? The most important one of the trilogy as far as I'm concerned.'

All rubbish as far as Ruth is concerned but, driving back along the misty Saltmarsh road, she kept having a ridiculous compulsion to look in her mirror to check that no one was sitting on the back seat. Even now, as she cooks supper for herself and Tanya, she puts on the radio to stop herself wondering if she can hear breathing outside.

Ruth doesn't cook much (although she loves reading cookery books, preferably with pictures of Tuscan olive groves) and she slightly resents cooking for Tanya. It had been all right with Judy but preparing a meal for this stranger sitting on the sofa picking cat's fur off her black trousers, this is different and slightly stressful. Nevertheless Ruth cooks pasta and sauce and mixes a salad. She and Tanya chat in a desultory manner as they eat. Ruth learns that Tanya is twenty-five and has been in the police force four years, she is a graduate (sports science) and she thinks keeping fit is a moral imperative. Ruth listens to this in silence, helping herself to an extra piece of garlic bread. Tanya thinks Norfolk is 'very nice', her colleagues are 'very nice' and Nelson is also 'very nice'.

'Don't you find him a bit of a bully?'

'No. He's been very nice to me.'

He's been nice to me too, thinks Ruth, and look where that got me. She looks out of the window and thinks of Nelson and that night, four months ago, when he turned up unexpectedly at her front door. The sun is setting over the marshes and the birds wheel into the air, shifting black clouds against the deep blue sky.

'Beautiful view,' says Tanya politely.

'Yes, isn't it?' says Ruth. She thinks of the Saltmarsh and its secrets: the hidden causeway, the henge, the bodies buried where the land meets the sea. Last year she had nearly died on the marshes. She had thought that the danger was over and that she could live quietly for a while. But somehow danger seems to have found her again.

Tanya eats a tiny amount of pasta, pausing between each mouthful. Ruth has finished her second helping before Tanya has eaten her first. They drink water ('I'm on duty') and Tanya reacts to the offer of pudding as if Ruth had tried to sell her drugs. Ruth eats a slice of chocolate cake and wonders what the hell they are going to talk about all evening. Perhaps they can just watch TV.

She is about to suggest this when, without warning, the lights go out. Tanya jumps up, alert at once.

'It's OK,' says Ruth, 'it's only the fuse. It does that occasionally. The box is out the back.'

The fuse box is in a small outhouse in the back garden. Ruth's neighbours, the weekenders, have converted their outhouse into another bathroom but Ruth's just contains rusty gardening equipment, a defunct exercise bicycle and the remains of a rotary washing line.

'I'll go,' says Tanya.

'Don't be silly. It's right by the back door. Anyway, you'd never find the box. There's no light in the shed.'

Ruth puts on her shoes and opens the kitchen door. It is dark outside and a fresh, salty wind is blowing. She steps into the garden, feeling for the side of the shed with one hand. She can feel the flint wall, the rotting wood of the door. She reaches out to touch the handle.

And encounters living flesh.

CHAPTER 27

Ruth screams. She is aware of a smell, lemon and sandal-wood, and then the world goes black. She is fighting for breath; she can't see or feel anything. She falls to the ground, scraping her knee on stone.

'Ruth!' Tanya's voice, muffled but close.

Something is pulled from over Ruth's head and she can see again. The night sky looks extraordinarily bright after the previous total blackness. Ruth is kneeling on the floor by the shed and Tanya is standing beside her, holding a heavy black cloth.

'What happened?' Tanya sounds very shaken. Whether it is concern for Ruth or fear of what Nelson would say if anything happened to her, Ruth doesn't know.

'I came out. I was feeling for the wall and I felt . . . a person. Someone was standing there, right by the wall. I touched them. Their face, I think. I heard them breathing. Then it all went black.'

'They threw this over you.' Tanya indicated the black cloth. 'It's weighted at the bottom,' she says.

'That's why I couldn't get it off.' Ruth struggles to her feet.

Now that the fear has subsided, she feels rather foolish. There is something infinitely ridiculous about being wrapped in a cloth, like a budgie in a cage.

Tanya pushes open the shed door. 'Is there anyone there?' she calls, her voice admirably steady. No answer but Flint nearly gives them both a heart attack by jumping heavily from the roof, landing with a thump on the grass.

'Let's get you inside,' says Tanya. 'I'll come back out here with a torch.'

But Ruth doesn't want to stay indoors on her own, so she follows Tanya back out into the garden. Tanya flashes her torch around the tiny shed. Its beam illuminates the collection of rusty iron and plastic, the fuse box on the wall, the festoons of cobwebs – but nothing else. She gestures towards the fuse box, all the switches have been pushed down.

'Someone did that deliberately,' she says, 'and look at the doorway. No cobwebs there.'

She shines her torch downwards and there, on the dusty earth floor, between a shovel and the plastic strings of the washing line, is a single footprint.

'Bingo,' says Tanya.

Avoiding the print, Tanya switches the power back on and, immediately, light from the house streams into the garden. She spends a few more minutes examining the footprint before saying, 'OK. Let's go in. I've got to call the boss.'

While Tanya rings Nelson, Ruth feeds Flint who has been meowing loudly for the last five minutes. She can just hear muttered snatches of conversation. 'No ... just now ... no sign of ... perpetrator escaped ... thorough search ... print ... seems a bit shaken ... no ... yes, sir.'

'He's on his way,' says Tanya as Ruth comes into the sitting room. She sounds nervous. Ruth thinks it must be extremely stressful to work for Nelson. And she could never imagine calling another adult 'sir'.

Nelson arrives in ten minutes, bringing with him a colleague from forensics. By this time, Tanya and Ruth are sitting in front of the television mindlessly watching a programme called *Your top fifty advertising icons from the 70s*. Ruth's knee is hurting and she is longing to be in bed. Tanya sits on the edge of the sofa, fiddling with her mobile.

'Nice to see someone's got time to watch telly,' is Nelson's opening gambit.

'Yes, we're just having a nice quiet evening,' Ruth retorts. She doesn't feel ready for Nelson's brusque irony. Tanya, though, blushes.

'I thought it would calm Ruth down,' she says, 'she's a bit upset.'

'I'm not the slightest bit upset,' snaps Ruth.

Nelson strides out into the garden, followed by Tanya and the forensics man. Ruth stays inside. She knows she should be bustling about making tea, being terribly grateful for all this police protection but instead she feels cross and tired and, despite what she said to Tanya, extremely scared. It is one thing to be afraid of the creature in the night, another actually to touch its face, to feel its breath. The danger has come closer, almost to Ruth's very door and, yes, she is very upset indeed.

Ruth sits on the sofa with Flint on her lap watching as the Smash aliens fill the TV screen. She has turned the sound off but she can hear their tinny voices in her head, reminding her of cosy evenings spent watching TV with her parents: *Tomorrow's World*, *Man About the House*, *Upstairs Downstairs*. No wonder they put all these nostalgia programmes on the TV, just the thing for saddoes like her. Funny, at the time, she didn't realise that she was living through the golden age of telly; you watched what was on, that was all. There were just the three channels for most of her childhood, no remote control, switching channels meant actually getting up from your seat. They didn't call it 'switching', she remembers, they called it 'turning over'. 'Shall we turn over, Daddy?' her mother would ask when *Top of the Pops* came on. How Ruth had longed to watch *Top of the Pops* with all those sinful transvestites gyrating to the devil's music. Turning over implied only two choices – BBC1 or 2. Ruth's parents had thought that ITV was somehow common – maybe that's why they had watched *I, Claudius*, despite it being so disgusting. Full of sex and violence it may have been, but it was on BBC2 and so somehow safe.

Lying on the table is the black cloth which, only an hour ago, was bundled over her head. Ruth leans closer to examine it, careful not to touch. It is heavy black material, almost oily-looking, and, as Tanya said, it is weighted along the hem, as if it has been specially made to hang down over something.

'Looks like something you'd put over a statue,' says a voice behind her. Nelson has come back in, bringing with him cool air and an almost palpable sense of action, of getting things done. Despite herself, Ruth feels a lot safer when he is in the house.

'What do you mean, over a statue?' she asks.

'You know,' says Nelson, slightly defensively, 'like when they cover the statues in church on Good Friday.'

Ruth thinks of Father Hennessey. *What about the Holy Ghost? The most important one of the trilogy as far as I'm concerned.* 'I'm happy to say I've never been in church on Good Friday,' she says. Not one with statues anyway. Her parents think statues are sinful, evidence of evil Catholic idolatry. Ruth is no fan of Catholicism but she remembers churches in Italy and Spain, rich with incense and mystery, statues and paintings illuminated by hundreds of glowing candles. Idolatry maybe, but a lot more interesting than the empty brick building, rather like a public lavatory, where her parents get to grips with being Born Again.

'Or a plinth,' says Tanya, appearing at Nelson's side, notebook at the ready.

'Plinth?' Nelson sounds impatient.

'It's like the cloth they use to cover the plinths at the museum,' says Tanya.

30th June
Day of Aestas

*Two black crows in the garden. My lucky number in the date. An
even number of pips in my breakfast grapefruit. When I sacrificed
(a blackbird) the head came off sweetly, easily, and the blood ran
swiftly into the earth, forming the letter S. S for Sacrifice. A very
good omen.*

CHAPTER 28

At nine o'clock sharp, full of a Full English Breakfast, Judy Johnson presents herself at the convent. She is told that Sister Immaculata is feeling slightly better and that she can see Judy in fifteen minutes 'when we've tidied her up a bit'. Dreading to think what this entails, Judy sits down to wait in the reception area, beside a plaster statue of the Virgin Mary, eyes rolling ecstatically up to heaven.

'Good morning, Miss Johnson.' It is the Sister, all starched veil and professional kindness.

'Detective Constable Johnson,' says Judy.

'I beg your pardon.' Titles are important, thinks Judy. The Sister would lose all her authority if addressed as Miss Whatever, would become just another middle-aged woman in a funny outfit. But as Sister Mary of the Sacred Heart she has power, albeit of a rather specialised kind.

'Sister?'

'Yes.'

'I wonder ... could you tell me ... what is wrong with Sister Immaculata?'

'Wrong?' The Sister raises her eyebrows. 'She has cancer,

Detective Constable Johnson. Inoperable. She has months, maybe weeks, to live.'

This time, Judy interviews Sister Immaculata in a conservatory overlooking a windswept rock garden. The nun is perceptibly weaker, her breath rattling in her chest, her hands shaking. Only her eyes remain alert – they regard Judy with suspicion, even, perhaps, fear.

'Detective Constable Judy Johnson,' Judy introduces herself. 'Do you remember me?'

'Of course I do. I'm not daft, you know.' Judy is rather relieved to hear the aggression in the old woman's voice. It will make her task easier.

'Sister Immaculata, your real name is Orla McKinley. Is that right?'

A pause. 'Depends what you mean by "real".'

'Your baptismal name.'

'Yes. What of it?'

'In 1951 you were living with the Spens family on Woolmarket Street.'

Another, longer pause. Sister Immaculata twists the ever-present rosary tightly around her hand. In the rock garden two seagulls fight over a crust of bread.

'I was working there as a nanny,' Sister Immaculata says at last.

'Annabelle Spens' nanny?'

'Yes.'

'Annabelle died in 1952, didn't she?'

Sister Immaculata looks at her but says nothing. The rosary beads are still.

'Did you stay on after Annabelle died?'

'Yes. They were kind. They let me stay.'

'Did you look after Roderick?'

'Roderick was fourteen. Hardly a child.'

'Sister Immaculata . . .' Judy leans forward. She knows everything depends on getting this old, dying woman to speak to her. She puts all her persuasive powers into her next words, even offering up a prayer for good measure. Please God, let her tell me the truth. 'Sister Immaculata, we found a little girl's body buried under the front door. I need you to tell me, is there any way that the body could be Annabelle's? Please. It's very important.'

At first she thinks that she has failed. Sister Immaculata says nothing and the rosary beads start to move between her fingers. But then, with a sound halfway between a sigh and a sob, the words start to pour out.

'It was wrong. It was evil. I knew that but I loved him, you see. Strange what a poor excuse that sounds, but I loved him. At the time, that was everything. I covered up for him. I knew it was a sin. A black sin. I've tried to atone but the sin catches you up in the end.'

'Sister,' Judy presses her hand, 'what sin? What did you cover up?'

Sister Immaculata looks at her and now her eyes are awash with tears. 'He killed her,' she says, 'and I covered up for him.'

Nelson is not having a good day. His computer has gone Trappist again, Clough has disappeared for a late breakfast or early lunch and Tanya is nowhere to be seen. He wishes Judy were here. She has one outstandingly good quality as a police officer – she is always where you want her to be. Except now, of course, when she's in bloody Southport. As a child, Nelson once spent a holiday in Southport. Long, wet walks along the seafront, a B and B where you got one slice of toast for breakfast and weren't allowed to touch any of the thousands of knick-knacks grinning evilly from the shelves. Never again.

He's also tired. He didn't leave Ruth's until past midnight. She'd seemed all right, shaken obviously but still feisty. It's one of the things he really likes about Ruth. She's tough. Some people would have been hysterical last night because, let's face it, someone had come right up to her house, intending to kidnap her, assault her or worse. But Ruth had been her usual, defiant self. She'd been quite acerbic when Tanya had (tactlessly) suggested that she was upset. Tanya is never in a million years going to understand someone like Ruth Galloway. He's not sure he understands her either but he does admire her. Admire her? queries a weasely voice in his head. Is that all? Nelson stamps firmly on any thoughts about his feelings for Ruth. He's already had to put up with the sight of Michelle sorting out piles of Rebecca's old baby things to give to Ruth. He doesn't need any more complications, thank you very much.

'Sir?'

Tanya's head appears around his office door. He tries to discourage the rest of her from joining it.

'What is it?'

'I've found Annabelle Spens' dental records.'

This is different. His tiredness vanishes and rearranges his face into something more welcoming.

'Good work, Tanya. Show me.'

Praise makes Tanya expansive. 'Well, it was really you saying about there being some fancy dental work done. I thought, maybe they didn't get it done locally. So I contacted the London School of Dentistry. They've been around since 1911, used to be at the London Hospital but it's now part of St Bartholomew's. Anyway, they had her records. They faxed them over a few minutes ago.'

She pauses for praise but Nelson just holds out his hand for the records. He scans the pages, frowning, then looks up.

'It's not her.'

'What?'

'Did you look at the records?'

'No . . . I just brought them straight to you.'

'Well, you remember our skull has a filling. Unusual in such a young child. According to this, Annabelle Spens didn't have a filling in her head.'

Ruth is on her way to meet Cathbad. He rang yesterday and suggested meeting at the Roman site and having lunch at the Phoenix. Now, Ruth considers that Cathbad will provide the perfect antidote to the darkness of the last few days. Cathbad may talk about being open to the 'dark side' but there is, in fact, something curiously comforting about him. Also Max has told her that they have unearthed a carving which could be a 'Janus Stone', a depiction of the old two-faced God himself. She looks forward to introducing Cathbad to Janus.

Ruth drives fast, listening to one of her more cheerful Bruce Springsteen tapes. None of that 'Badlands' stuff, the highway travelling to nowhere, the dead-end towns with no jobs 'on account of the economy'. This is the 'Dancing in the Dark' years, unsubtle guitar riffs and souring sax solos. Ruth is tired (she didn't get to bed until one and then hardly slept) but she is happy that the thought of a genuine Roman find can lift her spirits and help her forget that someone is trying to kill her.

Well, not forget exactly, she looks about her as she gets out of the car and she jumps when a skylark rises vertically out of the undergrowth, its song spiralling into the sky. She also keeps one hand on her mobile phone. Nelson is on speed dial – the first sign of anything lurking in the bushes and she'll be onto him. But, in the daylight, it's hard to believe in murdered children, sacrificial offerings or the cult of the witch-goddess.

It starts to rain as she climbs the grass bank; fine, warm rain that is refreshing rather than otherwise. The site is deserted, the trenches neatly covered with tarpaulins. There is no sign of Cathbad. Max had said that she would find the Janus Stone in the far trench. As she sets out across the uneven ground, the rain gets heavier and she wishes she had brought a coat. Lifting up the wet tarpaulin, Ruth sees the stone immediately. It is a round piece of what looks like granite, about twice the size of a human head. It looks mis-shapen and sinister lying there on the meticulously raked earth. Was it from a statue or did it have some other func-tion? Even from where she stands she can see that both sides of the stone have a face, neither of them particularly friendly.

'Janus,' says a voice above her. 'Janus. The guardian of the doorway.'

CHAPTER 29

Judy hardly dares to breath. She knows it is vital that Sister Immaculata goes on speaking so she prays that no one else comes into the conservatory, that no well-meaning soul offers them tea or coffee, that the elderly nun doesn't become too weak to continue.

'Who killed her?' she prompts gently.

But when Sister Immaculata turns to look at her, Judy sees that the old woman is no longer there. The eyes, full of anguish and brimming with tears, are the eyes of Orla McKinley.

'I was only twenty-three,' she says. 'He called me his Jocasta. I was twenty when the baby was born. Too young. I didn't know. I was only an ignorant girl from County Clare. He was so much cleverer. He knew all about history, about Ancient Rome. About the gods. About the terrible things you had to do to placate them.'

'The baby,' prompts Judy, a cold hand starting to close around her heart.

'My baby,' says Sister Immaculata, her face shining now with some remembered light. 'My Bernadette.'

'You had a baby?'

'A little girl. I had her for three years. And then he killed her. He said the gods demanded it.'

The cold has now spread through Judy's entire body. 'Christopher Spens killed your baby?' she whispers.

Sister Immaculata does not seem to hear. 'He said that the gods needed a sacrifice. We had to make the walls safe again. Annabelle had died, he said, because the walls weren't safe. We had to offer the gods something precious. That's why he killed her, he said.'

'So he killed your baby *as a sacrifice*?'

'It was his baby too,' says Sister Immaculata sadly, 'that didn't seem to make a difference though.'

'It was his baby too,' echoes Judy.

'I knew it was wrong.' Sister Immaculata grasps Judy's hand. 'I knew it was wrong. A sin. And sin catches up with you, doesn't it? That's what the sisters used to say, back home in Ireland. Well, I sinned. With him. And I got pregnant and had the baby. Born in sorrow, that's what they say. A bastard. Well, she paid the price, didn't she? My Bernadette.'

'How did he kill her?' Judy knows she must get the whole story. She'll have to come back and take a proper statement but somehow she knows that this chance might not come again. Sister Immaculata has kept her secret for over fifty years and now she is choosing to talk. She mustn't stop now.

'I was washing clothes in the laundry,' says the nun wearily, 'the maids had the morning off. When I went to check on her she was dead. Stabbed in her cot. There was blood over the walls, the covers, the floor – everywhere. He wanted me to put my hands in her blood. It was part of the ritual, he said.'

'What did you do?' asks Judy in horror.

'I covered up for him,' says Sister Immaculata sharply, 'didn't I tell you?'

'How?'

'I disappeared. He buried the body in the garden. Said he would dig her up later and put her under the door. An offering to Janus. The head would go in the well, he said. I left. I left that day, went back to Ireland. Everyone thought I'd taken Bernadette with me. That crazy unreliable Irish girl, they would have said. I did it to protect him.'

'But why?' Judy almost wails.

The nun looks at her with a curious expression, almost of pity, on her face. 'I still loved him, you see. That was the worst thing. He'd killed my baby and I still loved him. I think now that was the biggest sin of all.'

'So you went back to Ireland?'

'I went back and I became a nun. What else can you do when you've committed a mortal sin? Then, years later, Father Hennessey came to the convent. He was looking for sisters to work in his children's home. When he told me where it was, I knew. God had sent him. It was my chance to be near Bernadette again. I used to talk to her. At night. I used to walk in the grounds and talk to her. They were the happiest years of my life.'

'Did Father Hennessey know?'

'Oh no. He suspected. Not about Bernadette but he knew I had a secret. He tried to get me to tell him. The truth will set you free, he used to say. Free! I'll never be free.'

As she says the last words, her head slumps forwards on her chest.

'Sister Immaculata?' Judy bends over the huddled figure. She is still breathing, harsh uneven breaths, but her eyes are closed.

Instantly the Sister is at their side.

'You'd better go now,' she says to Judy.

Outside, on the seafront, Judy takes great gulps of salty air. It is as if she can feel the nun's painful struggle for breath inside her own lungs. She shakes her head, wanting to rid it of the image of the baby, the blood-soaked cradle, the terrified mother, the crazed father, the knife gleaming in his hand . . .

She forces herself to think logically, to switch off the horror film now running on a continuous loop in her brain (she can even smell the house – lavender polish and lilies and the sour undercurrent of blood). She is a police officer and she has a job to do. Judy shelters in the porch of one of the Gothic hotels to ring Nelson. It is raining and a sharp sea wind is blowing along the deserted promenade. Typical English summer weather.

He answers on the first ring and she tells the story as unemotionally as she can.

'Jesus.' She can hear Nelson's sharp intake of breath and knows that he, too, is not unaffected. Not that he would ever show it, of course.

'Christopher Spens got the nanny pregnant and then killed her baby as an offering to the gods?'

'That's what she said, sir.'

'Do you believe her?'

'Yes.'

Another pause and then Nelson says slowly, 'That would explain why the body under the doorway shared DNA with Roderick Spens. They did share a common male ancestor – they both had the same father, Christopher Spens.'

'Do you want me to come back, sir?'

'No. Stay where you are. I'll come up tomorrow and we'll take a proper statement. She's unwell, you say?'

'She's dying.'

'We'd better be quick then,' says Nelson callously. 'You stay in Southport another night. Enjoy yourself.'

This last, thinks Judy, as she walks along the promenade in the rain, might prove a tough assignment.

Nelson puts down the phone. Judy's story is almost unbelievable and yet he does believe it. As soon as he saw the little body, arranged so carefully amidst the stones and the rubble, he had known that something evil was afoot. Whether the child was Elizabeth Black, Annabelle Spens or Bernadette McKinley, something terrible had happened to that little girl and the memory of it still haunted that house, hung in the air around the swing and the wishing well, clung to the wallpaper, was imprinted in the black and white tiles. All traces of the house may now have vanished but Nelson knows one thing; he would not live in one of Edward Spens' luxury apartments for a million pounds.

He jumps when his phone rings again. An impatient voice, a woman, educated and possibly Asian.

'This is Doctor Sita Patel.'

'Who?' Nelson's mind is blank.

'You rang me. About Sir Roderick Spens.'

'Oh yes.' This is what Nelson had promised Whitcliffe. That he would check with Sir Roderick's GP about his state of health, ask whether being involved in a police investigation, however peripherally, would upset his delicate mental balance (Whitcliffe's words).

Nelson explains as best he can. There is a silence at the other end of the phone.

'I don't understand,' says Doctor Patel crisply, 'Sir Roderick Spens does not have Alzheimer's.'

'He doesn't?'

'His mind is remarkably sharp. Sharper than yours or mine I daresay, Detective Chief Inspector.'

Nelson clicks off his phone, thinking hard.

'Interesting God, Janus.'

'So I understand.' Ruth looks up from the mosaic.

'A minor deity, of course. Like Nemesis, Morpheus and Hecate.'

'The minor deities all seem to be baddies,' says Ruth lightly.

'You could say that.'

Judy's options for the afternoon seem to be: amusement arcade, shopping centre, an endless cream tea at one of the endless hotels or going back to the B and B to stare at the wallpaper (pink with green trelliswork). In the end, she decides to go to the cinema. Inside one of those multiplexes, you could be anywhere. The same worn purple carpet, the same smell of popcorn, the same posters, the same Pick 'n'

Mix with what look like the same fingerprints on the chocolate Brazils.

She hasn't been to the pictures for ages. She and Darren like such different films, she usually waits until things are out on DVD. But a film is just what she needs to stop the slideshow in her head, to rid her mind of Sister Immaculata's words: *There was blood over the walls, the covers, the floor – everywhere. He wanted me to put my hands in her blood.*

The foyer is deserted and Judy dithers for ages between a thriller and a girl-fest about bridesmaids. In the end she opts for the thriller. She has been going out with Darren since they were both seventeen and he has started to make noises about marriage. Judy, to her own surprise, finds herself violently opposed. The idea of prancing down the aisle in a huge white dress seems alien, offensive and, above all, *embarrassing*. Judy hates being the centre of attention. It's one of the things that makes her a good detective.

There are only four people in the cinema. An elderly couple, a single man who looks so like a pervert that he could be an undercover policeman – and Judy. She sits near the back, eating Revels and feeling rather guilty. Going to the cinema is no way for a person of working age to spend the afternoon. But, in the cinema, there is no afternoon. Just as you could be anywhere, it could be anytime. She knows that when she leaves the light will hit her like a blow. It is always dark in multiplex world.

The thriller is quite entertaining though she had forgotten that Americans mumble so much. She wants to lean forward like an old lady with an ear trumpet, '*What* did you say, young man?' And the music is loud enough to pin her back against her seat. It has been a long time since she has been to a club or anywhere that plays loud music. She is used to the gentle murmur of her iPod. She really must get out more.

Gradually, though, she starts to get into the plot which involves the FBI, a conspiracy to kill the president and, rather inexplicably, aliens. She is just drifting into zombie-like enjoyment when one of the characters mumbles something about 'my kid sister, Jocasta'.

Jocasta.

What is it about that name that rings alarm bells in Judy's mind? Ignoring the on-screen attempts to blow up the Empire State Building (the genre is post-9/11 apocalypse), she runs the last few hours through her internal scanner. Judy has an excellent memory – another reason why bloody Nelson should promote her. Jocasta . . . Jocasta. There. She has it.

I was only twenty-three. He called me his Jocasta.

The next minute, Judy is stumbling out of the cinema, oblivious to the fact that she will now never know whether Todd, Brad and Shannon manage to save the planet. In the foyer, she sits on the dusty, popcorn-strewn steps and rummages for her BlackBerry. She keys Jocasta into the search engine and there it is: 'Jocasta was a famed queen of Thebes. She was the wife of Laius, mother and later wife of Oedipus . . .'

Mother and later wife of Oedipus.

Oedipus had inadvertently married his mother, hence the complex. Why would Sir Christopher, a much older man, call Orla 'his Jocasta'? Judy scans further back in her memory, to the Spens family tree that she had scribbled in her notebook. *Roderick: born 1938.* If Orla/Sister Immaculata is seventy-five now, she must have been born in 1933. When the baby died, she was twenty-three. Roderick would have been eighteen. *He called me his Jocasta.*

Judy dials Nelson's number.

But Nelson ignores the call. He is staring at a six-word text message: *I'm going to kill your daughter.*

30th June
Day of Aestas

I got my knife and went indoors. All was quiet. The mother was washing clothes in the laundry, the maids had the morning off. I went into her room. The blinds were drawn and the light was pinkish, like the light on the inside of your eyelids.

Her eyes are blue, like mine. I've never noticed that before. Her lips move as if she's about to say something. She doesn't say much (another sign of her backwardness) but it looks as if she's about to say something now. I decide I'd better speak first.

'Hallo,' I say.

''Lo,' she replies.

CHAPTER 30

Nelson is running, faster than he has ever run in his life. Twice in his police career his life has been in danger and, even at the time, he'd been quite pleased at how he'd handled this. The knowledge that he might have been about to die had sharpened his reactions, made them cold and precise. He had not been scared so much as angry and determined not to let the perpetrators get away with it. But this, this is something else altogether. His heart is leaping in his chest, huge shuddering movements that make him feel sick and dizzy. He lurches as he runs, coordination shot, breath coming in shallow, painful spasms. His daughter. Someone is going to hurt one of his daughters. It is as if they have already cut out his heart.

He reaches his car and looks at his watch. Three thirty. Think. Focus. He forces himself to take deeper breaths, gripping the steering wheel. Like this, he is no good to anyone. Where should Laura and Rebecca be at three thirty? Just leaving school. If he hurries, he can be there in five minutes.

If he hurries ... Nelson leaves a trail of bemused and terrified road users behind him as he drives, mostly on the wrong side of the road, to the girls' school on the outskirts of King's Lynn. The siren is blaring and he barely slows down for anything, red lights, junctions, pedestrians, anything. Finally, he screeches to a halt beside the school, mounting the kerb, scraping the side of the car against the wall.

The rain has stopped and teenage girls are pouring out of the school gates, all wearing purple sweatshirts and short black skirts. His heart leaps every time he sees a girl with long brown hair but there are so many of them, so many slim girls with minuscule skirts and long, wavy hair, but not one of them is his. His heart pounds harder than ever and he can hear himself making a moaning sound under his breath, almost a whimper. Please God, he prays madly to the God whom he has ignored for most of his adult life, please God make them be all right.

And then, in a knot of purple sweatshirts, he sees Paige, Rebecca's best friend, ambling along without a care in the world, chatting to a plump girl with hair dyed a virulent pink.

'Paige!' Nelson's bellow makes every head turn in his direction. 'Paige!'

He races up to her, grabbing her arm. He is aware how mad he must look. Rebecca's nice, respectable father, a policeman, who is popular amongst the girls for his bad karaoke turns and his willingness to offer lifts, turning into this raving lunatic with staring eyes and trembling hands.

'Paige! Where's Rebecca?'

Paige backs away, staring. She seems incapable of speech. Her mouth hangs open and he can see the gum inside it. He is suddenly filled with a murderous rage that this girl, this imbecile, should be safe while his darling daughters are in danger.

'Where's Rebecca?' he repeats, trying to make his voice calmer.

'I dunno. She's got an after-school club, I think . . .' She is still backing away, her eyes round. Nelson closes his eyes, trying to still the demons inside him. Unexpectedly, the pink-haired girl comes to his aid.

'Drama club,' she says brightly. 'They're doing *Fiddler on the Roof*. Room C9, Block 3.'

Nelson is running again before she has finished speaking. Sliding over the wet turf of the playing field, scattering a game of hockey ('Look out!'), crashing through the main doors to Block 3. Christ, why do schools have so many doors? He runs through endless corridors, door after door banging behind him. He shouts 'Rebecca!' and the sound bounces off the glass and plasterboard and a photo-montage of 'School Journey 2007'. Room C9, the girl had said. Maddeningly, the rooms do not seem to be in any order: A12, B1, B7, D15. He stops and starts to double back, heart pounding harder than ever. He grabs a passing arm, 'C9,' he pants. The owner of the arm, a middle-aged man, looks uneasy.

'Who are you?'

'Rebecca Nelson's father. *Where is she?*'

And then, behind the man's corduroy back, he sees a door miraculously labelled 'C9'. Thrusting the man to one side, he launches himself through it.

The large room contains a makeshift stage, a hassled-looking teacher, a few gum-chewing girls and, wonder of wonders, miracle of miracles, his daughter. Ignoring everyone, Nelson enfolds the outraged Rebecca in a fierce hug.

'Thank God. Thank God.'

'Dad! Get off!'

'Rebecca,' he holds her at arm's length, 'where's Laura? Where's your sister?' If anything happens to Laura, he will always feel guilty that he came to find Rebecca first.

'I've got no idea. Dad! Let me go! What are you playing at?'

'We're going home.'

'I don't want to go home. I'm playing Tzeitel.'

'Come on.'

Without letting go of Rebecca's arm, he shouts 'Sorry' to the now frankly terrified teacher and propels them both out of the room.

In the corridor, he stabs Laura's number into his phone. Straight through to answerphone. He tries again, hardly noticing the four missed calls from Judy Johnson. He looks at his watch. Four o'clock. Michelle won't be home before six. Where is Laura? His darling eldest daughter, so correct and well-behaved always (like one of the girls in Little Women, Michelle used to say). Where can she be?

'Does Laura go to any clubs on a Thursday?'

'I dunno.'

'Keep ringing her,' Nelson thrusts his phone into Rebecca's hand, 'we're going home.'

Ignoring Rebecca's litany of complaints, threats and slurs on his parenting (he's had plenty of practice), Nelson drags her back through the school and across the now deserted playing field to the place where his car is rammed up against the wall.

'Dad! Your car!' For the first time, Rebecca sounds shocked.

'Keep phoning.'

Laura will have gone home. It's not unlike her to get home first, put the kettle on and cook supper for everyone. An angel, that's what she is. Nelson's eyes are wet when he thinks what an angel his eldest daughter is. Rebecca has always been the rebellious one and, besides, Rebecca is sitting beside him, safe and sound, so he doesn't need to sanctify her. But Laura, Laura is out there somewhere with a madman on her trail. Perhaps he has already found her, perhaps he has . . . Nelson rams his foot down on the accelerator.

'Dad! Are you trying to kill us?'

'Keep phoning.'

He takes the turn into the drive on two wheels. Michelle's car isn't there but then he wouldn't expect her to be home yet. Will she kill him for not phoning her first? No, Michelle would want him to do what he is doing – save their daughters' lives.

'Laura!' yells Nelson, bursting in through the front door.

A silence during which Nelson thinks that he can hear his heart breaking. And then, a faint noise, like a rat scrabbling, directly overhead.

'Laura?' Nelson starts to climb the stairs.

'Dad! Don't!' Rebecca grabs his arm. He looks at her, uncomprehending. He tries to shake Rebecca off and, as he does so, notices two things: Laura's flowery backpack lying beside the front door and a pair of man-size trainers next to it.

'Dad?'

And there is Laura at the top of the stairs. Not dead but gloriously alive, wearing a dressing gown tightly belted around her waist.

'Laura! Sweetheart!' He bounds upstairs to hug her. She's safe. Thank God, she's safe. Thank you God. I'll go to mass next Sunday. She's alive. They're both alive ... A dressing gown?

He loosens his grip, takes in Laura's dishevelled appearance, Rebecca's attempts to make herself invisible, the scuffling sounds still emanating from one of the upstairs rooms. Quick as thought, he kicks open the door to Laura's bedroom.

And finds a youth, half-dressed, trying to climb out of the window.

CHAPTER 31

It takes about a second for Nelson to revert from distraught father to aggressive policeman. He slams the window shut and addresses the cringing boy, 'Get your clothes on, sunshine, and get out of my house. If I ever see you here again, I'll lock you up.'

At the foot of the stairs, Rebecca and Laura are staring up at him, clinging together for support.

'Did you know?' he asks Rebecca. 'Did you know what she was doing?'

'No. Honestly!'

He knows she is lying but there is no time to do anything about that now. He is already phoning Sergeant Clough. 'Cloughie. Someone's threatening my girls. I need some protection over here right now.' Glancing at his phone, he sees there are now six missed calls from Judy.

'Get in the sitting room,' he tells the girls.

'I want to get dressed,' says Laura.

Nelson experiences a spasm of – what? Revulsion, anger, sadness? His daughter, his angel, was about to have sex with that gangling idiot upstairs. He hears the front door slam.

At least he is gone, maybe he won't come back. Maybe he was just in time to save his daughter's virginity. And then he thinks: who am I kidding? Of course he wasn't in time; he is months, perhaps years, too late.

'Who was he?' he asks.

'His name's Lee,' says Laura sulkily. 'Mum's met him,' she adds, as if this makes it all right.

A fresh horror strikes Nelson's heart. 'Does your mother know . . .?'

'No!' Laura's shocked response somehow reassures him. At least Laura has had the decency to hide her sex life from her parents. At least Michelle isn't colluding with her daughters behind his back.

'I want you both to stay downstairs,' he says.

It is gradually beginning to dawn on Rebecca that there is more to her father's behaviour than the usual parental paranoia.

'Dad,' she says, 'what's going on?'

'Nothing,' Nelson starts to dial Judy's number.

'You said someone was threatening us.'

'Just some nutter,' says Nelson, trying to sound reassuring. 'There's nothing to worry about, I promise you.'

Both the girls now look completely terrified. They huddle together on the sofa and Rebecca automatically switches on the TV. Nelson is about to shout at her to turn it off but then he thinks that maybe they could do with the soothing mindlessness of MTV or *Hollyoaks*. Certainly, Laura and Rebecca both relax slightly when the screen is filled with loud Americans exchanging complicated handshakes.

Then the doorbell rings and they both scream.

'It's only Cloughie,' says Nelson. 'Stay here!' he barks, slightly ruining the calming effect.

But it isn't Clough. It's Cathbad. He is wearing what Nelson calls his 'semi-Druid' costume; jeans and T-shirt covered by a tattered purple cloak. But his expression as he grasps Nelson's arm is devoid of any play-acting. He looks in deadly earnest.

'Nelson. I think something's happened to Ruth.'

Judy presses 'redial' again and again as she runs through the rainswept Southport streets. Why the hell isn't Nelson answering his phone? Passing pensioners and glum-looking tourists turn to stare as she races past them. Probably no one has moved that fast in Southport for the last fifty years. When she arrives at the convent, she is wild-haired and out of breath, still punching redial with one finger.

'Can . . . I . . . see . . . Sister Immaculata please?'

'I'm sorry, it's out of the question.' The nun at the door looks faintly accusing. 'She's had a very bad turn. The doctor's with her now.'

'I'll wait,' pants Judy.

'She won't be seeing anyone else today.'

At first Nelson hardly takes in what Cathbad is saying. Then, slowly, the wheels turn in his head and his whole body is suddenly icy cold. Ruth . . . his daughter. I'm going to kill your daughter. Could whoever sent this message possibly know that Ruth is carrying his daughter inside her? He goes so pale that Cathbad looks concerned.

'Are you all right?'

'What's happened to Ruth?'

'We were meant to meet at the Swaffham site. But when I got there there was no sign of her. And I found this in one of the trenches.'

He holds out Ruth's phone.

'You'd better come in,' says Nelson.

The girls hardly look up as the cloaked figure passes through the sitting room. They are deeply involved in some rubbish involving American high school pupils, loud rock music and vampires. Nelson and Cathbad talk in the kitchen, amongst Michelle's gleaming work surfaces and the cork-board groaning with invitations, shopping lists and school timetables. It seems almost impossible that evil should come here, into this sunny family room, but they both know that it has; they both feel its shadow.

'I went to her cottage,' Cathbad is saying. 'It's completely deserted.'

'The university?'

'No one there. Her office is locked.'

Nelson picks up Ruth's phone. His was the last number she dialled. He looks at his own phone, six missed calls from Judy Johnson and, before that, one from Ruth Galloway.

It is a shock when his phone rings again. Judy Johnson.

'Johnson. What is it?'

'Roderick Spens sir. I think he was the father.'

'What?'

'Sister Immaculata. I thought the baby was Sir Christopher's but now I think it was Roderick's. He would have been about fourteen or fifteen when it was conceived. Sister Immaculata, Orla, would have been twenty.'

'She had an affair with a fourteen-year-old?'

'I think so. Sister Immaculata said he called her his Jocasta. Jocasta was the mother of Oedipus.'

'Classical scholar, are you now?'

'I looked it up.'

'Have you confronted this Sister Immaculata?'

'She's too ill to speak to me.'

Nelson remembers Dr Patel saying that Sir Roderick's mind was 'remarkably sharp'. He remembers that, when Ruth texted to say that she was expecting a girl and he had rung her back, Sir Roderick had actually been in his office, dithering about and pretending to be a sweet little old man.

'Are you still there, sir?'

'Yes. Good work, Judy. Keep trying to see the nun. I'll call you later.'

He clicks off the phone. Cathbad leans forward and Nelson sees not the fey Druid but the scientist, the man who would, incredibly enough, have made rather a good policeman.

'Nelson,' he says. 'I think Max Grey has kidnapped Ruth.'

30th June
Day of Aestas

I hadn't expected this. Socrates may favour dialogue but I don't. The last thing I needed was a chat with the infant. Apart from anything else, my time was limited. The maids would be back at midday and the mother could come in at any moment.

Then I had a brainwave. 'Keep quiet,' I said, 'I've got a surprise for you.'

I bent over the bed. I had hoped she was asleep but she wasn't. Her eyes were open and she looked at me.

She obeyed my order, even putting her finger to her lips. I'm obviously born to command. In fact, I think I've got quite a gift with children.

'Lie still,' I said. And I pulled the knife out of my pocket.

I raised the knife. She laughed. Sacrilege! I lowered the knife slightly and looked at her. Then she started to cry.

CHAPTER 32

When Ruth opens her eyes it is still dark. She is not scared at first. Instead she feels rather sleepy, soothing memories rocking to and fro in her head: picnicking with her mother and brother in Castle Wood, listening to the radio with her dad, floating in the sea, hair streaming back amongst the seaweed, sleeping on a beach in the sun. Even when she realises that she is, in fact, lying tied up on a narrow bed, she is not immediately filled with terror. The pleasant memories persist along with the gentle rocking motion. Then, as if in an effort to rouse her, the baby in her womb kicks. Ruth is suddenly wide awake, struggling to sit upright. Her hands are tied behind her back so this is a difficult feat, but she manages it. By her head there is a small round window but through it she can see only grey and green, merging and separating like colours in a kaleidoscope. The whole thing is so horribly like a dream that she actually closes her eyes again and wills herself to wake up. But when she opens her eyes it is all still there, the rope (now digging painfully into her wrists), the window onto nothingness, the strange see-sawing movement.

Desperately she tries to remember what has happened. She was in the trench, looking at the Janus Stone. She can see the two stone faces looking up at her, sinister and impassive. Then someone spoke to her. Who was it? She remembers that she wasn't scared, just curious and slightly annoyed at the interruption. She remembers getting out of the trench and going to look at something in a car. Then something must have frightened her because she tried to ring Nelson. After that – nothing.

'Ah. You've woken up.'

Ruth turns and sees what should have been clear all along. She is in a boat, very like Max's boat. Hang on, it *is* Max's boat. She can see the stuffed dog, Elizabeth's dog, grinning at her from the bed. She is lying on the galley seat. The sink and cooker where once Max cooked her a gourmet meal, are opposite her. The herbs are still swinging picturesquely from the ceiling. And, standing on the step leading down from the deck, is Sir Roderick Spens. What's he doing here?

'Can you help me?' she says. 'I'm tied up.'

Inexplicably Roderick lets out a high-pitched giggle. 'Tied up? So you are. Dr Galloway's busy. She's tied up.'

Ruth does not know what is happening but she knows that she is suddenly very scared. And Roderick's face, so mild-looking with its faded blue eyes and fringe of white hair, is the scariest thing of all.

'Let me go,' she says, trying to sound authoritative.

'Oh I can't let you go,' says Roderick, still sounding gently amused. 'You have what I want, you see?'

'What?'

'You have Detective Inspector Harry Nelson's baby. You lay

with him and now you're with child. You're carrying his daughter. That's what I want.'

Ruth stares, cold with horror. The archaic language 'lay with him ... with child' only serves to heighten the horror. Somehow this old man knows her secret, that she is carrying Nelson's baby, and he is going to use this knowledge in some terrible way.

Still smiling, Sir Roderick approaches and Ruth sees the dull gleam of a knife.

'I want the baby,' he repeats.

Nelson stares at Cathbad.

'What do you mean?'

'Max Grey. I think he's got something to do with Ruth disappearing.'

When Cathbad appeared in Nelson's office (was it only yesterday?), he had had some actual information about Max to go with his sixth sense. Apparently Cathbad had been speaking to a fellow Druid who lives in Ireland. 'He knew Max Grey from a long way back, when he lived in Ireland. He described him in detail. Only he called himself by a different name entirely. And Pendragon—'

'Who?' Nelson had asked, wincing as if in pain.

'Pendragon. My friend. He said that this Max Grey character was a real troubled soul. Full of inner violence.'

Whilst admiring the Druid networking system, Nelson had, at the time, dismissed this as mere new age fancy. But now he says with real urgency in his voice, 'Why do you think he's involved?'

'Today, when I couldn't find Ruth, I rang him. No answer.

I contacted his students. He hasn't been seen all day.'

'Where does he live?'

'On a boat, apparently. Moored near Reedham.'

'Come on then.' Nelson reaches for his phone. 'Let's pay him a visit.'

Ruth screams, so loudly that it startles both of them. Roderick stops and looks at her quizzically.

'Why are you frightened?' he asks.

'Why do you think?' shouts Ruth. 'I'm stuck here on a boat with a madman. A madman with a knife.'

Roderick looks quite hurt. 'I'm not mad,' he says. 'I've got a first in classics from Cambridge.'

From what Ruth has seen of Oxbridge graduates, the two are not mutually exclusive. But she knows that her best hope is in getting Roderick to speak to her. She tries to make her voice calm and reasonable, as if she is having a cosy chat with another academic.

'I did archaeology at UCL,' she says. 'They've got a good classics department.'

'University College London,' muses Roderick. 'A very respectable university. You must be a clever girl.'

Ruth attempts a simper. 'Are you a classicist?' she asks, trying to sound suitably admiring.

'I am a Roman.' His eyes are glittering. Cataracts or madness? At least he sits down on a small stool opposite Ruth, and lowers the knife. 'I realised that at an early age. I was born at the wrong time. I belong in the age of discipline and self-reliance, of sacrifice and the pure libation of blood. Of the old gods.'

The old gods. Ruth thinks of the body buried under the door, the head in the well, the black cockerel. She remembers the feeling that the house on Woolmarket Street belongs to an older, darker, time.

'Of course,' Sir Roderick is saying, 'I don't do much these days. I belong to the historical society and, of course, I'm a trustee of the museum.'

The museum. Alarm bells go off in Ruth's head and in quick succession she sees the model baby, the two-headed calf and the black drapery that was thrown over her head. In the same moment, she recognises the smell, lemon and sandalwood. The scent that emanates discreetly from Sir Roderick Spens.

'My father was a great classicist,' Roderick goes on, 'Christopher Spens. Have you heard of him?'

Something tells Ruth that she had better say yes.

'He was a great man. A great headmaster. Wrote many books about Ancient Rome. But he never got the recognition he deserved. He died a broken man. Never got over my sister's death.'

'Your sister died?' Ruth remembers Nelson saying something about Annabelle Spens. Could Roderick's sister be the child buried under the door?

'Of scarlet fever, yes. Nothing was ever right again. My mother stayed in her room all day crying. My father spent every hour at the school, never seemed to want to come home. He knew the house was cursed, you see. That's why I had to kill the other baby, you see. To lift the curse.'

Ruth's whole body is suddenly stone cold. 'What baby?' she whispers.

'My baby,' says Roderick carelessly. 'I lay with one of the servants. An ignorant Irish girl but comely enough.' His voice thickens.

'And she had a baby?'

'Yes, that's what happens, you see.' He leers at her. 'I was only a boy, of course. She took advantage of my adolescent urges. She said she loved me. She was a poor thing really. But she had a child, a girl. She called it Bernadette.'

It. Despite everything, Ruth feels tears rush to her eyes. The baby, stabbed, beheaded and buried under the door was Sir Roderick's child. And to him she is still 'it'.

'What about the mother?' she asks.

'Oh, she went back to Ireland. The land of saints and scholars.' He gives that chilling giggle again. 'I buried the body in the garden but when the pater had the arch and the columns built I dug it up and buried it in the hole under the new doorway. An offering to Janus, y'know. Protect our walls and all that. I put the skull in the well. It seemed the right thing to do.' He smiles complacently.

'But what have I got to do with all this?' asks Ruth. Even if she gets free, will she be able to get past Sir Roderick? He is old but he looks fit. And he has a knife.

'That detective, Nelson, he's too close to the truth. I've told my son that I've got Alzheimer's. He was only too ready to believe that I was going senile. Fits in with what he and his brainless wife already think about me. Anyway, he speaks freely in front of me. Doesn't think I understand. I got him to take me to the site. I saw you digging there and I knew you would find out the truth. Then, when I was at the police station, I overheard your call. When DCI Nelson rushed out, he left his phone behind. Very careless.' Giggle. 'I read your message and I knew. You were having his baby. So, unless he calls off the investigation, I'm going to kill his daughter. It's only fair after all.'

'It's not at all fair!' Ruth bursts out, in spite of herself.

Roderick ignores her. He continues speaking, in a self-satisfied tone. 'I saw you at the Roman site. I was there with the Conservative Association. They'd hired a minibus. Very civilised. Then, when I saw you at the house, I made the connection. I thought I'd try to scare you off. I wrote your name on the stone with the blood of a cockerel. Strong magic. I knew the archaeologist from Sussex would find it and tell you. I thought the dead baby was a nice touch. I knew you'd be there that day because you'd had dinner with him the night before.'

'You're well-informed,' says Ruth, between dry lips.

'My granddaughter works on the site,' answers Sir Roderick airily. 'She tells me all the comings and goings.'

'Your granddaughter?'

'An uncouth girl. But useful. Then, of course, when Nelson wanted to do the DNA testing, I knew he'd make the link between me and the body. That's why I had to act. I knew you'd go to the Roman site, to see the stone. I waited for you every morning. I knew you'd come eventually. You were so kind, offering to get something from my car for me. As you were bending over, I hit you over the head with my car torch. A perfectly serviceable tool for the purpose. Then I drove you to the boat.'

'How did you get me on board?' Ruth remembers the jolly barbecuing families at the marina. Surely one of them will have noticed a man carrying a prostrate body on board. And, come to that, how did Roderick manage to carry her?

'I wrapped you in a carpet. Like Cleopatra.' Another giggle. 'I parked my car by the boatyard and one of the men very kindly helped me with my burden. Remarked how heavy the rug was.'

'Where are you taking me?'

'To a house where I have the necessary equipment for libations, et cetera.' He could be any elderly eccentric talking about his hobby. Except for the knife in his hand and the deranged glint in his eye.

'No one will think of looking where I'm taking you,' continues Sir Roderick. 'Nelson will know he's been beaten by a better man.'

'Have you told him?' If Nelson knows, he will be on his way. He will move heaven and earth to save her, she knows that. Oh please let him have told Nelson.

'I sent him a text message. A crude form of communication but effective.'

'You should call him again.' The police can trace text messages, can't they?

'*You're* going to call him.'

And, in a worryingly swift movement, he is at her side, holding out a phone with one hand and, with the other, keeping the knife at her throat.

Nelson leaves as soon as Clough arrives to keep an eye on the girls. 'Never fear, Uncle Dave is here,' are Clough's opening words as he settles down on the sofa to watch the American high schools kids battling with the undead.

'For Christ's sake, keep your wits about you,' growls Nelson.

'You can rely on me, boss.'

Nelson reaches forty miles an hour before he has backed out of the close but, beside him, Cathbad is calm and serene. He is the only person Nelson has ever met who is not terrified by his driving.

It is nearly six o'clock. Rush hour time. The roads are thick with traffic and when they reach the outskirts of Norwich Nelson puts the siren on and they weave madly between lanes, forcing other drivers up onto grass verges and scattering bollards like ninepins.

Cathbad hums a Celtic folk song.

Outside Reedham, the road is blocked because of an accident, stationary traffic in both directions. Nelson thumps the steering wheel.

'Look at the map,' he tells Cathbad, 'find a short cut.'

Cathbad points to an unmade-up road on their left. A pile of abandoned tyres squats by a broken gate. It looks like it couldn't possibly lead anywhere.

'Try that way.'

'Why?'

'I've got a good feeling about it.'

Nelson swings to the left. The Mercedes bumps along rutted tractor tracks, occasionally descending into vast, muddy puddles.

'If my suspension's buggered, I'll blame you.'

Cathbad keeps humming.

The lane takes them past deserted barns, abandoned cars and, inexplicably, a smart bungalow offering Bed and Breakfast. Finally, Nelson crashes through overhanging trees and encroaching hedgerows to come to a halt, with his front wheels hanging over the edge of the river bank. He turns wrathfully to Cathbad.

'It's a dead end. You—'

But Cathbad is pointing through the trees, where a church tower is just visible.

'Reedham,' he says vaguely.

'How did you—'

'The flow,' says Cathbad, 'you have to go with the flow.'

But Nelson is already striding off along the river bank.

At the marina, they find the boat owners in the middle of a party. The wine is flowing and sausages are grilling on the barbecue. Reggae music blasts from one of the boats, a low cruiser called *Dreadlock 2*. Nelson shoves his warrant card in the face of the large man cooking sausages.

'I'm looking for a boat called the *Lady Annabelle*.'

The man looks blank and there are some giggles, hastily suppressed.

'I know the *Lady Annabelle*,' says a voice from the reggae boat. A tall man with waist-length dreadlocks smiles up at them. 'It's owned by that professor, isn't it?'

'Do you know where it's parked? Moored?' asks Nelson impatiently.

'Sure.' The man sounds as if he has all the time in the world. Nelson grinds his teeth though Cathbad looks approving. 'Just along the moorings. To the left.' He gestures. 'You can't miss it. It's the last boat.'

'Peace,' calls Cathbad over his shoulder as he and Nelson march towards the wooden gate.

'Peace and love,' calls back the dreadlocked man.

But at the end of the moorings they find only a frayed rope. The *Lady Annabelle* has gone. From the marina they can hear Bob Marley singing about redemption. The river flows past them, dividing into its two directions, mysterious in the evening light. Midges gather around their heads.

'What now?' asks Nelson.

'We trust to the flow?' suggests Cathbad.

Luckily for Cathbad's continuing existence, Nelson's phone rings at that moment. He snatches it up. Number unknown.

The voice, though, is very well-known indeed.

'Nelson?'

'Ruth!'

Her voice sounds high and strained, like someone much younger. She speaks without pausing or allowing him to answer.

'Nelson, you have to call off the investigation or he'll kill our baby and me too. He's serious, he's the real ringslinger. Please Nelson. Save our baby. I can't tell you where we are. Please Horatio. Save us.'

The phone is clicked off.

Nelson is shaking. He tries to dial the station, get them to trace the call, but his fingers just won't work. Cathbad grabs his arm.

'What did she say?'

Nelson just shakes his head. His baby, his unknown beloved baby is in danger. And Ruth – headstrong, feisty Ruth – sounding like a child herself. Ruth, who could be about to die.

'You've got to remember her exact words,' Cathbad tells

him sternly. 'Tell me and I'll write them down. Come on, Harry. You can't go to pieces now.'

Dully, Nelson relates Ruth's exact words. They sound odd but he is pretty sure that he has remembered them correctly. Cathbad writes them down while Nelson rings the station, trying to get a trace on the call.

When he has finished, he looks at Cathbad who is squatting down, frowning at the dirty scrap of paper in front of him. To Nelson's relief, he doesn't mention the 'our baby' part, instead he says, '"He's the real ringslinger". What did she mean by that?'

'I don't know.'

'And why did she call you Horatio? Is Harry short for Horatio?'

'No.'

'She's giving us a clue,' says Cathbad. 'Well done, Ruth. Attagirl. We just have to work it out. Ringslinger. Ringslinger. There was a Hroerekr Ringslinger, a mythical king of Denmark. Erik used to talk about him.'

'What was his name?' It sounds like gargling to Nelson.

'Hroerekr. Roderick in English.'

'*What?*'

Cathbad looks up in surprise.

'That's it!' shouts Nelson. 'She's telling us that it's Roderick. Sir Roderick Spens.'

Briefly, he tells Cathbad about the Spens family. When he gets to the part about Annabelle Spens, Cathbad stops him.

'What was the boat called?'

'*Lady Annabelle*.'

'Could it belong to the Spens family?'

'Of course! Max Grey is a friend of Edward Spens. He told me when I interviewed him. Edward must have lent him the boat. That's why Ruth called me Horatio. To remind me of the other Nelson. The famous one. The Admiral. She's telling us that she's on a boat.'

'And what about Max Grey?' asks Cathbad. 'Where's he got to?'

'I'm here,' says a voice at their feet.

30th June
Day of Aestas

. . . *The infant screams and keeps on screaming. Even the knife in her chest doesn't seem to stop her. Clearly the child is possessed of an evil spirit. Closing my eyes and muttering a prayer to the Lady, I stab and stab. When I open my eyes there is blood over the bed, the walls, everything.*

She is dead but the screaming goes on.

CHAPTER 33

'Why did you call him Horatio?'

'Harry's short for Horatio,' lies Ruth. 'He doesn't like people to know. I called him that so he would know it was me.'

Roderick nods, satisfied. Ruth holds her breath, hoping that he doesn't query 'ringslinger' but perhaps Roderick regards it as an example of young people's slang (he has already lectured Ruth at length on the decline of literacy amongst the youth of today) because he doesn't comment further. Ruth knows it's a long shot but maybe Nelson would be sufficiently intrigued to Google Ringslinger and find the Danish king, the grandfather, according to Erik, of Hamlet. Cathbad would have known, she thinks, but she has no idea where Cathbad is.

'You're a fallen woman,' says Roderick chattily, removing the knife from Ruth's neck. 'Just like the Irish whore.'

Ruth says nothing. If she hadn't been tied up, she would have kicked him in the balls.

'You knew Nelson was married but you still lay with him. You're a whore.'

'If you say so.'

'Well,' says Roderick as if they have just finished a cosy chat over the cucumber sandwiches, 'I'd better get back to the helm.'

Max is, in fact, sitting in a dinghy. With the ease of long practice, he ties the boat to the landing stage and scrambles ashore.

'I think Roderick Spens has kidnapped Ruth,' he says. 'I went to the site this morning. I though she might be there, to see the Janus Stone, but it was deserted. I was going to ring you but I got a call from the boatyard to say that someone had taken the *Lady Annabelle*. An elderly man. He was loading something heavy on board. They thought it was suspicious.'

'Did they say where he was going?' asks Cathbad.

Max looks dubiously at Cathbad, whose purple cloak is wet and muddy from the trek along the river bank.

'Cathbad's helping with the enquiry,' says Nelson brusquely. 'We need to know Ruth's whereabouts. We think she's in serious danger.'

Max still looks suspicious but he answers quickly enough, ' They said he was asking about the height of Potter Heigham Bridge.'

Nelson and Cathbad look at him blankly.

'It's a bridge over the Thurne,' says Max. 'Very low. Lots of boats get stuck. If they're going that way, I think they're heading for Horsey Mere. The Spens family have got a cottage there.'

More blank looks.

'It's a little-known stretch of waterway,' says Max, 'on the North Rivers.'

'Which way will he go?' asks Nelson.

Max points to the fork in the water. 'If he's going to the North Rivers, he'll go that way. Along the Yare to Yarmouth.'

'Can we catch him at Yarmouth?'

Max looks at his watch. 'The boatyard said he went past at four o'clock. He'll be through Yarmouth by now.'

Nelson looks at his watch. It is half past seven.

'Can we catch them by road?' he asks. 'I drive fast.'

Max shakes his head. 'Our best bet is to try to get to Potter Heigham before them. He'll have to take the canopy off the boat before it can get under the bridge. That'll slow them down a bit.'

'Let's go then,' says Nelson.

The boat is moving. The rocking motion becomes unpleasantly violent and Ruth is afraid that she will be sick. She can't be sick. She needs to escape from this lunatic with his frightening Victorian language and his terrifyingly modern knife. He killed his own child, now he wants to kill her baby. Well Ruth is not about to let that happen.

If she can just get across to the other side of the boat, she can reach the kitchen cabinet where there are sure to be knives and other sharp implements. It's so close, just an arm's length away. If she can get herself free, she thinks she should be a match for Roderick Spens, knife and all.

Gingerly, she rolls over so that her legs, tied tightly together, are on the floor. Then, without warning, she is hit by a wave of nausea so intense that she knows she must be sick. It is awful having her hands tied behind her back because she can't move her hair out of the way. All she can do is tilt her head as far away as possible so that the vomit doesn't land on her feet. She continues to retch feebly until her stomach is empty and then she lies back on the bench with her eyes shut. She hopes that Roderick hasn't heard her but the noise of the engine is surprisingly loud. She realises that they must be travelling fast. If so, that might be a good thing. It might alert the river police, other sailors, anyone.

She lies still, listening. Above the engine noise, she can hear Sir Roderick singing snatches of opera. Nutcase. Slowly she slides her legs over again and tries to stand. Another spasm of nausea grips her stomach but she isn't sick again. She waits, breathing hard, and then, holding on to the edge of the table behind her, starts to hop towards the knives.

They find Sir Roderick's car by the boatyard. This is hardly difficult as it is a maroon Rolls Royce with the licence plate SPENS2.

'Jesus,' says Nelson. 'He was hardly travelling incognito.'

'He's not supposed to drive at all,' says Max. 'Edward says he has Alzheimer's.'

'Edward is wrong,' Nelson tells him.

Max chews his lip. 'Even so, Sir Roderick has always been strange. When we were at university, Edward used to mention his father doing odd things. Being obsessed with certain Roman gods, offering sacrifices and such like. He once broke into Fishbourne Roman Palace and started strewing herbs and flowers around. Edward used to worry about him.'

'With good reason,' says Nelson. 'I'll get some uniforms down to look at the car. I'll call the river police too.'

'They're going to the North Rivers,' says Max.

'So?'

'The river police don't cover the North Rivers. There's a ranger but they've only got one car and they don't work at night.'

'Jesus.' Nelson raises his eyes to the heavens and curses the day that he ever heard of Norfolk, the river, or Ruth Galloway. Max watches him narrowly. 'Come on,' he says at last, 'we've got to get to Potter Heigham before they do.'

Three hops and she's there. She leans against the sink, feeling ill and faint. Her head aches, presumably where Roderick whacked it with his 'perfectly serviceable' torch. Probably right on the spot where she hit it once before, when Roderick left a model foetus in the trench as a 'warning'. If she gets out of this alive, she swears she is going to kill him.

Opening the sink drawer with no hands will be the next problem. She looks around for anything sharp left lying around but everything is irritatingly tidy. Damn Max and his anal archaeologist habits. Where *is* Max anyhow? How come Roderick has got his boat? The truly dreadful thought, which has been hovering at the back of her mind for hours, now pops, fully formed, to the surface. What if Max is in league with Sir Roderick? After all, Max and Edward Spens were friends at university. Max could easily have helped Roderick leave those grisly offerings at the site. Max could even have given him the idea. He is another classicist, another fan of the Roman gods. He knows all about Hecate, all about Janus and Nemesis and the rest of the bad guys. Could Max really be plotting to kill her?

No, it can't be true. Max came back because he was drawn

to the place where he had lived with Elizabeth. No. She mustn't let herself think like that. Roderick must be acting alone. He is mad enough, God knows.

But where *is* Max?

The drawer has an obligingly protruding handle. Ruth bends down and takes it firmly between her teeth. Then she pulls. It's surprising how much it hurts but the drawer opens and inside Ruth can see at least three sharp knives, one with wonderful serrated edges. She turns round, trying to get her bound hands into the drawer.

'Oh no you don't,' says a voice behind her.

When they reach the car, mist descends. Literally, one minute they can see the car parked precariously on the river bank, see Reedham behind them and the unmade-up road in front and the next, nothing. Just thick white fog, billowing up in clouds from the water, leaving them, seemingly, alone in the world.

'River mist,' says Max. 'Comes down in seconds.'

'This will make it easier for Spens to avoid detection,' says Nelson.

Max nods. 'You can't see a thing on the river in a fog like this.'

'Is it safe to drive a boat?'

'You don't drive a boat.'

Nelson snorts impatiently and Max hurries on to say, 'No. When visibility's this poor, you shouldn't be on the water at all.'

There is a silence where they all think of Roderick – old, unpractised, almost certainly mad – sailing, in a thick fog, towards a low bridge and dangerous waters, with Ruth on board.

'Come on,' says Nelson. 'We've got to catch him.'

The journey to Potter Heigham, with visibility down to a few metres, is a terrifying one. Nelson can't see Max who is in the back, the subordinate's seat, but Cathbad seems perfectly calm, even, at one point, closing his eyes. Nelson himself is rigid with tension. He has to rescue Ruth. He can't let himself even contemplate the idea that he may be too late.

They almost drive straight past the boatyard, which is set back from the road, a long low jetty surrounded by boats. Nelson gets out of the car and immediately steps in a muddy puddle.

'Jesus.'

'We're right by the bridge here,' says Max, nimbly avoiding the water. He gestures but they can see nothing, only thick grey clouds merging with the grey water. The lights from the boatyard are hazy and spectral, will-o'-the wisps in the fog.

At first, the boatman refuses to let them rent a boat.

'Visibility's too bad. You'll never get through the bridge or see the posts on the other side.'

'Post markers,' Max explains, 'they tell you which way to go. Towards the sea it's red on the right, green on the left.'

Nelson impatiently waves his warrant card in the boatman's face. 'Police. We have a trained pilot with us.'

'Helmsman,' mutters Max.

The boatman still looks worried but he leads them along the river bank. A dozen low, white boats are chained to mooring posts. They look flimsy in the extreme, just two seats in front and two at the back, low in the water, more like remote control toys than anything built for full-size adults.

'They're electric,' says Max, seeing their faces, 'ideal for this stretch of water.'

'Electricity is good,' says Cathbad. It seems the first time he has spoken in hours.

'Why?' asks Nelson.

'It's silent.'

Sir Roderick is standing halfway up the step, slightly above her. Making a split-second decision, Ruth butts her head at him, hitting him squarely in the stomach. He falls sideways, with a startled 'oomp' of surprise, and lands on the bench. But the force of the collision makes Ruth stumble too and, with her hands and legs tied, she can't right herself. She can hear Roderick stumbling about, breathing hard. She hasn't knocked him out then. She rolls onto her knees, struggling to get enough leverage to stand. But her leg muscles aren't strong enough. If only she'd been to the gym even once since her induction session. She tries again, rocking to and fro to try to get some momentum.

Then her head explodes with pain and everything is dark.

The fog is now so thick that they can hardly see each other. The boatman's face is a wavery white disc on the river bank and Max, in his dark jumper, has vanished altogether. The boatman gives them life jackets but Nelson and Max just throw theirs into the bottom of the boat. Cathbad, though, ties his carefully over his purple cloak. The flimsy structure rocks alarmingly as the three men get on board.

'We need to balance ourselves,' says Max. 'Cathbad, you stay on the same side as me.'

'So I weigh as much as both of you together,' mutters Nelson but he climbs into the front seat beside Max. Cathbad sits behind them, shivering in the exposed part of the boat. Ahead of them they can see nothing. When Max turns on the lights, all they do is reflect the mist back to them, light motes dancing in smoke.

'This is madness,' says Max, turning the key in the ignition.

'Just drive,' growls Nelson.

Max does not dare to correct him.

When Ruth wakes, her first thought is that she must be dead. She feels dreamy and uncoordinated, as if her limbs do not belong to her. Then, looking out of the porthole, she sees only greyness, neither land nor sea. No water, no trees, no other boats – nothing. This is one of those near-death moments; the long tunnel that leads – where? The bright light and your departed loved ones welcoming you home? The operating table and the painful recall to life? Then the word 'fog' comes into her mind and she breathes a sigh of relief. It is all right. She is not dead. It's just a river fog.

Then, painfully, her body starts to come back to her. Her head is pulsating with pain and the familiar sick feeling rises in her stomach. But the nausea is good because it reminds her of her baby. She has to survive for the sake of her daughter. Hang on in there, sweetheart, she tells her, I'll get us out of this.

Then she sees it. A nail in the wall, holding up a Glories of Norfolk calendar. A proper honest-to-goodness solid nail, not just a pin tack. Carefully, Ruth loops her hands over it and starts sawing away at the rope. The calendar swings wildly but the nail holds. In a few seconds her hands are free. Quickly, she unties her feet, swallowing down another wave of sickness. Then she opens the sink drawer and selects the serrated knife. She waits for a second, weighing the knife in her hand, then turns back to the step and pushes the hatch to the upper deck. It is locked. Ruth pauses, breathing heavily. Can she force the hatch open or is there another way out?

Suddenly she falls backwards as a terrible noise rocks the boat, as if the sky is being ripped off the world.

Nelson, Max and Cathbad hear it too. They recoil, as if from a physical blow. Max cuts the engine, Cathbad flings an arm up over his face.

'What the hell was that?' he breathes.

'The sound of a boat going under the bridge,' says Max grimly.

'The *Lady Annabelle*?'

'I think so. There were no lights. Why would anyone be out on a night like this with no navigation lights?'

'Have they run aground?' asks Nelson.

Max listens. 'No. I think they're through. That was the sound of the hull hitting the side of the bridge.'

'Will it have damaged the boat?'

'Yes,' says Max sadly.

'Good,' says Nelson, 'then we've got more chance of catching them. Can you get us through the bridge?'

'I'm going to try,' says Max.

For a few seconds the boat is in complete darkness. Ruth sits crouched on the floor wondering what the hell is happening. The noise continues, like a thousand nails scraping along a blackboard. Then, as suddenly as it started, it stops and the light outside the window is grey once more. Ruth stands up and looks around the boat. At the end is Max's bed, neatly made, with Elizabeth's dog on the pillow. Above the bed is a hatch that looks as if it slides open. Ruth tries to think about the geography of the boat. If she gets out of the hatch can she possibly edge around the side of the boat and take Roderick by surprise? It will be dangerous, the fog is thick and Ruth is not exactly agile at the best of times, even if she wasn't four months pregnant. But she has to try.

She climbs onto the bed and tries the catch. To her delight the hatch opens easily, sliding back to create a hole big enough to climb through. Gingerly, she sticks her head out. The air is cold and the mist seems almost solid, as if it will take an effort to cut through it. Come on, Ruth, she tells herself, you can do it. It's only a bit of fog, what harm can it do you? But the grey world outside fills her with dread. And she is afraid, horribly afraid, of the elderly monster at the helm of the boat. She begins to shiver so violently that her teeth chatter and it is only by a massive effort of will that she forces herself to move. You owe it to the baby, she tells herself, you have to get her to safety.

This last thought is strong enough to get her foot on the edge of the hatch.

She finds herself standing on the very front of the boat, the prow. Luckily it is flat though it rocks slightly beneath her feet. Can Sir Roderick see her? She doesn't think so. She can hardly see her own hands as they feel for the side of the boat. Thank God there is a handrail. Slowly, quietly, she begins to crawl towards the stern.

They sense rather than see the bridge. A feeling that some large, solid structure is nearby. Then, without warning, they are plunged into darkness. Nelson sees Max's knuckles white on the wheel and hears Cathbad's sharp intake of breath. Then the greyness is around them again.

'Well done,' says Nelson to Max. 'Where are we now?'

'Heading towards Horsey Mere,' says Max.

'And they're here too?'

'They must be right ahead of us.'

It is like voyaging into the afterlife. They have left behind the solid world and entered into a dream state, moving silently between billowing white clouds. There is nothing to anchor them to their surroundings: no landmarks, no sounds, no earth or sky. There is only this slow progress through the endless whiteness, the sound of their own breathing and the lap of the water against the sides of the boat. Nelson, looking at his phone, is not surprised to see that he has no signal. It would have seemed incredible if anything as prosaic as a mobile phone signal could have penetrated this unearthly fog. It is nine o'clock but it could be any time, day or night. There is no moon and no sun, just the grey nothingness all around them.

'It's like crossing the River Kormet into the Land of the Dead,' says Cathbad dreamily.

Max looks round and Nelson sees his eyes gleam through the mist, 'Yes, or the River Styx. Interesting how many mythologies involve river crossings.'

'Spare us the lecture,' says Nelson, who is leaning forward, trying to force the boat onwards through sheer effort of will. 'Can't we go faster than this?'

'No,' says Max. 'We'll be into Candle Dyke soon. I don't want to miss the markers.'

But the dream world gives nothing away.

Sir Roderick appears as if by a particularly malign form of magic. One moment she is moving carefully along the side of the boat, one hand on the rail, whiteness in front and behind, and the next she sees his red face, white hair and wide, surprised eyes. He is standing holding the wheel and Ruth knows that now is her moment. She has the advantage of surprise. Jumping forwards, she launches herself at him.

The wheel slides out of his hands but, for an old man, his reactions are remarkably quick. He throws up an arm and hits Ruth in the face. She stumbles and the knife clatters to the floor. Unmanned, the boat drifts slowly to the left. Ruth scrabbles about frantically for the knife and breathes a sigh of relief when her fingers close around its wooden handle. But when she straightens up she is looking into the barrel of a gun.

CHAPTER 34

At first Ruth assumes that the gun is a fake. There is something polished and old-fashioned about it and, after all, Roderick is an old man, a feeble old windbag who likes to go on trips with the Conservative Association. So, with the gun pointing at her, Ruth says, in a reasonably calm tone, 'Don't be silly. Keep your eye on the boat.'

Roderick's answer is to fire the gun in the air. The shock of the report, coupled with the acrid smell of gunpowder, almost make Ruth vomit again. Like Roderick, the gun may be antique but it is still deadly.

'There you are, my dear,' says Roderick smugly, 'I'm not just a silly old man with a gun, am I? I know how to shoot. I got my Blue at Cambridge.'

Ruth had heard enough about Cambridge to last her a lifetime. Quite suddenly her fear crystallises into anger and she finds herself shouting back, 'I don't care where the hell you went to university. Just let me get off this bloody boat!'

Roderick's answer is to approach her, still smiling, and place the muzzle of the gun firmly in her stomach.

'Be impertinent again, my dear, and I'll shoot your baby dead.'

There is a silence. The boat continues to drift to the left and, in one corner of her mind, Ruth hopes that it will run aground or hit another bridge or something. But the rest of her mind is concentrated feverishly on the madman who is threatening her life – and the life which she now realised is dearer than her own. She stares into Sir Roderick's filmy eyes. There must be something she can say, something that will divert him, will make him see what he is doing, would make him see her as another human being. But then, she remembers, this is a man who killed his own daughter, in cold blood when he was still a teenager. There is no reason to believe that he has learnt humanity in the intervening years.

They continue to look at each other when, suddenly, as if from miles away, Ruth hears a distinct shout of 'Ruth!'

Sir Roderick is momentarily distracted. As he turns away, Ruth shouts, 'Help!' as loudly as she can. Her voice echoes back to her uselessly, deadened by the fog. Sir Roderick wheels back round to face her and Ruth shoots her hand upwards and knocks the gun from his grasp.

'Bitch!' spits Sir Roderick, attempting to hit her across the face. But Ruth is on her knees looking for the gun. She can't see anything but she knows it is here somewhere. Her fingers touch tarpaulin, polished wood, brass and then, miraculously, the cold muzzle of the gun. She stands up and faces Sir Roderick.

'Keep away from me or I'll shoot.'

Sir Roderick laughs, a genuine guffaw this time, probably born of a lifetime of despising women.

'Shoot! Women can't shoot.'

Ruth pulls the trigger.

It was Nelson who had shouted. He hears the first gunshot and yells wildly into the fog though he has no idea where the sound has come from. Then, suddenly, Cathbad calls, 'Look out!' and the *Lady Annabelle* looms out of the mist, heading straight towards them. The little boat now looks vast, a huge black shadow, silent and menacing.

'Ruth!' shouts Nelson again.

He hears someone shout back but can't make out any words. Then he is almost thrown overboard as Max veers frantically to the left, trying to avoid the larger boat.

'What's he playing at?' Nelson yells at Max, his face wet with spray.

'I don't think there's anyone at the helm,' Max shouts back.

Is Sir Roderick dead then? Is he, even now, fighting desperately with Ruth? He cannot allow himself to think that Ruth might be dead. Ruth and his unnamed, unknown, daughter.

'We're in Candle Dyke now,' says Max, and Nelson is suddenly aware that there is space all around them. Before, although they couldn't see the river bank, they knew it was there but now there is nothingness, just a sense of expanding water and silence. The *Lady Annabelle* has vanished again and, high above, they hear the call of seagulls.

'Where the hell have they gone?' yells Nelson.

Then the second gunshot echoes across the water.

That's it. Ignoring Cathbad's warning shout Nelson jumps

straight into the river. He has no idea where he is going, he just knows that he can't stand to wait for one second longer, a useless bystander, hearing sounds of gunfire and doing nothing. Somehow he just has to get nearer. He has to get to Ruth.

The water is freezing and the fog seems to have got into his eyes, blinding him, making him choke and gasp. For a few seconds he knows he is going to drown, then some survival instinct makes him strike out, struggling through the black water, his heavy clothes dragging him down.

Then, suddenly, it is in front of him. The hull of the boat, as huge and unattainable as a skyscraper. Treading water, he yells, 'Ruth!'

He hears Max shouting but his voice seems to come from miles away. Nelson can only think about the obstacle in front of him. He has to get on the boat, he has to save Ruth. God knows what that bastard will have done to her. He beats uselessly against the *Lady Annabelle*'s metal sides. He can see a rail about a foot above him but there is nothing to grab hold of. He flails wildly and falls back, going under then rising, spluttering, to the surface. As he does so, something heavy hits the water just a few inches away from him.

It is a body, he is sure. He hears how heavily it falls and he knows, without any doubt, that the body will be dead when it hits the water. For a moment, he feels nothing. His entire body, his entire self, is numb. Even as he swims towards the dark shape in the water, he knows that it is all over. He knows that she is dead.

Max has been desperately following in the electric boat. He

sees Nelson reach the *Lady Annabelle* and try to get a hand-hold on her side. Max swings the smaller boat round, attempting to get alongside. Next to him, Cathbad is silent for once. He had shouted 'Harry!' when Nelson went overboard. Once, Max had thought that Cathbad loved Ruth. Now he isn't so sure.

The *Lady Annabelle* is still coming towards them and Max has to act quickly to save his boat from being rammed. He can see Nelson bobbing in the water and then he hears a splintering crash and sees a body falling.

'Oh no,' Cathbad whispers.

'Hold tight,' says Max. He swings the electric boat round almost at a right angle and somehow he is beside Nelson, who is supporting the body in a lifeguard's hold, barely keeping his head above water.

'Hang on, Nelson,' Max shouts, 'I'm here.'

With Cathbad's help, he hauls the body into the boat. It is frighteningly heavy; a dead weight. Then Cathbad helps Nelson in; he is shivering and crying, he seems to have completely taken leave of his senses.

Max is bending over the body. He looks up and suddenly the mist clears, revealing a full moon like a baleful eye.

'It's not her,' he says gently.

CHAPTER 35

It is June the twenty-first, the longest day. In the evening Max is holding a party at the Roman site to celebrate both the summer solstice and the end of the dig. Cathbad will be there, complete with dowsing rod, mistletoe crown and oak staff. Ruth is also invited, along with most of the staff from the archaeology department. But Nelson, though invited, is instead on his way to Sussex to visit Father Patrick Hennessey.

He is not quite sure why. Over the phone, he told Hennessey that he wanted to 'clear up some loose ends' but, in truth, all the loose ends in the case of Bernadette McKinley have been well and truly laid to rest. Two weeks ago, Father Hennessey himself conducted the funeral service for the little girl who died over fifty years ago, at the hands of her father.

Bernadette's mother was not at the funeral. When Judy turned up at the convent, on the morning after her interview with Sister Immaculata, she was told that the nun had died in the night. 'Did she see a priest?' Father Hennessey asked urgently when he was told. Yes, Judy said, Father Connor was with her at the end and administered the last rites. Judy knows, and Nelson knows too, the importance of this. Sister Immaculata may have confessed to Judy but this is not the confession that would matter most.

Although neither parent could be present, the little dusty church was not quite empty for the short ceremony. Nelson was there, as were Clough and the newly promoted Detective Sergeant Judy Johnson. Ruth, Max and Cathbad also attended, the latter dressed quite conservatively in a black shirt and jeans. Irish Ted and Trace were also there, Trace wiping her eyes on the sleeve of her lacy purple top.

Edward and Marion Spens sat in the front row, staring straight in front of them. 'After all,' said Edward afterwards, rather unsteadily, to Nelson, 'she was my half-sister. It just seems unbelievable that . . .' His voice trailed off. Nelson sympathised with the unspoken words. Almost unbelievable that Edward's father turned out to be a murderer who killed a child while in his teens and attempted murder again as a seventy-year-old? Almost unbelievable that the crime lay buried for over half a century, while the killer's son planned to dig up the land for profit? Almost unbelievable that, on the same site, a children's home would provide a refuge for hundreds of children and yet two would run away, one dying soon afterwards? All of it is unbelievable, yet all of it is only too true. Nelson grasped Edward Spens' hand briefly then walked away through the tombstones. There was nothing else left to say.

At the church gate he stopped and spoke to Trace, who was still mopping her eyes.

'I've just been speaking to your uncle.'

She looked up at him. 'How did you know?'

'It wasn't difficult,' said Nelson though, in truth, the connection escaped him for a long time, even after he saw the names on Judy's family tree. Charlotte Spens, children Tracy and Luke. Though, of course, Trace's surname isn't Spens, which made it less obvious. Still, her presence explained why Sir Roderick was able to know so much about what went on both at the Swaffham dig and at Woolmarket Road.

Trace looked shell shocked, much as her uncle had done. 'I can't believe that Grandad . . . Mum quarrelled with Uncle Edward, you see, so we didn't really see the rest of the family. But I'd always liked Grandad. He always seemed such a sweet old thing. We used to talk about history, about the Romans. It was something we had in common.'

'Let's hope it's the only thing,' said Nelson soberly, turning away to talk to Ruth.

Ruth had looked pale and tired but otherwise in good enough health. Her pregnancy was now obvious, even in the unflatteringly baggy black suit.

'Are you OK?' he asked.

'Fine,' she smiled rather shakily. 'I'm glad we had this funeral. It feels right.'

'Yes,' Nelson agreed, 'it feels right.'

He was about to say more when Clough bore down on them, suggesting a visit to a nearby pub. 'It's the proper thing to do after a funeral. Ask any Irishman.' In the background, Irish Ted was nodding vigorously.

'I'd better get back to work,' said Ruth. 'Goodbye, Nelson.'

And she had leaned over and kissed him on the cheek. It was their first physical contact since their child had been conceived.

When the police boarded the *Lady Annabelle* that night in

early June, they had found Ruth sitting huddled on the deck, holding the gun. 'I killed him,' she kept saying, 'I killed him.' Nelson, had he been there, would have told her to keep this thought to herself. But Nelson was, at the time, sitting in an ambulance wrapped in a silver foil blanket and babbling about his daughters. The reinforcements, two police cars and an ambulance, had arrived almost as soon as Max pulled Sir Roderick's dead body out of the water. The *Lady Annabelle* had drifted harmlessly onto the river bank. The policemen, local boys, boarded the boat easily, leaving their squad car parked in the reeds, its lights flashing eerily in the mist.

Ruth was convinced that she had killed Sir Roderick Spens. After all, didn't she pull the trigger and see him fall, arms flailing helplessly, through the wooden railing of the boat? But the post-mortem (performed by an indecently cheery Chris Stevenson) showed that there were no bullet wounds on Sir Roderick's body. Cause of death was a blow to the head, probably sustained when he fell. The bullet was later found, wedged into one of the *Lady Annabelle*'s bench seats. Ruth was relieved but the verdict does not alter her fundamental belief that she was the cause of the old man's death. She had wanted to kill him. Isn't intent to kill the same as murder?

This is something that Nelson could discuss with Father Patrick Hennessey. He knows, as he joins the traffic edging over the Dartford Bridge, that his visit is about more than police business. The Woolmarket Street case is closed. Whitcliffe is, if not happy, at least satisfied that none of the details have made it to the press (though the local papers did report the death of Sir Roderick Spens in a boating accident). Edward Spens is going ahead with the building development. 'Life must go on,' he said sententiously to Nelson, as if Nelson might be about to dispute the fact. He plans to call the apartment block 'Bernadette House'.

But Nelson knows, in his heart, that nothing is over. They may know who killed Bernadette, they may know what happened to Elizabeth Black (forensics have uncovered the bones buried in the school playground – Father Hennessey will have another funeral to conduct) but the feelings stirred up by the deaths of these little girls (Annabelle Spens too) are not so easily buried. Fathers and daughters, this is the phrase that keeps running through Nelson's head. He will shortly be the father of three daughters. This is the thought that now keeps him awake at night, the thought that has sent him speeding down the motorway towards the retired Catholic priest.

Confession? He hasn't said the word aloud to himself but when he greets Father Hennessey and the older man suggests a walk in the secluded part of the garden, he knows that this is what he has come for. Once a Catholic ... he smiles grimly to himself. Father Damian would be proud of him.

At first they discuss the Woolmarket Street case.

'Have you any idea why Sir Roderick Spens did this terrible thing?' asks Father Hennessey.

'Edward Spens found his diaries,' says Nelson, following the priest down a path overgrown with lavender and lemon balm. 'He kept a diary from when he was a child. It's all there, the murder and everything. Weirdest thing you ever read. Like a cross between Adrian Mole and Jack the Ripper.'

'He must have been a very troubled soul.'

'Troubled? Yes.' Nelson gives a bark of humourless laughter. 'But he managed to go through life without anyone suspecting. I mean, Edward Spens knew his father was odd. That was why he lived with them, to keep him out of trouble. But he never suspected that he was a murderer.'

'And yet it came to light in the end,' murmurs Hennessey. 'Evil can't stay hidden for ever.'

They have reached a sunken garden, out of sight of the house. They sit on a low bench, still warm from the sun. In front of them is a fountain, a mere trickle of water descending from the mouth of a stone fish. The dappled light overhead turns the spray into a hazy rainbow, yellow, green and blue.

Father Hennessey turns to face Nelson. 'Why did you want to see me, my son?'

Nelson takes a deep breath. 'I wanted to ask your advice.'

Hennessey inclines his head but says nothing. The silence trick. Nelson recognises it but that doesn't stop him from falling into the trap and singing like a bird.

'I'm a married man, Father. I love my wife and I love our two daughters.' He pauses. Those terrible few hours when he thought his daughters were in danger have impressed on him just how much he does love them. He would do anything for them, even (at Michelle's insistence) invite Laura's boyfriend for Sunday lunch.

'I love my wife,' he repeats, 'but a few months ago I . . . slept with someone else. I'm not making excuses, I knew it was wrong, but it was at a very difficult time . . . for me and for the other woman. We just came together, didn't think about the consequences. But now she's pregnant. She's expecting my baby, a girl. And I don't know what to do.'

Nelson stares at the fountain, the water falling endlessly into the stone bowl. Father Hennessey's voice is calm.

'You say you love your wife. Do you love this other woman?'

Nelson is silent for a moment and then he says, 'I don't know. I care about her. I care about her and the baby. I want to look after her.' He laughs, rather harshly. 'My wife does too. That's the weirdest thing. She knows this woman and wants to help her. With the baby and everything. My wife wants to befriend the woman who's having my baby. You couldn't make it up.'

'Love is always a force for good,' says Hennessey gently. 'Your love for your wife and daughters, for this woman and her unborn baby. Even your wife's kindness towards her. These are all good things.'

Nelson turns towards him, his eyes are wet. 'How can it be good? If my wife finds out, our marriage will be over.'

'Are you sure about that?'

'You think I should tell her then?'

'I can't give you advice,' says Hennessey, 'although I know that's what you want. I can only tell you that a baby is always a blessing, love is always a blessing. You care about these people, you will find a way.'

Nelson nods. He stares ahead, watching the light play on the water. He hardly notices when Father Hennessey puts his hand gently on his head and murmurs a blessing before walking away, back to the house.

Evening and Max's party is in full swing. The lonely hill, where once the Roman occupiers had huddled together against the cold Norfolk wind, is now full of people. Someone has set up speakers by one of the trenches and Leah's uncle has brought barrels of beer and cider from the pub. Irish Ted and Trace are dancing amongst the mounds of soil and stones. Ruth sees Clough, wearing a Manchester United shirt, cut in and dance with Trace, showing surprisingly good hip action. If Clough has come, why isn't Nelson here?

Ruth wanders away. She feels tired and wishes there was somewhere to sit down. Another five months of this! At least the baby seems to have suffered no adverse effects from that terrible night on the *Lady Annabelle*. Ruth has had a check-up and another scan and the baby was fine, dancing happily in the grey clouds of Ruth's womb. 'A large baby,' the technician had said. Typical. Nelson gets her pregnant with a giant baby and then buggers off. She will definitely insist that she supports Arsenal.

Ruth herself has recovered rather more slowly. She still can't shake the idea that she killed Roderick Spens. In her dreams, she sees herself pulling the trigger and Roderick's face disintegrating in a horrific shower of blood and bone. The actual events, with Roderick falling almost in slow motion, the wooden rail splintering and the long wait before the body hit the water, seem less real than the nightmare. She didn't kill him but she wanted to. And this, she knows, is the reality. She knows that she would have killed a man to save herself and to save her baby.

'Ruth!' She looks up to see Max approaching. So far he has been circulating, showing the ability to schmooze required of any successful archaeologist (one reason, perhaps, why Ruth will never reach the top in the profession). He has chatted heartily with Phil, hand in hand with a glowing Shona (the deadline of the final examiners' meeting is still a month away), grasped the hands of all the volunteers and spent an intense fifteen minutes with the local press. He will go far, there's no doubt about it.

Ruth has been happy to watch Max from a distance. The last thing she wants is to talk to the press – or to Phil. Her own relationship with Max, the bond she feels with him, has been strengthened by Max's appearance on that fateful night. It was Max who turned up in the police car to tell Ruth that he, Cathbad and Nelson had been following her in an electric boat. He told her about Nelson's kamikaze dive into the water. 'When he thought you were hurt, he just went crazy.' They had looked at each other and Ruth knew that Max knew that Nelson was the father of her baby. Neither of them said anything though. Max held Ruth's hand all the way to the hospital.

Now he is smiling. The dig has been successful. He will be going back to Sussex to write up the results. Even the *Lady Annabelle* has been saved and Edward has offered him the use of the boat whenever he wants. Somehow he doesn't think Ruth will be joining him on board.

'It's a great party,' says Ruth.

'You know what party animals archaeologists are.'

Ruth looks over to where two earnest women are discussing Roman pottery, and smiles.

'Let me know when the hard drugs start circulating.'

'I've got something to show you,' says Max.

Ruth looks at him warily. She feels that she has had enough surprises to last her a lifetime. But Max is smiling and the party is going on all round them. Surely the underworld is far away.

Max takes her hand and leads her to his car. The front window is slightly open and on the back seat is a large black dog. When the dog sees them it goes mad with delight, wagging its entire back end. It is a slim, slinky animal with a whiskery, smiling face. Ruth finds herself smiling back.

'Do you remember the breathing you heard on the site? I said I thought it might be a dog?' asks Max, leaning in to pat the now delirious dog. 'Well, this is her. She's a stray, been hanging round the site for weeks, so I thought I'd take her in.'

'A dog is for life . . .' says Ruth, pointing to the car sticker.

'Well, exactly. And I think I need some company.' Max's face darkens momentarily but lightens when the dog leaps through the window and flings herself on him.

'She wants to join the party,' says Ruth, who is thinking that the dog is more gregarious than she is. A party animal.

'I'd better put her on the lead,' says Max. 'She might get overexcited with so many people about.'

'What's her name?'

'Claudia.' Max grins. 'It's a suitably Roman name and she does have claws, as I know to my cost.'

Ruth pats the leaping, wriggling dog. 'Will you have room for her in Brighton?'

'Yes, I've got a garden and I'm looking forward to long walks on the seafront. It'll keep me fit.'

He looks pretty fit already but Ruth does not say this. Max hands her Claudia's lead (slightly to her alarm) and rustles around in the boot of the Range Rover.

'I've got something for you.'

He emerges with a carrier bag which he hands to Ruth.

'What . . .?'

'Look inside.'

Ruth looks and sees another dog. A stuffed one this time, rather battered by the years, but still smiling.

'Elizabeth's dog,' says Max, rather thickly. 'She called it Wolfie. I thought your baby should have it. It's ridiculous me keeping it, after all.'

Ruth looks from the stuffed dog to Max, holding Claudia on the lead, and her eyes suddenly fill with tears.

'Thank you,' she says. 'I'm very honoured.'

'No doubt Nelson will say it constitutes a health hazard,' says Max, more briskly, 'but I'm sure you won't listen to him.'

'Why change the habit of a lifetime?'

They rejoin the party and Ruth unbends sufficiently to dance with Irish Ted. In the distance, she can see Cathbad building the inevitable bonfire.

'You're a good mover for a pregnant lady,' says Ted.

'Thank you.'

He smiles, gold tooth glinting, and Ruth remembers what she has always wanted to ask him. Leaning forward, she whispers, 'Why are you called Irish Ted?'

'Don't tell anyone,' whispers back Ted. 'I am Irish but I'm not really called Ted.'

It is past midnight but the bonfire is still glowing. Ruth walks slowly down the hill. She is exhausted but it was a good party. Cathbad has danced in honour of the Sun God, Max has finished his dig and gained a companion, and she isn't going home alone. She smiles at the woman walking next to her. It had been Cathbad who suggested that she invite her mother – 'Gaia the Earth Goddess, you know. The eternal mother. It's all linked' – and, rather to Ruth's surprise, her mother had readily accepted. She has spent the evening talking to Max about mosaics, singing madrigals with the Druids, and dancing with both Clough and Ted. Now, she puts an arm round Ruth.

'Tired?'

'A bit.'

'We'll go home and have a nice cup of tea. Then you should go to bed. You need your sleep when you're pregnant.'

Roman mothers, thinks Ruth, were probably saying the same thing to their daughters on this same site, two thousand years ago. Come in and sit by the hearth, have some herbal infusion and pray to Hecate for a safe delivery.

Everything changes but nothing is destroyed.

ACKNOWLEDGEMENTS

Special thanks must go to my aunt Marjorie Scott-Robinson who has been an invaluable source of information on Norfolk, ghosts, tides and the best way to get a large boat under a low bridge. For this and for all the laughter and encouragement – Marge, thank you.

There are, as far as I know, no Roman remains at Swaffham but there is a wonderful Roman site nearby, at Caister St Edmund. Similarly, though Norwich is rich in wonderful houses, Woolmarket Street is fictional. Norwich Castle does indeed house a magnificent museum but the exhibits I mention are (apart from the teapots) imaginary.

Thanks to Andrew Maxted, Matthew Pope and Lucy Sibun for their archaeological expertise. Particular thanks to Lucy for her insights into life as a forensic archaeologist. However, I have only followed the experts' advice as far as it suits the plot and any resulting mistakes are mine alone. Thanks also to Graham Ranger for his unforgettable description of the 'smell' of crime.

Heartfelt thanks to my editor Jane Wood, my agent Tif Loehnis and to all at Quercus and Janklow and Nesbit. Love and thanks always to my husband Andrew and to our children Alex and Juliet.

WHO'S WHO
IN THE DR RUTH GALLOWAY MYSTERIES
MYSTERIES

Dr Ruth Galloway

Profession: forensic archaeologist

Likes: cats, Bruce Springsteen, bones, books

Dislikes: gyms, organized religion, shopping

Ruth Galloway was born in south London and educated at University College and Southampton University, where she met her mentor Professor Erik Andersen. In 1997 she participated in Professor Andersen's dig on the north Norfolk coast which resulted in the excavation of a Bronze Age henge. Ruth subsequently moved to the area and became Head of Forensic Archaeology at the University of North Norfolk. She lives an isolated cottage on the edge of the Saltmarsh. In 2007 she was approached by DCI Harry Nelson who wanted her help in identifying bones found buried on the marshes, and her life suddenly got a whole lot more complicated.

Surprising fact about Ruth: she is fascinated by the London Underground and once attended a fancy dress party as The Angel Islington.

Harry Nelson

Profession: Detective Chief Inspector

Likes: driving fast, solving crimes, his family

Dislikes: Norfolk, the countryside, management speak, his boss

Harry Nelson was born in Blackpool. He came to Norfolk in his thirties to lead the Serious Crimes Unit, bringing with him his wife Michelle and their daughters, Laura and Rebecca. Nelson has a loyal team and enjoys his work. He still hankers after the North though and has not come to love his adopted county. Nelson thinks of himself as an old-fashioned policeman and so often clashes with Super-intendent Whitcliffe, who is trying to drag the force into the twenty-first century. Nelson is impatient and quick-tempered but he is capable of being both imaginative and sensitive. He's also cleverer than he lets on.

Surprising fact about Nelson: he's a huge Frank Sinatra fan.

Michelle Nelson

Profession: hairdresser

Likes: her family, exercising, socializing with friends

Dislikes: dowdiness, confrontation, talking about murder

Michelle married Nelson when she was twenty-one and he was twenty-three. She was happy with her life in Blackpool – two children, part-time work, her mother nearby – but encouraged Nelson to move to Norfolk for the sake of promotion. Now that her daughters are older she works as a manager for a hair salon. Michelle is beautiful, stylish, hard-working and a dedicated wife and mother. When people see her and Nelson together, their first reaction is usually, 'What *does* she see in him?'

Surprising fact about Michelle: she once played hockey for Blackpool Girls.

Michael Malone (aka Cathbad)

Profession: laboratory assistant and druid

Likes: nature, mythology, walking, following his instincts

Dislikes: rules, injustice, conventions

Cathbad was born in Ireland and came to England to study first chemistry then archaeology. He also came under the influence of Erik Andersen though they found themselves on opposite sides during the henge dig. Cathbad was brought up as a Catholic but he now thinks of himself as a druid and shaman.

Surprising fact about Cathbad: he can play the accordion.

Shona Maclean

Profession: lecturer in English Literature

Likes: books, wine, parties

Dislikes: being ignored

Shona is a lecturer at the University of North Norfolk and one of Ruth's closest friends. They met when they both participated in the henge dig in 1997. On the face of it Shona seems an unlikely friend for Ruth – she's outgoing and stunningly beautiful for a start – but the two women share a sense of humour and an interest in books, films and travel. They also have a lot of history together.

Surprising fact about Shona: as a child she won several Irish dancing competitions.

David Clough

Profession: Detective Sergeant

Likes: food, football, beer, his job

Dislikes: political correctness, graduate police officers

David Clough ('Cloughie' to Nelson) was born in Norfolk and joined the force at eighteen. As a youngster he almost followed his elder brother into petty crime but a chance meeting with a sympathetic policeman led him into a surprisingly successful police career. Clough is a tough, dedicated officer but not without imagination. He admires Nelson, his boss, but has a rather competitive relationship with Sergeant Judy Johnson.

Surprising fact about Clough: He can quote the 'you come to me on my daughter's wedding day' scene from The Godfather off by heart.

Judy Johnson

Profession: Detective Sergeant

Likes: horses, driving, her job

Dislikes: girls' nights out, sexism, being patronised

Judy Johnson was born in Norfolk to Irish Catholic parents. She was academic at school but opted to join the police force at eighteen rather than go to university. Judy can seem cautious and steady – she has been going out with the same boyfriend since school, for example – but she is actually fiercely ambitious. She resents any hint of condescension or sexism which can lead to some fiery exchanges with Clough.

Surprising fact about Judy: she's a keen card player and once won an inter-force poker competition.

Phil Trent

Profession: professor of Archaeology

Likes: money, being on television, technology

Dislikes: new age archaeologists, anonymity, being out of the loop

Phil is Ruth's head of department at the University of North Norfolk. He's ambitious and outwardly charming, determined to put the university (and himself) on the map. He thinks of Ruth as plodding and old-fashioned so is slightly put out when she begins to make a name for herself as an advisor to the police. On one hand, it's good for the image of UNN; on the other, it should have been him.

Surprising fact about Phil: at his all boys school, he once played Juliet in *Romeo and Juliet*.